ONE OF MANY

"Believe me, you are just one of many," she said, hoping to nettle him. "I am practiced at lovemaking, as you have probably guessed."

"I'm not surprised," he murmured, wondering why he was so angry. "You know too much about men not to have learned it in the bedroom."

"That does not mean that I will welcome any unwanted attention from you," she said hurriedly, hoping she hadn't given him the wrong impression. "I choose my men carefully."

"Go to sleep, San Antonio Rose—you are safe with me. I have never been one to fancy another man's leavings, especially not if that man is Santa Anna."

No one could make her as mad as Ian. "I never invited you to my bed, and I never will. I pick and choose whom I take for a lover."

He turned his back with a jerk, and she smiled. She had gotten under his skin at last, even if she had told a lie to do it.

Other *Leisure* books by Constance O'Banyon:
TEXAS PROUD

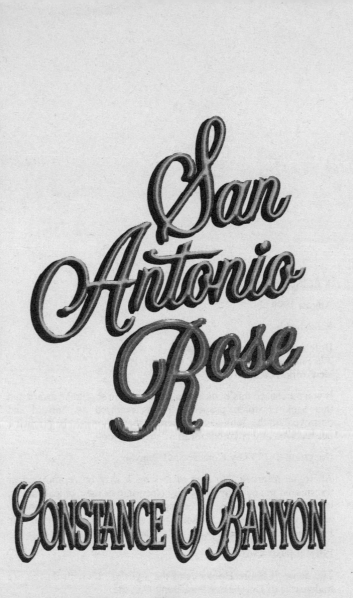

San Antonio Rose

Constance O'Banyon

LEISURE BOOKS   NEW YORK CITY

A LEISURE BOOK®

August 1999

Published by

Dorchester Publishing Co., Inc.
276 Fifth Avenue
New York, NY 10001

ISBN 0-8439-4563-X

Printed in the United States of America.

To Evelyn Rogers, a very special friend with an enormous talent and a caring heart to match. I know if I asked you to walk a mile with me, you would walk two. That kind of friend is hard to find and is to be treasured. And Jay Rogers, what a guy!

Donna Rusch—Coffee Pot—who has a loving and generous nature. It is a pleasure to know you—you always make me smile.

And to Haley Elizibeth Garwood, who is a wonderful writer. Thanks for your many E-mails that cheered me on while I was pushing a tough deadline. You said I could do it, I believed you, and I did it.

Acknowledgments

Dr. R. N. Gray. No one knows more about Indians in Texas than you do. I could listen to you for hours. Thank you for sharing your knowledge with me, and for setting me straight on Chief Bowels, the red-headed Cherokee chief.

Thanks to my uncle, Henry Hoyle, for introducing me to Dr. R. N. Gray.

AUTHOR'S NOTE

Whenever delving into history it is inevitable that there will be many conflicting reports on any given subject. This is true of Texas's fight for independence. The one true fact that is consistent throughout is that there were heroes on both the Texas and Mexican side—honorable men who were willing to die for what they believed. My main source of information came from an eyewitness journal meticulously kept by one of Santa Anna's own officers, Jose Enrique De La Pena. I found his account to be invaluable.

There are several different opinions on Sam Houston's height, ranging from six feet four inches to six feet six inches. I have chosen to believe he was six feet four inches which would have still allowed him to cast a tall shadow. Sam Houston was named Co-lonneh by his adopted Cherokee father, who was head chief of the western Cherokee tribe—in English the translation means "The Raven."

There are numerous writings, rumors and legends concerning an unknown woman who kept Santa Anna occupied at San Jacinto, allowing Houston time to launch a surprise attack that ended in the dictator's defeat. Some accounts called her the Yellow Rose. My account names her Emerada de la Rosa—the San Antonio Rose.

Lastly, I chose to deal indirectly with the Battle of the Alamo since the true accounts speak for themselves and need no help from me. However, all the world needs a hero, and I have mine in the man who gave America one of its finest heroic letters. For those Americans who have never read the letter, I would like to share it with you:

The Alamo—Feb. 24, 1836

To the people of Texas and all Americans in the
world—fellow citizens and compatriots—I am
besieged by a thousand or more of the Mexicans
under Santa Anna—I have sustained a continual
bombardment and cannonade for twenty-four hours
and have not lost a man. The enemy has demanded a
surrender at discretion, otherwise, the garrison are to
be put to the sword if the fort is taken—I have
answered the demand with cannon shot, and our flag
still waves proudly from the walls. I shall never
surrender or retreat. I call on you in the name of
liberty, of patriotism and everything dear to the
American character to come to our aid with all
dispatch. The enemy is receiving reinforcements daily
and will no doubt increase to three or four thousand
in four or five days. If this call is neglected, I am
determined to sustain myself as long as possible and
die like a soldier who never forgot what is due his
own honor and that of his country—victory or death!

WILLIAM BARRET TRAVIS
LT. COL. COMDT.

Lay the proud usurper low,
Tyrants falling every foe,
Liberty's in every blow,
Let us do or die!

—Robert Burns

Chapter One

Nacogdoches, Province of Tejas—1835

The woman emerged from the mist like a ghostly figure. She was dressed all in black, and she rode an equally black horse. She was so well covered that only her eyes were visible, and she hoped they reflected none of the apprehension she was feeling.

Emerada de la Rosa knew that she was treading on dangerous ground, and every instinct she had cried out for her to turn around and ride away.

But she had made up her mind; there was no turning back now.

She squinted her eyes to see through the thick fog that shrouded the land like a spiderweb. The air was so thick and humid that it was difficult for her to take a deep breath.

She slowed her horse to ford a narrow stream, then rode up the banks to top a small hill. The thick grass muted the sound of her horse's hooves, but the jingle of the bridle interrupted the silence as she guided her mount down the hill to the bivouac camp that lay almost hidden by scrub bushes and dense tree growth.

Suddenly, from out of nowhere, a guard stepped in front of her, his rifle pointed at her heart. "Identify yourself," he demanded.

She raised her chin defiantly and matched the young sentry stare for stare. "My name is not important," she said with a slight Spanish accent. "It is enough for you to know that Sam Houston is expecting me. Take me to him at once."

Although her voice was soft, the words were a command.

The guard nodded and lowered his gun. "Be you the San Antonio Rose?"

"*Sí*," she said, "I am."

"I was told to expect you. Follow me." He led her to a log cabin that was set apart from a row of tents. The guard paused, rapped on the door, then pushed it open, calling to someone inside.

"She's here, General."

Emerada dismounted and briskly stepped inside the cabin. The guard closed the door behind her.

She inspected the man that the Indians called *Co-lon-neh*, a name he'd been given by his adopted father, a chief of the Western Cherokees. Most people, his friends and enemies alike, used the English translation, which meant "the Raven." The legendary tales of the man's exploits were no less amazing than Houston himself. He was an imposing figure, casting a long shadow at six-foot-four. His eyes were soft blue and his expression was meant to put her at ease. But she wondered what turmoil went on behind those disarming eyes.

"You are taller than I thought, Señor Houston," Emerada said, lowering the shawl that had hidden her face from him.

He noted that her gaze swept over him without the apprehension that most people experienced on meeting him for the first time. He had always appreciated a beautiful woman, and she certainly was a beauty, with her ebony hair and dark brown eyes fringed by long lashes. She came only to his shoulder, and he guessed that because she was a dancer she would have a trim body beneath the layers of clothing she wore.

He was suspicious of this young Mexican woman who had sent a message that she wanted to meet with him on a matter of importance, but he hid his distrust behind a finely honed diplomatic manner.

"The San Antonio Rose. I must say that I was intrigued when I received your letter. You implied that you had something to discuss that would be beneficial to us both."

"*Sí*, I do. I hope you will think so, too."

His fierce gaze fastened on her face. "What can the San Antonio Rose have to say to me? Surely you have enough admirers that you don't need to add the heart of an old warhorse like myself?"

Trying to keep her anger under control, Emerada glanced around the cabin to make certain that they were alone. The door leading to what must be his bedroom was closed, so she lowered her voice. If someone was in that other room, she didn't want to be overheard.

When Houston indicated that she should be seated, she dropped down on a wooden stool and fixed him with a disapproving glower. "I did not come all this way to pry compliments from you, señor."

His face was expressionless as he asked, "Why did you come?"

"Your feeble army faces dangers that you do not yet comprehend. You need all the help you can get if you are to defeat Santa Anna. He not only outnumbers you, but his men are seasoned and well trained—yours are not."

Houston drew in a less than tolerant breath. "Why should the San Antonio Rose wish to help me?"

"My reasons for helping you shall remain my own . . . for now."

"I know nothing about your personal life,

16

and, on making inquiries, I found no one else seems to know much about you either. Should I trust my life, and those of my men, to a woman with no known identity?"

"I am here to offer my assistance to your cause, but that does not mean I am willing to share my life story with you. Just because you do not know my true identity does not make me less able to help you."

"Tell me then why I should trust you."

She matched his intense stare. "Is it your wish that you and I should bicker like two old women in the marketplace?"

After a long moment of silent confrontation, the stark planes of Houston's face eased into a grin. "I will listen to what you have to say and then judge whether or not you can help me."

"If you want to know about Santa Anna's movements, you will need to rely on someone who can get in and out of his camp without suspicion—is that not right?"

Houston's voice had an edge to it when he asked, "And that would be you?"

She nodded. "I put myself at great risk to come here today. What would I have to gain by misleading you?"

"What would you gain by betraying Santa Anna? He is your president, is he not?" Houston asked. "Why should I believe that you're willing to champion *my* cause?"

"Let it be clear from the beginning that I feel nothing for your cause, Señor Houston,"

Emerada said heatedly. "As I told you, my reasons for helping you will remain my own."

Sam Houston walked the length of the cabin and back, stopping before her. He saw many conflicting emotions reflected in the fiery depths of her eyes: pain, disillusionment, obstinance, and pride. In some ways she reminded him of his wife, who was a revered Cherokee princess.

"If it's money you want, señorita, I can assure you that our treasury is all but depleted," Houston said guardedly, his eyes probing deeper into hers with the intent to intimidate her, to discover her flaws.

She merely returned his probing glance with one of unrelenting pride. "To suggest that I would do this for money is an affront to me, señor. I did not come here to be insulted, and I do *not* want your money!"

His hand went to his chin and he rubbed it over a day's growth of beard thoughtfully. Despite her profession, she was obviously highborn. She spoke English well, but with a slight Spanish accent that puzzled him, because some of her words were tinged with a French pronunciation. She bore herself in a haughty manner, and he deduced that she was one hell of a woman. He could also tell that she was accustomed to getting her own way.

What did she really want from him? he wondered. "Suppose I decide to believe you. What can one woman do to help our cause?"

"You know I am a dancer?"

He nodded. "Your fame has preceded you, but we do not need dancers in my army."

Emerada proudly tossed her head and glared at him before continuing. "Sometimes a woman can be a far more effective weapon than a gun."

Houston realized that he had allowed her beauty to disarm him, and that gave him even more reason to mistrust her. He was locking horns with a woman of superior intelligence, and he had to be wary. "Why is that, señorita?"

"I do not know why they do it, but men always seem to tell me their deepest secrets—you Americans, as well as my people. For instance, I know that your ragtag army numbers in the hundreds, rather than the thousands. I know that it is comprised totally of volunteers, who could desert you in battle if they so choose, and they probably will. I also know that you need a miracle to keep Santa Anna away until you can muster a larger force to stand against him."

Houston's mouth twisted cynically. "Hell, señorita, everyone knows that. Are you asking me to believe that you can perform a miracle that will keep Santa Anna away until I can meet him as an equal?"

"No. I am not a miracle worker. It will take more than a woman to keep the dictator from running up your tail, Señor Houston, but I can give you information."

His glance traced the delicate lines of her

face, and he was tantalized by her beauty. "The question that comes to mind is, if you help me, what will you want in return?"

She lowered her eyes and her chin quivered with raw emotion. "I will tell you what I want when the time is right. For now, I ask only that whatever passes between us be kept secret. I must have your word that no one, and I do mean no one, will learn about our arrangement—that is, should we come to an understanding today."

Houston was silent for a moment while he studied the tip of his boot. When he looked back at her, he smiled. "Very well. I accept your terms. At least for the time being."

"And no one will know of our arrangement," she pressed.

"No one." He could see the relief in her eyes. "But I am still not sure that I trust you."

She shrugged. "You are not called the Raven without reason. I would have no respect for you as a leader of men if you blindly put your trust in a scheme such as I have just offered you. However, I believe that as time passes you will come to appreciate that I can be of value to you."

"And how do you know that you can trust me?" he asked as his mouth slid into a grin.

"We will just have to trust each other. I will start now by telling you that Santa Anna intends to cross the Rio Grande with a large army very soon."

"I already know this."

"*Sí*, but you don't know where he will cross, or where he will amass his troops. I can learn this for you."

There were several maps spread on the rough wooden table, and she moved to stand over them. After a moment of reflection, she pointed to a spot. "Here is where I expect him to cross, and I intend to be there to meet him."

Houston glanced down at the map. "If you can do this, you would indeed be helpful to me."

"There is more," Emerada said, searching the map and pointing to Nacogdoches. "There is a Cherokee tribe near here."

"Yes. I know Chief Bowles very well. You are indeed well informed."

"If you have any influence with the Cherokee, it would be wise for you to seek them out. I have it on good authority that Santa Anna has sent someone with orders to persuade the Cherokee to attack your troops. Ignore this warning, Señor Houston, and you shall have a war on two fronts."

He nodded, his gaze focused on the map. "If what you say is true, and I am beginning to believe it is, you have already been a help to me."

Emerada wrapped her shawl about her head. "I must leave now. You will hear from me only if I have something important to report. You shall know if the message is from me if it bears my seal, a single yellow rose."

She extended her gloved hand to him, and

Houston raised it to his lips. "Until next time, señorita."

Without ceremony, she swept out of the cabin, leaving a puzzled Sam Houston to ponder her words.

Emerada descended the steps and stood for a moment, noticing that a brilliant sun had burned the fog away, leaving the sky bright and clear. Her attention was drawn to several riders entering the camp, and she tossed the scarf about her lower face so she wouldn't be recognized. She had almost reached her horse when a sudden gust of wind ripped the shawl from her head and sent it flying.

A man had just come out of the tent that adjoined Houston's cabin, and with a quick move he caught the shawl and walked slowly toward her. He wore a gray uniform, and the gray-frocked coat had red piping down the front and around the collar. His black boots were thigh-high and his black slouch hat was turned up at a rakish angle and fastened with a red cockade. The man's piercing eyes were the bluest that Emerada had ever seen, and they seemed to cut right through her as if probing her deepest secrets.

His lip curled in distaste, and there was an edge to his voice as he held the shawl out to her. "Have you lost your way, señorita? The enlisted men are bivouacked by the river."

The man's insult stung Emerada deeply, and

her anger rose like molten lava. "Your men are safe from me, Colonel Ian McCain. As are you. I would prefer the lowest dregs of your army over you."

"So you know who I am. I am flattered," he said in a tone that implied just the opposite.

Emerada allowed her gaze to slide over the colonel. Although she'd never met him, he fit the description that others had given her. He was tall and lean, with dark hair and broad shoulders. He was undeniably handsome, and he was reputed to be favored by the ladies, but he was too arrogant for her liking. She slid her shawl into place and bestowed her haughtiest glare on him.

"Do not be flattered. I have heard nothing good of you, Colonel Ian McCain. The best that has been said of you is that you are sometimes referred to as the Raven's Claw."

And with that she turned away.

In her haste to depart, she tripped on a protruding root and, to her horror, went flying forward. To her further dismay, Ian McCain grabbed her in his arms. For a moment—or was it an eternity?—she stared into fathomless blue eyes that seemed to catch the glow of the sunlight in their depths. The touch of his hand on her arm was electrifying. Emerada felt in that moment that her fate had somehow been linked to this man. But that was foolish. He had insulted her, and she didn't even like him.

Ian steadied her, his arms circling her shoulders. He smiled rakishly. "So, you would throw yourself in my arms. Now, I *am* flattered."

She shoved against him, glaring at his audacity. "Your misplaced humor is exceeded only by your arrogance, señor." She stepped quickly away from him and wrapped her shawl about herself once more. "Good day, Colonel McCain."

Ian McCain had artfully been put in his place. In amazement, he watched the woman mount her horse, and he continued to watch until she disappeared behind a hill.

Puzzled, he turned toward Sam Houston's headquarters. He was certain that the woman had come from the general's cabin, and he wondered who she could be. He shrugged. It was none of his concern if Houston took his diversion where he found it. But the commander was sometimes too trusting when it came to women, and there were enemies and spies everywhere—even female ones.

Ian found Houston with his head bent over his map.

"Ah, Ian, I'm glad you're here. I want you to do something for me."

"Yes, sir."

"Did you see the woman who just left?"

"I certainly did, sir. Who is she?"

"She claims to be the San Antonio Rose. I want to know if she is indeed the dancer. Find out everything you can about her and report back to me as soon as possible."

Ian nodded. "As you wish, sir."

"No other comment, Ian? Aren't you curious? She's about the prettiest little gal I've ever laid eyes on."

"If there's anything you want me to know, you'll tell me, sir. I assume she didn't come here to dance for you."

"As much as I would have liked to see her dance, no. I can't tell you anything more than I have at the moment, because I have given my word. Dress yourself so you'll blend in with the Mexicans." Houston looked worried. "You'll find her in Presidio del Rio Grande, Mexico. I don't have to tell you what can happen if the wrong people find out who you are. You speak Spanish like a native, and you are the best man I have for sneaking in and out of enemy camps. It's those damned blue eyes of yours that worry me—they'll stand out among the Mexicans."

Ian grinned. "I'll do my best not to get caught, sir."

Houston suddenly looked like a man who carried the weight of the world on his shoulders. "This mission must be kept in the strictest confidence. It's imperative that I know who she is. Since you have a way with the ladies . . . " He shrugged. "Well, you'll know what to do."

Ian shook his head. "I don't think this one likes me very well. I'm afraid I insulted her a moment ago when I mistook her for a camp follower."

"Put that aside for the moment. We're soon going to have one hell of a war to fight, and there are immense hurdles to cross."

When Ian would have replied, Houston held his hand up to silence him. "I know what you're thinking. What kind of a war is this when I'm forced to send my best officer to spy on a dancing girl?"

Ian smiled slightly. "It had crossed my mind, sir."

Houston nodded. "Before you find the woman, I have another mission for you. This one won't be as pleasant. Find Chief Bowles, and speak to him for me. He knows you by reputation and because I have spoken of you to him." He bent over the map again and pinpointed an area with his finger. "Just ride south and follow the Angelina River. You'll know the village when you come to it."

"Isn't Bowles the chief of the Cherokee?"

"Yes. Are you afraid?"

"I'd be lying if I said no, sir."

Houston laughed. "What's the matter— afraid they'll spoil your pretty face and the women won't think so well of you?"

"I think I'm more afraid of the San Antonio Rose than I am of your Indians, sir. She was fearsome to tangle with."

"Amen to that. And pretty, too." Then Houston became serious. "Speak to the chief with my voice; remind him that we are brothers." A grin swept over his face. "With any luck you'll get to him before one of his braves kills you."

"You are a comfort, sir."

"If you fail, Ian, we're likely to be attacked from the front by Santa Anna, and from the rear by the Cherokee." Houston opened a trunk and removed a saber with an ivory and silver handle. "Give Chief Bowles this gift from me."

Ian saluted, turned on his heel, and left abruptly. The Indians were not what occupied his thoughts as he mounted his horse and left the encampment. He was thinking about dark brown eyes in the face of a beautiful woman. He wondered what was so important about her that it would merit the general's marked attention. He knew it wasn't sexual, or Houston would have handled the matter himself.

The woman occupied Ian's thoughts long after he'd left the camp behind.

Chapter Two

Ian McCain rode at an all-out gallop after he left Nacogdoches. He crossed a small stream that was so clear he could see catfish swimming in and out of the shadows and occasionally darting out of the water. When he rode up the embankment on the other side, he spotted a doe, two fawns, and a buck with a twelve-point antler. When they saw Ian, they bounded into the thickets and disappeared.

Texas was a land of plenty and promise for those hardy enough to withstand the hardships that went along with that bounty. He'd found it exciting from the first day he arrived. If he could choose anywhere to live, it would be Texas. But the land was going to have to be won first, and therein lay the real problem:

Santa Anna and his army stood between him and his dream.

By the next day, Ian had located his first Indian trail. It stretched through the pinewood like an unraveled thread and then disappeared among a thick growth of trees.

When he reached the woods it was hard going, and he often had to hack his way through. He also had to contend with pesky gnats and mosquitoes. Later he came upon a soggy bayou and carefully maneuvered his horse along a narrow strip of hard ground to keep from sinking into the mire.

It was late afternoon when Ian reached a clearing that brought him within sight of the Cherokee village. With his keen sense of observation, he became aware that there were several Cherokee braves following him. They stayed just far enough behind him to keep out of sight.

Wisely, he made no move for his gun and kept his hands in sight, resting them on his saddle horn. If he appeared threatening in any way, he knew he would never reach the village alive. He was certainly not going to do anything to provoke the Indians.

When he reached the river, three Indians suddenly rode up beside him, silently observing him, their stark expressions suspicious and dangerous.

One of them spoke to him in English.

"Why do you intrude on our land, whiteface? You are not welcome here."

Ian was surprised that the three Indians wore leather boots and clothing made of homespun cloth. He had expected them to be dressed in buckskin and wearing moccasins. Still keeping his hands in sight, he answered, "I was sent by the Raven to speak with Chief Bowles."

Invoking Houston's Indian name brought an instant change in the warriors' attitudes. One of them nodded, his dark eyes still distrustful. "Ride beside us. Do not reach for your weapon."

Ian nudged his mount forward, and the Indians closed in around him—one on either side, and the other behind. Silently they rode across the Angelina River and up the embankment on the other side.

When they entered the village, Ian had another shock. This tribe lived in log cabins rather than lodges or tepees. Smiling, healthy-looking children ran along beside Ian, while the women stared at him with curiosity. Ian noticed that the furrowed land was tilled and ready for planting. This tribe was not nomadic if they planted gardens. In fact, they were not at all what he'd come to expect Indians to be like.

His Indian guides directed him to the center of the village, where a man with long red hair was hoeing his garden. Ian was taken by surprise—a white man living among the Cherokee?

The man leaned on his hoe while observing Ian with a blank look on his face. Finally he propped his hoe against the cabin and walked toward Ian.

The cold-eyed look he received from the redheaded man was enough to chill the blood of any man, and Ian felt a prickle of uneasiness. It was apparent that this was no ordinary man, and there was something unnerving about him. In every way except his coloring, he resembled an Indian.

"Why do you come among us, American?" the redheaded man asked in surprisingly good English. "You were not invited into my village."

Ian's jaw tightened, as did his shoulder muscles, when he stared into a pair of the blackest eyes he'd ever seen. It was difficult to judge the man's age, although he did have some gray hair scattered among the red. He bore himself erectly and had an air of nobility about him—and there was something very dangerous about him.

"Tell me, white man, why are you here?"

Ian shifted his weight uncomfortably, causing the saddle leather to creak beneath him. "I have come to speak to Chief Bowles on behalf of General Houston. Will you take me to him?"

The deep wrinkles about the man's mouth smoothed, and he smiled. "I am Chief Bowles.

31

If you were sent by my brother, *Co-lon-neh*, then you are welcome. What is your name?"

Ian tried to hide his shock behind a stiff expression. Houston, with his sense of humor, probably thought it was a good joke to let him find out that the chief of the Cherokee was more white than Indian, at least in appearance.

Although the chief had relaxed his stance, Ian still had a prickly feeling along the base of his spine. "I am called Ian McCain."

After a scrutinizing stare, the chief nodded. "I have heard of you. You are the Raven's Claw. Come," he said in a commanding voice. "Walk with me to the hill, and I will hear what you have to say."

Chief Bowles turned to the warriors who had escorted Ian into the village and spoke rapidly to them in their own language.

Ian imagined the chief told his braves not to follow them, since they immediately stepped back a few paces. However, their dark eyes still studied him with distrust, and one of them kept his hand on the hilt of his knife.

Ian paused by his horse. "Before we walk to the hill, may I give you the gift that *Co-lon-neh* sent you?"

The old man's eyes brightened expectantly, like those of a child anticipating a treat. "It is always good to have something from a brother I hold in regard."

Ian reached across his saddle for the sword, grasping it by the handle and turning to hand it to Chief Bowles. This set in motion a fierce re-action from two of the warriors, who leaped protectively in front of the chief, their knives drawn and ready to strike. The chief spoke to them rapidly, and they grudgingly moved away.

Ian proffered the sword across his arm in military fashion to demonstrate that his intentions were not hostile.

The chief grinned as he examined it from hilt to point as they walked along. "I like this very well. You can tell *Co-lon-neh* that I will remember him when I touch this wonderful sword."

"I hope that sword offered to you in friendship today will never be used to draw the blood of Sam Houston or his army."

They had reached the foot of the hill, and the chief halted to look at Ian quizzically. "Why would this sword ever be used to spill my brother's blood?"

God, help me say this right, Ian prayed silently.

"Chief Bowles, it has reached our ears that men from the Mexican government have spoken to you about joining them in their fight against us. General Houston was much distressed by this rumor. It is a false rumor, isn't it?"

The Indian looked thoughtful. "There is truth here, but only a little." He slid the sword back into the fringed leather scabbard and gave his full attention to Ian. "I was approached, here in my village, by several men from Mexico. But I sent them away when I learned that they wanted me to fight against my blood brother." His voice took on a serious tone. "To the Cherokee, it matters little who claims Tejas. All we want is to keep this part that belongs to us. If you have come to ask me for help, I have not considered going to war at this time. So I give you the same answer I gave the Mexicans."

"That is not why I am here. The Raven has not authorized me to ask you to send your warriors into battle. His only request is that you do nothing to harm our fight for independence."

"Tell my brother that I will do nothing to hurt him or his worthy cause." Chief Bowles nodded. "If he fights the Mexican government, he must be on the side of right."

"Then I can tell General Houston that you will not raise this sword against him?"

"Have I not said so?"

"I know your word is good because the general has told me that you are a man of honor."

The chief sized up his young companion. "You are a brave man, Raven's Claw. You boldly ride into my village when my warriors could have slain you. I favor a brave man above all other kinds."

They stopped at the top of the hill, which gave a wide view of the river winding its way peacefully through the fertile land. A warm breeze played through the pine trees carrying with it an aromatic scent.

Ian dragged his gaze away from the landscape and turned his attention to the chief. "Yes, bravery is to be admired. But I must add yet another virtue to that—for what is bravery without honor?" Ian mused aloud. "The most evil of men can be brave, but if he is without honor, that makes him unworthy of himself and a danger to everyone else."

"Your words are spoken with wisdom, and I see the mark of greatness on your brow. It is good that you stand at *Co-lon-neh*'s side, for he has turbulent times ahead. He will need more like you with him when the war comes."

Ian nodded solemnly. "The Raven has loyal men who follow him, but they are not great in number."

The chief's gaze went out over the land, and he pointed his finger in every direction. "As far as you can see in any direction is our land, but there are those who would take it from us. We want to be brothers with all white men, but they will not have it so. Soon I fear we will have to fight to survive."

Ian could feel the old chief's pain, and he knew that what he had predicted would one day come to pass. "My people always seem to want what the Indian has. I hope that day never comes, but like you, I fear it will," he admitted with regret.

The tired old eyes moved across the land almost caressingly. "Once my people were all around me, as many as grains of sand on a seashore. With the passing of seasons, and the coming of the white man, my people are growing fewer in number. Soon we shall be no more."

"It is sad to think that, Chief Bowles. But I fear that your predictions are not without merit. I hope the time will never come when you and I will face each other in battle."

Chief Bowles looked at Ian with a trouble expression. "Had you said to me that the day cannot come when we would war with the white man, I would not have believed you. But you spoke the truth to me, and for this I will always remember you, Raven's Claw."

Ian nodded. "I must leave now. I hope we shall meet again in friendship, Chief Bowles."

"Let it be so," the old chief said. He watched the young American walk away, assessing his character as a man. *Co-lon-neh*'s young soldier was a proud man with much honor. He hoped the young warrior would not fall in the inevitable battle. But *Co-lon-neh*'s forces were gravely outnumbered.

He feared *Co-lon-neh* and his claw would both perish beneath the Mexican sword.

Chapter Three

Presidio del Rio Grande, Mexico
February 12, 1836

The sound of hundreds of thundering hooves echoed through the small village, causing the people to look to the south in apprehension. Just four days before, an advance guard of Santa Anna's army had passed through the village, and people had been forced to dodge clamoring hooves to keep from being trampled beneath them.

Now more troops were passing through the village, and the inhabitants were beginning to wonder if it would ever end.

It was said that Santa Anna's mission was to put down the insurrection in Tejas—an insurrection that was spreading and gaining momentum because of a handful of malcontents who declared themselves free and independent of Mexican rule.

The long column of soldiers was an ominous sight, with their flags waving, pennants unfurled, and colorful banners snapping in the wind. The mounted cavalry wore dark blue tailcoats with metal buttons that shone in the sunlight—they appeared formidable, equipped with rifles, swords, and long lances.

It was easy to distinguish *Generalísimo* Antonio López de Santa Anna, *El Presidente* of all Mexico, from the others. He rode at the head of his troops, arrayed in ornamental battle gear. His chest was covered with medallions and ribbons, and on each shoulder, he wore gold loops and heavily fringed epaulets.

As the cavalry approached, villagers scattered through the dusty streets, hurrying to their homes, bolting their doors, then positioning themselves at windows to watch the glorious spectacle from a safe distance. When the first riders reached the center of town, they didn't slacken their pace. Fruit and vegetable stalls were overturned; chickens scattered, squawking, their feathers flying through the air. Following the cavalry, an endless stream of infantrymen, wearing dark blue coats trimmed in scarlet, marched past. They looked neither left nor right as they stepped in time.

The villagers were relieved when the calvary

had finally passed through without stopping. Then to their amazement, they saw Santa Anna dismount before an inn and hand the reins of his horse to an aide-de-camp. With easy grace, he stepped into the small inn, followed by an entourage of five officers and three aides.

The fathers and husbands of the village hid their daughters and wives, admonishing them to stay out of sight, for it was known that *El Presidente* favored a well-turned ankle.

Was it possible that he, too, had come to their village to watch the San Antonio Rose dance?

Night shadows crept across the rooftops at Presidio del Rio Grande. The streets were crowded with a loud, enthusiastic group of men. A crush of humanity was pushing and shoving to find a place at Cantina El Paraíso. Many brawls broke out among the crowds because there wasn't enough room inside for everyone.

Many of the men had traveled for days just for the chance to see the beautiful San Antonio Rose dance. They hoped that when they returned to their own villages they would be able to brag to their *amigos* that they had actually seen the legendary beauty. Her fame had spread throughout Mexico, and it was said that the men who were fortunate enough to see her dance fell in love with her.

Emerada stood at the top of the stairs, her body trembling with fear. The day she had waited for had come at last—Santa Anna was in the village, and she prayed that he would come to her performance tonight.

She glanced down the stairs at the smoke-filled room, searching for Domingo. When she saw him leaning inconspicuously against the wall, seemingly blending in with the rest of the men, she drew in a relieved breath.

What would she do without Domingo? He was always there, looking after her. He was a tall man, with arms and legs like tree trunks. His once black hair had long ago turned to gray, but that did not keep people from giving him a wide path when he passed by. One look at him had discouraged many would-be suitors when they'd tried to approach Emerada.

Domingo had no past that he could remember, except the knowledge that Comanches had killed his whole family. Emerada's father had once told her that at a very young age Domingo had appeared at Talavera Ranch when it had belonged to her grandfather. Her grandfather had settled him in the bunkhouse, where the vaqueros had befriended him. Somehow, when Emerada was born, Domingo had attached himself to her as protector, and he still filled that role.

Suddenly the soft strum of a guitar filtered through El Paraíso, and Emerada took several quick swallows and raised her castanets, clicking them in time with the music.

Everyone fell silent, and each head turned toward the stairs.

She stood so still that she looked like a statue, her only movement her fingers controlling the rapid, melodic sound of the castanets. She was tall for a woman, and her body was slender and curvaceous. She was dressed all in red, from the tip of her dancing shoes to the mantilla that shimmered like a precious jewel as it covered her waist-length hair. Her dress fit snugly about her voluptuous body, and the many-tiered train cascaded to the floor behind her in graceful folds.

Suddenly two other guitars joined in the riveting melody, and the San Antonio Rose raised her head, her magnetic gaze moving over the crowd and drawing gasps from many onlookers.

Emerada moved so gracefully down the stairs that it appeared she was floating. When she stepped onto the stage, she arched her delicate arms above her head and clicked the castanets to set a tempo that was immediately imitated by the three guitarists. Forcefully she tapped her feet, moved her hips, and captured her audience in spellbinding ecstasy.

As Emerada tossed her dark hair, her eyes flashed, and she bewitched every man, making each feel as if she danced for him alone. She was luminous and radiant; each movement she made was calculated to inflame her audience with passion.

* * *

Ian sat hunched in a corner, a large sombrero concealing the upper part of his face and his blue eyes. He'd been waiting in the cantina for hours, mingling with the locals and asking questions about the San Antonio Rose. No one seemed suspicious of his motives, and he finally learned that her name was Emerada, although no one could tell him what her last name was or where she came from.

As Ian had waited for Emerada to appear, he heard glowing accounts of her talent and beauty. Now, as he watched her, he was inclined to agree with her admirers. He was as captivated by the dancer's hypnotic allure as everyone else in the audience. She was beautiful, and she knew just how to use that beauty to enslave the men who already worshiped her.

Surprisingly, as Ian watched the dancer he felt a knot of excitement gathering within him. Emotions boiled, igniting a deeper passion with each move she made. As much as he fought against his attraction to her, he was as affected by the San Antonio Rose as any of the other poor fools in the room.

Suddenly there was a commotion at the door—mumbling voices and men pressing forward as Santa Anna himself entered with a flourish. His officers were shoving aside a knot of people, clearing a path for the general who was also president of Mexico.

Ian pressed his body against the wall and positioned his hat at an angle so he could observe the sudden disruption without drawing attention to himself. Houston could not have known when he asked Ian to find out about the dancer that the search would lead him to the Mexican president—or had he?

His jaw clenched as he glanced back at the dancer. She must be aware that Santa Anna had arrived, but she didn't miss a step when he sat down at the front table after his officers had roughly expelled the three men who'd occupied the chairs.

Emerada could feel Santa Anna's eyes on her, so she began to perform for him alone. She removed her filmy red mantilla and tossed it into the crowd, where a fight broke out among those who wanted to possess it.

She tapped her feet and flung her head back so that her hair flowed about her waist like a dark, silken curtain. Her arms arched over her head, and she twirled gracefully. Gathering her gown, she raised it high enough to show her ankles, and a roar of approval rippled through the room. With sensuous movements, Emerada edged closer to Santa Anna, her gaze locked with his.

She discovered that Santa Anna was a handsome man, but of course he would have to be. She thought of all the young girls who had succumbed to his charms, much to their regret when he deserted them. She must not forget that he was greedy, ambitious, unscrupulous, and a man who could kill without remorse. She suspected that he could also be very charming—she was depending on that.

The guitarists slowed the melody and played plaintively. Emerada's hands gracefully moved to match the tapping of her feet. Then the guitarists fell silent, and Emerada dropped into a curtsy.

The cheers were deafening, and a tribute of flowers was thrown onstage. Emerada chose a single yellow rose and turned to the stairs she had descended earlier.

She held her breath, wondering if Santa Anna was going to send someone after her—he just had to!

"Excuse me, señorita." A voice spoke up behind her. "May I speak to you?"

She turned to find one of Santa Anna's aides behind her. She bestowed her most haughtiest stare on him. "I am very weary, señor. And I do not talk to soldiers."

"*Señorita, perdóneme.* You misunderstand my intentions. His Excellency has asked if you will please join him at his table," the officer said, graciously bowing.

Emerada met the dictator's gaze, and he stood up and smiled at her, his expression one of expectancy. She gathered her courage and went back down the stairs. The day she had waited and planned for had come, and she prayed that she would have the courage to do what she must do.

As Emerada approached Santa Anna, her smile was alluring, her body arched, and she allowed her gown to slip off her shoulder to reveal the merest hint of soft breasts. Although she wore the expression of a seductress and her eyes held an invitation, she was trembling, not with awe for the dictator, as any onlooker might think, but with loathing. She detested the part she was playing, and what she would be forced to do to gain the confidence of this man whom she despised above all others.

Emerada reminded herself that Santa Anna was no fool. She was playing a dangerous game that might cost her her life. But no matter what the cost, no matter how much she had to degrade and humiliate herself, she would play this game to win!

Nothing must go wrong!

She dropped into a low curtsy, and before she could rise, she felt Santa Anna's hand on her arm, guiding her upward.

"*Bravísima, señorita. Magnífica!* You are even more wonderful than I have heard," the dictator said with passion. "I am honored to have seen you dance."

Emerada studied him for a long moment. He was a handsome man in spite of his flamboyant uniform. His eyes were soft and deep brown, showing no evidence of the cruelty he was capable of. She moved forward, allowing him to hold a chair for her, a chair that had been hurriedly vacated by one of his officers.

"Thank you, *Presidente*." She could not bring herself to smile at him: "You are more gracious than I had heard." Her words sounded more biting than she had intended.

Santa Anna frowned for a moment as he absorbed her words, wondering if he'd just been insulted. Then, when she looked up at him coquettishly, his amused laughter joined hers.

She was daring and bold—just the way he liked his women. He congratulated himself when he saw how deeply she was affected by his presence. Before the night was over, the San Antonio Rose would be his to do with as he desired.

"Did you know that I came out of my way so I could see you perform, my beauty?" He raised her hand and kissed her fingertips lingeringly, while staring deeply into her eyes. "It was worth it. Will you not dance for me again?"

Emerada shook her head. "I would rather talk to you, *Presidente*. I have heard that you are a fascinating conversationalist."

He smiled. "Whether that is true or not, you can judge for yourself, señorita. But this place is much too public. Do you not have somewhere that we can be alone?"

She lowered her lashes. "No, not alone, *Presidente*. It would not be proper for me to be alone with a man, even you." She acted demure, but it was less of an act than anyone would have guessed. Emerada had never been alone with a man before. "But would you do me the honor of dining with me in my room?"

Santa Anna stood and helped her to stand, thinking she'd been an easy conquest. The rumormongers would have it that she would not be easily won. The gossip that had reached his ears was that San Antonio Rose never entertained a man in private. He smiled, feeling pleased with his prowess. "That is what I desire above all else. Let us go there now."

She drew her hand from his. "You must not come to my room until I make myself more presentable for you, and my maid will want to make certain the food is worthy of you. When I am ready, I will send my man to you. His name is Domingo."

Santa Anna bowed, his eyes on the plunging neckline of her gown. "Do not keep me waiting too long, beautiful one."

She blushed prettily, while stepping away from him. "I look forward to dining with you, *Presidente*."

Ian was not near enough to hear the conversation between Santa Anna and the dancer, but it was easy to guess what they were saying by their behavior. It was apparent that Santa Anna and the woman knew each other very well—probably intimately.

47

Tonight had been his good fortune. He'd never expected that his investigation into the woman's personal life would lead him to the Mexican dictator. He sank back into the shadows and watched the woman move up the stairs. Her hips swayed gracefully, and he found himself wondering what it would feel like to hold that body next to his.

Ian shook his head to clear it of such thoughts. Houston had good reason to be suspicious of her—a hell of a good reason!

He'd bet his life on the fact that Santa Anna and the dancer were lovers.

Emerada's expression was grim as she hurried down the back steps of the cantina to the hotel, where she had a suite of rooms. The streets were deserted, and she encountered no one on her way. When she finally reached her suite, she closed the door and leaned against it, trying to stop her heart from pounding. She was frightened, and she had every right to be. Santa Anna was a dangerous man. What if she couldn't go through with it? What if . . . ?

Josifina Gomez came out of the bedroom and hurried toward her charge. "Emerada, what has happened? You are so pale. Are you ill?"

"I have had a shock, nothing more."

Josifina gripped the neck of Emerada's low-cut gown, pulling it back onto her shoulders. "It is bad enough that you must dance in a public place: must you also dress like a woman of the streets?" She tossed her hands in the air as if invoking divine guidance; then she crossed herself and looked upward. "What your sainted mother would say about your actions, I cannot guess. If she is watching, she will know I have had no part in this thing that you do."

"Must we go into that again?" Emerada sighed. She'd heard all this many times, and she was in no mood to be lectured tonight.

"Where is Domingo? Why is he not with you? I told him never to leave you alone. This is not a decent town for a properly brought up young lady to be seen without an escort."

"I only came up the stairs alone. Besides, I sent Domingo to saddle our horses and gather supplies. Later I will want you to pack my small valise."

Josifina looked at Emerada suspiciously. "You are going to see that American general again. Do not deny it; I know you are, while I fret and worry if you will come back alive. When will all this end?"

Emerada was weary. All she wanted to do was fall across the bed and go to sleep. She certainly didn't want to argue with Josifina, and she did not want to entertain the Mexican *Presidente*.

"I do what I have to. I do not like it any more than you, Josifina. But you know it is something I must do if I am going to help bring down Santa Anna."

The older woman clicked her tongue. "What makes you think you can succeed where others have failed? Heed me well, Emerada: this will cost you your life if you continue. How can I keep my promise to your mother to keep you safe if you recklessly endanger your life?" Josifina declared forcefully.

"I myself did not know if it could be done until I met the American general. Houston may just be the man who can help me destroy Santa Anna."

"Domingo can carry your words to this Houston. You do not need to go. I will tell him this when he gets back."

Emerada was still pondering her meeting with Santa Anna, and Josifina's words failed to reach her. She looked into the concerned eyes of the woman who had been her *niñera* when she was small, her duenna when she was older. Now Josifina took care of her, not as a servant, but lovingly, and sometimes high-handedly.

Josifina still wore the old Spanish-style clothing. She was dressed in a plain black gown and a black mantilla fastened with a large pearl clip. She was slightly built, and her back was stooped with age, but although she looked fragile, she could be a formidable adversary.

Other than Emerada's Aunt Dilena, who was in Paris, Josifina and Domingo were the only people left from her old life. She didn't know what she would do without their care and concern. And she would need them more as the days passed.

"Josifina, he's here," Emerada said at last.

The older woman's face drained of color and she gasped audibly. She didn't need to ask who was here—she knew. Every step Emerada had taken for the last year had been skillfully calculated and meticulously planned for her meeting with Santa Anna. Josifina had dreaded the time when her charge would finally come face-to-face with the man who had ordered the death of Emerada's family.

"You saw him—spoke to him?"

"*Sí.*" Emerada let out a pent-up breath. "I invited him to dine with me, and he accepted." She avoided Josifina's eyes, knowing they would be disapproving and accusing.

"You know that man had no respect for women! Has he not scattered his seed all across Mexico? Has he not left many a young girl with a broken heart and a ruined reputation?"

"I am not some innocent who can be swayed by his high office or empty promises." Emerada kicked off her red dancing shoes, trying to hide her nervousness. "Help me dress in my silk gown. Hurry. He will be here soon."

Ian slipped out of the cantina and stood in the shadows just outside the door. He waited and watched, his senses alert. Soon his vigilance was rewarded; Santa Anna appeared, surrounded by his entourage. He paused so near Ian that had Ian been so inclined, he could have reached out and touched the dictator. He clung to the shadows as Santa Anna spoke to his men.

"I will not be needing you tonight. Wait for me back at camp."

One of his officers stepped forward and uttered a hesitant protest. "But, *Presidente*, assassins are everywhere. It is not safe for you to—"

Santa Anna smiled instead of chastising his officer for daring to contradict his orders. "You are right, of course. You and one of the other men come with me and watch for enemies. I will send you away later." He chuckled. "Possibly the only person I have to fear tonight is the beautiful San Antonio Rose, and the danger there will be to my heart."

Ian's hand went down to rest against his ivory-handled knife. It would be so easy to kill the dictator right then. However, good sense prevailed. Houston had told him to watch the woman, and that was what he would do.

Chapter Four

A pale moon hung over the village, creating shadowy recesses between some of the buildings where Ian could hide. Staying within the darkness, he followed Santa Anna and his two soldiers from a safe distance. When the Mexican president entered the Las Lomas Hotel, Ian slipped in behind him, taking care not to be seen.

The hotel was shabby; the once bright yellow walls were crumbling and flaking, and the brick floor was cracked and broken in places. The outer room was empty except for a man and a woman who were arguing with the Mexican clerk about a room. The man patiently tried to explain to them that there was not a room to be had in the village because so many outsiders had come to watch San Antonio Rose dance.

When Santa Anna moved past them, the three people gawked at him, but he paid them no heed.

Ian watched a huge Mexican man escort Santa Anna and his soldiers up the stairs. When he decided it was safe, he went up himself, hugging the shadows. He stood for a long moment before the door Santa Anna had just entered.

Suddenly the door was wrenched open and the big man came out, positioned himself in front of the door, and gave Ian a suspicious glare.

Ian got the feeling that the giant man was one of the dancer's servants, rather than one of Santa Anna's men. Frustrated, he went back downstairs. It wasn't likely that the man would leave his post.

Ian left the hotel and stood out front, searching the upstairs windows. He had to find another way to observe what was going on between the dancer and Santa Anna.

Emerada entered the room with a flourish of apricot silk and gave Santa Anna her brightest smile. Santa Anna's two aides were standing stiffly by the door, as if they were at attention.

"Señor," she said to Santa Anna, "you do me great honor." She dipped into a graceful curtsy.

"I am honored that you have agreed to dine with me."

The dictator's dark eyes sparkled, and he took her hand, raising it to his lips. "It is I who am honored, señorita. Will you please give me leave to call you by your Christian name—I can't very well call you San Antonio Rose all night, can I?"

A numb calmness seemed to descend upon Emerada. She had practiced this evening so often in her mind that her instinct now took over. "My name is Emerada, sir."

"Ah, Emerada. A beautiful name for a priceless beauty. *Sí*, it suits you."

"You are too kind, señor."

"You must call me Antonio—I insist on it. There is no reason for the two of us to be so formal, is there?"

She laughed and reached for the wooden box on the stand, opened it and offered him a cigar, and struck a match for him. Moistening her lips with her tongue, she pursed her mouth slightly as she blew out the match, catching his attention by her provocative action.

"I do not know you well enough to call you by your Christian name, señor. We are, after all, strangers. And I would never take such liberties with one as exalted as yourself."

Santa Anna laughed, delighted with the stunning beauty. She was witty and intelligent, with just the right amount of humility. "Before tonight is over, I will no longer be a stranger," he said meaningfully.

"You must be weary after your long ride," she said, fearful of the passion that suddenly flared in his eyes. She offered him a chair, and when he was seated, she took the stool at his feet. "Let me help you to relax. Perhaps, just for tonight, you can forget about fighting and war."

He puffed on the cigar and motioned for his men to move to the other side of the room. "Yes, I am weary. I am not unlike Napoleon, misunderstood and troubled by ingrates who do not appreciate what I do for them."

"I have heard it said that you are very like Napoleon. Please, tell me why that is."

"It is simply because I will not consider any military plan that is contrary to the great man's strategy. Using his plans has won many a battle for me."

Emerada thought it best not to point out that the great man, Napoleon, had lost his final battle and died in exile—a fate she hoped Santa Anna would also share. "It must be a troublesome burden," she answered, feeding his inflated ego. "It is easy to see that you are destined for greatness."

He nodded and stubbed out the cigar. "These are demanding times, but a man with my responsibilities must lead, while others can only follow."

She nodded. "It takes a man of great vision

and courage to ride at the head of an army—a man of destiny, like yourself."

His hand moved up her arm. "So true. You have great compassion and understanding." His hand moved across her bare shoulder. "A beautiful woman can do much to make a man forget his agonies, if only for a little while."

Josifina entered the room, her dark eyes sparking with anger. "If you please, dinner is ready." She slammed down a soup tureen so forcefully that the liquid spilled onto the table.

Santa Anna glared up at her. The servant's bristly manners inflamed his anger. "Watch what you are about, clumsy old woman. If I had been near you, I would have been burned," he said in a furious voice.

"Forgive Josifina, sir," Emerada intervened quickly, knowing how impulsive Josifina could be, and how she might very well tell Santa Anna just how she felt about him. Emerada stood so that her body was between the dictator and Josifina. "The hour is late, and she has labored tirelessly, preparing this fine meal for you. Can you not overlook her shortcomings?"

Santa Anna smiled, his anger dissolved, urged on by a pair of soft brown eyes. "Were you so certain that I would dine with you tonight that you had your maid go to so much trouble?"

Emerada lowered her lashes. "I was not sure, but I hoped you would."

* * *

Ian had scaled the outside wall and now watched through a window, observing the interaction between the dancer and the Mexican president. He was not aware at first that his eyes lingered on the woman, sweeping across her bare shoulders to the neckline that plunged downward to reveal the curves of her breasts. The bodice of her gown was so tight, it appeared that with the least touch, her breasts would come spilling out. He jerked himself up swiftly when he began fantasizing about stripping her gown off, touching her, kissing those full lips—

What in the hell was the matter with him? Was he as besotted as the men who had mobbed the town to see the dancer? To regain his composure, he glanced at Santa Anna. Though he could not hear their conversation, it wasn't hard to see that the man was smitten by the San Antonio Rose. But then, who wouldn't be? She was like no other woman he'd ever seen. His eyes moved back to her. He wondered how long she'd known Santa Anna.

Were they lovers? Of course they were. Ian could tell by the way they acted that they knew each other very well indeed.

Ian's eyes narrowed. If the dancer was on such good terms with the dictator, then she must be a threat to Texas's fight for independence. Houston had been right in suspecting her.

Ian was watchful all through the meal, observing how Santa Anna and the woman spoke intimately with each other. It was clear to him that neither of them noticed what they ate.

When they had finished eating and moved to a sitting area near the window, he ducked back, smiling. Now he could hear what they were saying to each other.

"Pity you have somewhere you must go tonight," Santa Anna said ruefully. "Are you sure you cannot stay? I had envisioned the two of us—"

Emerada interrupted him. "Unfortunately, my plans were made long ago and cannot be delayed. But another time—"

He pulled her to him and would have kissed her, but she wedged her arm between them. "There is no hurry, señor. We will meet again."

When Emerada braced her hand against his shoulder, she heard the rustle of paper. Determined to see what secrets he was hiding, she pressed herself back against him, tentatively sliding her hand inside his breast pocket.

Santa Anna, thinking that she was relenting, held her even tighter, unaware that she removed the document and slipped it behind her back.

She was relieved when she saw that the two men at the door were discreetly looking in the other direction to give them privacy.

Now she had become a thief, Emerada

thought. But to steal from such a man was no sin—she was sure of that.

"If only I had not given my word," Emerada said as she pulled away from Santa Anna with a feigned look of regret.

"When will you return from this thing you must do?" he asked in the same petulant tone of voice a small boy would use when he hadn't gotten his way.

"I hope it will not be long. I am anxious to get to know you better."

"Ah, señorita, I am on my way to battle. You must come to me wherever I am." He leaned forward and whispered in her ear. "I will not be hard to find. Look for me between here and San Antonio de Bexar."

She nodded and quickly stood up, her eyes issuing a promise of things to come—promises she hoped she would never have to keep. "I will find you, *Señor Presidente*."

There was a profound look of regret on his face. "Until we meet again, Emerada."

Ian had been listening to the conversation. *So*, he thought, *her name is Emerada. But Emerada what? Why does she keep her true identity a secret?* Perhaps she was a spy for Santa Anna, as well as his lover. Houston must be told at once.

In his haste to leave, Ian stepped too near the ledge and almost lost his balance. The noise attracted Santa Anna's attention, and he moved to the window. "Who's there? Guards,

guards, take this man. I want to question him
at once!"

Ian considered jumping to make his escape,
but the roof was too high, and he didn't fancy
broken bones. There was nowhere for him to
go. So he pulled his hat lower across his face
and returned to the window, surrendering to
the inevitable.

Emerada watched as Santa Anna's soldiers
dragged the intruder through the window and
slammed him against the wall. She stepped
back several paces, wincing when one of the
soldiers wrenched the man's arm behind him
and spun him around. His wide-brimmed hat
fell off, and for a brief moment she looked into
piercing blue eyes. It was Ian McCain! What
was he doing spying on her?

Before she could react, he lowered his head
to conceal his identity. He must have known
she recognized him. He was dressed like a
Mexican peasant—but why? If Santa Anna discovered this was Houston's man, he would
have him shot!

Emerada was annoyed with herself for car-
ing what happened to Ian McCain, and angry
with him for exposing them both to danger.
She agonized over what action she should take.
If she unmasked him as a spy, she would win
Santa Anna's confidence.

She glanced at Ian and found him watching
her. In that moment, she knew that she could

not live with the guilt of his death if she could prevent it.

With a soft laugh, Emerada moved toward Ian, standing between him and the lamp so he would be in shadow and it would be harder for the others to make out his features.

"Pedro, you fool," she scolded. "How many times have I told you that I do not need you to protect me? You should have known that I would be safe with *el Presidente* and his soldiers to guard me."

She dislodged one of the Mexican's hands from Ian's arm and nodded for the other guard to release him. "This man is harmless. He has set himself up as my guardian and is only trying to protect me." Her voice became hard. "Run along, and do not bother me again tonight, Pedro."

Ian did not take the time to question why Emerada had come to his rescue—he thanked his good fortune that she had. Scooping up his sombrero, he clamped it on his head and hurried toward the door, taking care to hide his blue eyes.

"Just a moment," Santa Anna ordered. "You appear to be a strong young man. If you have so much energy, why are you not in my army?"

Emerada linked her arm through Santa Anna's and smiled up at him, drawing his attention away from the intruder. "Pedro is just a harmless fool. He would be no better a soldier for you than he is a guard for me. Let him go— do it for me."

Santa Anna looked doubtfully at the man who paused in the doorway. "Still, we need every able-bodied man to march against the treasonous dogs in Tejas." He glanced down at the beauty beside him, who looked at him pleadingly. "Very well, for you I will let him go." Santa Anna glared at Ian, who took care to keep his eyes averted. "You have this lady to thank for your freedom. Get out, and if I hear of you troubling her again, you will be shot!"

"*Sí, Señor Presidente*," Ian muttered, then moved out the door and down the stairs. His thoughts were troubled as he mounted his horse and rode out of the village. Why had the dancer helped him escape?

After Santa Anna's departure, Emerada took a deep breath and let it out slowly. She had accomplished her goal tonight. Santa Anna was interested in her, and if her luck held, she'd be able to move at will in and out of his camp.

"That man is gone, and you still have your virtue, which is a blessing, since he is known for despoiling young ladies," Josifina said with disgust. "I have warned you many times about him. There is danger in the game you play, Emerada—grave danger."

Emerada was accustomed to Josifina's grumbling, but she was right about Santa Anna—he was a dangerous man to cross. "I do what I must, and you know it."

Josifina's shoulders seemed to slump more.

"I know how you feel and why you do what you do. But you cannot bring back the dead."

Emerada's dark eyes glinted. "No, but I can avenge their deaths—and I will."

Without wasting any time, Emerada stepped out of her gown and into a leather riding skirt.

"If you must leave tonight, you will wear something warm—it has turned cold," Josifina insisted, going to the trunk and removing a hooded woolen poncho, which she held out to Emerada.

Obediently Emerada slipped the poncho over her head and walked to the door. "Do not despair if you do not hear from me right away. I will be gone for a few days. Just remember that I can shoot straight and I can take care of myself."

Josifina knew it would do no good to argue with Emerada when her mind was made up about something. "I will not allow you to go unless you take Domingo along."

"Sí. He is as fussy as you are, and it is not likely that he would let me go alone." Emerada came back and kissed Josifina on the cheek. "If anyone asks about me, tell them I am ill and cannot be disturbed."

"I know what to do. Go quickly and come back soon. I pray that God will guide you safely back to me."

Emerada threw her arms around the old woman. "Yes, pray for me, because I am afraid. I know what I must do, but I also know of the danger."

She left quickly, while Josifina dabbed tears from her eyes.

The danger was real; Emerada knew this. She was either committing treason, or she was a patriot, depending on whether one asked Santa Anna or Sam Houston.

She went quickly down a side street and found Domingo waiting for her beside their horses. Josifina had been right: It had turned bitterly cold and started to snow. It would be a long ride to Houston's encampment, but she was determined to confront him about sending his claw to spy on her!

As they rode out of the village, making a wide sweep to avoid Santa Anna's troops, the weather grew worse.

After they had ridden for an hour, the snow was whipped up by a strong wind. Domingo guided Emerada to a barn, where they would rest for the night. After he made her a bed in the hay and covered her with a woolen blanket, the old man sat near the door, keeping watch over her.

Emerada's last conscious thoughts were of piercing blue eyes. Anger burned within her. Ian McCain could have ruined everything for her tonight. She should have let Santa Anna have him. How dared the man spy on her! Her eyes narrowed. McCain had not taken it upon himself to watch her movements—no, Houston must have sent him.

McCain would soon feel the sting of her anger. And Houston, why had he betrayed her confidence? How could she trust him after this? But if she didn't have Houston to help her in her quest for justice, she would have no one.

Chapter Five

The unseasonably cold weather retained its grip on the land. The snow continued to fall, and snowdrifts made it impossible to keep to the road.

Emerada guided her horse through the high snowbanks and tried to follow Domingo's tracks.

Miserably, the two of them pushed on against the gale-force winds. It rarely snowed in this part of Tejas, and the winters were usually mild. It seemed as if God's hand had been set against them. As wretched as Emerada felt, she could only imagine how difficult it was for the Mexican soldiers, who were ill-equipped for such bitterly cold weather.

After five days of hard riding, they finally

reached Nacogdoches. By then the snow had melted, and a warm breeze revived the land.

Emerada dismounted while Domingo remained with the horses. She hurried toward the crude log cabin and moved up the rickety steps. Not bothering to knock, she pushed the door open and moved inside. No one was there. She removed her gloves while she looked around at the sparse furnishings—a table and five chairs, an oil lamp, and plank floors. There was a door to her right, and she supposed that would be Houston's bedroom.

She moved to the table and stared down at the map spread there. From the markings she saw, it was apparent that Houston already knew that Santa Anna had crossed into Tejas. No doubt his spy, Ian McCain, had reported to him.

She should have let Santa Anna kill him.

The outer door opened, and Emerada turned to see Ian enter. For a long moment they stared at each other.

Ian was the first to speak. "I'm glad to have this chance to thank you for saving my life." His expression looked anything but thankful— he examined her face so closely that she was sure she had no secrets left.

"I was just thinking about you."

Ian smiled and drew closer, reading the anger in her eyes. "Pleasant thoughts, I hope."

"I was thinking that I should have allowed Santa Anna to shoot you. What were you doing climbing up to my window and spying on me?"

"Did it occur to you that I was spying on Santa Anna, and you just happened to be with him?"

"Whatever you may think about me, I am not a fool. You came to Prisido del Rio Grande to spy on me and nothing more. You just happened to find Santa Anna there." She smiled in amusement. "Have you told Houston how you were caught sneaking around on a roof? Does he know that his spy—his claw—was so easily discovered?"

Ian had come to respect Emerada's intelligence, although he questioned her choice of lovers. Santa Anna was a philanderer, and it did not sit well with Ian that this woman gave in to the Mexican president's lustful urges. "I told him everything."

"Everything?" She gave him a mocking smile. "What could you have told him about me, I wonder?"

He moved to the table and rolled up the map. "Now what could I possibly need to know about you that I couldn't find out in any cantina?"

She had been removing her gloves, and he saw her hands close in fists. "You insult me, señor. If I were a man, I would shoot you dead!" She slapped her glove against her thigh. "Maybe I shall shoot you anyway."

He smiled. "If you were a man, I can assure you that this conversation would not be taking place, dancer."

Emerada buried her resentment for Ian Mc-

Cain deep, a practiced accomplishment she had developed over the last four years. Now was not the time to spar with him—she had more important matters to attend to. "I have come to see Houston. Is he here?" she asked, dismissing Ian by turning her back on him.

"Unfortunately, he is not."

She whirled around. "Where is he?"

"I cannot say," he said evasively. "Tell me what you want, and I'll see that the general gets your message."

"I do not talk to underlings," she said contemptuously. "Houston will not thank you if I came all this way to see him and you stood in my way."

He smiled. "No man would like to be denied your company, Emerada."

She glared at him, her breasts rising and falling with each breath she took. "I did not give you permission to use my name."

His eyes were piercing now, and his tone was hard. "Would you prefer that I call you San Antonio Rose?"

"No, señor, I would not."

"Then what *should* I call you?"

"You have no need to address me at all. I have no wish to speak to you." She moved to a chair and sat down. "I will wait here until Señor Houston comes back."

"Then you must be prepared to wait for several days. As I said, he's not here."

70

She stood up and paced back and forth. "When will he return?"

"I can't say."

"Cannot, or will not?"

He shrugged. "I can't say."

Emerada dropped down on the chair wearily. She had ridden for days through a blinding snowstorm to reach Houston, and now he wasn't here. "I will remain in town for two days. If he has not returned by that time, I shall have to leave."

Ian was suddenly struck by her soft beauty, and for a moment he could not speak. Pulling his thoughts together, he said, "Señorita, I would advise you to reconsider. There are very few women here, and none as pretty as you. Though I would like to think my men are all gentlemen, I can't ensure your safety."

She moved to the door and gave him a scornful glance. "I will look after my own safety. You cannot even find your way off of a roof without getting caught. Inform Houston, when he returns, that I want to see him." Without looking in his direction, she left the cabin.

After she'd gone, Ian stood there staring at the door, stung by her unfavorable opinion of him. Sparks had flown between them since their first meeting. She got under his skin as no other woman ever had. She was shrouded in mystery. One thing he knew: She wasn't a mere dancer, as she would have people believe. He would find out about her, no matter how mysterious she was, or how hard she tried to cover her tracks.

The room Emerada occupied above the general store was surprisingly comfortable and clean. It consisted of a small bed and two overstuffed chairs. The bed had a soft mattress and a brightly colored patchwork quilt. She couldn't wait to lie down and rest after her grueling journey. She rummaged in her small valise until she found a light cotton gown and quickly changed into it. After a short nap, she went to the window and stared out at the encampment.

She was glad that a warm breeze had swept across the land, melting the snow and washing the countryside with sunshine. Her view looked out on a parade ground, and she could watch the men training for war. She compared these ragtag men unfavorably with the Mexican soldiers, who were smartly dressed and marched in time—these men marched as if they were wading through a cow lot. Looking for something to admire about them, she admitted that she was impressed by their marksmanship.

She stood up straight and pulled away from the window when Ian McCain walked across the training ground. Tentatively, she parted the curtains and peered out again. Ian was too far away for her to hear what was being said, but laughter drifted to her—the recruits obviously liked the insufferable man!

She leaned forward, her gaze settling on Ian. He was all male, tall with a classic profile. She positioned her elbow on the window ledge, resting her chin on her hand, watching only him as he instructed the men on how to load their guns and fire them while running. He was a good shot, hitting the target every time.

Emerada wondered where he was from and what had brought him to Tejas. She could tell that he was a gentleman, even though he chose to treat her with disrespect. She was not very good at distinguishing the differences between Americans accents, but Ian's speech was similar to Houston's so she assumed that he must also be from the South.

After a while Ian left, and Emerada lost interest in the soldiers. She hurriedly dressed in her riding skirt, determined to escape the confines of the small room.

Later she rode along a country lane, taking in the beauty of the land. No matter where she traveled, Tejas would always be the home of her heart, although when this was all over she would leave and never return.

Sometimes she was so confused. Tejas belonged to Mexico, so that made Mexico her country, and yet she could not condone the government's treatment of its citizens, any more than her father had.

She sighed and set her mouth in a stubborn line. She knew what she had to do, and she would not stray from her chosen path. She would see her plan through to the end—either hers or Santa Anna's.

Emerada felt better after her ride. She left her horse with Domingo and went directly up the back stairs to her room.

It was stifling in the small bedroom. She pulled her blouse away from the waistband of her skirt and removed it. Next she slipped her skirt over her hips so she could wash her body, hoping it would cool her overheated skin.

She was startled when she heard a male voice coming from the chair in the corner, and she spun around to face the intruder.

"Honor dictates that I reveal my presence before you reveal too much of your . . . presence?"

Emerada grabbed her blouse and held it in front of her. "How dare you come into my room uninvited?"

Ian suppressed a smile and slowly drawled, "I beg your pardon. I did knock, but when you didn't answer, I tried the door, and it was open. You shouldn't leave your door unlocked, señorita. No telling who might wander in."

"Like you?" she asked vehemently.

"It was not my intention to intrude. I merely wanted to tell you that Houston is expected within the hour." Ian knew that he could have sent anyone to deliver the message, but he'd wanted to see her again. He had to admit that he was as infatuated by her charm and beauty as any inexperienced lad would have been. "I knew you wanted to be informed of his arrival."

Her grip tightened on the blouse. "You have given me the message; now leave!"

He smiled. "You have nothing to fear from me, little heartbreaker. I just wanted to tell you about Houston."

He reminded her of a caged animal as he prowled the length of the small room and stopped near her. Emerada drew back until she was pressed against the wall. "Please leave, señor. As you see, I am not dressed to receive a gentleman caller."

There was something in her gaze that astonished him—fear. Did she really think he would ravish her, or was it an act to show that she was innocent? He decided it was an act.

His lip curled in scorn. "I suppose a man would have to be a president to claim your affections?"

"In your case, it would not matter what your rank was," she replied angrily. "I would not have you."

His mouth twisted briefly, and he shifted his stance. "I believe I have been put in my place." He bowed his head and retreated to the door. "We shall meet again, Emerada—depend on it. And who knows, you may change your mind about me."

After he'd gone and closed the door behind him, Emerada found that her heart was flut-

75

tering like the wings of a trapped bird. She had never had such a strange reaction to any man. For some reason she could not understand, every time she encountered Ian McCain, she either wanted to scratch his eyes out or lay her head on his shoulder and tell him all her troubles.

What was wrong with her?

Emerada knew she couldn't trust him. She sensed that behind that polite smile there was something hard and dangerous. She felt a tightening in her chest. He wanted to destroy her—she could feel it. And he might just succeed if she wasn't careful.

Domingo waited by the horses while Emerada entered Houston's headquarters. She could see the tiredness in his eyes as he offered her a wooden chair.

"No, I won't be staying that long."

"I'm sorry I wasn't here to receive you. But urgent business called me elsewhere."

"I know," she replied, wondering if she should go on trusting him. "You were visiting with the Cherokees to enlist them in your fight."

He looked at her in astonishment. "How could you know that?"

"It is nothing so mysterious. My bedroom window overlooked your parade ground and I overheard two men talking. Did you have any luck with the Indians?"

He raised his hand and shook his head. "You probably already know the outcome of the meeting."

She shrugged. "I was not spying on your men, if that is what you think." She moved closer to him. "But you have been spying on me. I am not sure I want to help you because you broke trust with me."

Houston glanced up at her in surprise. "I can assure you I did nothing—"

Emerada held up her hand to silence him. "Do not try to tell me that your claw, or whatever you call Ian McCain, has not been spying on me. I know he has."

"Please be seated so I can explain. I didn't break my word to you." He looked sheepishly at her. "Though I did send Ian to find out about you, I did not tell him about the arrangement between us. He knows nothing about that."

She sat down, wanting to believe him because she needed him as much as he needed her. "Are you being truthful with me?"

"As God is my witness. You have to admit that you gave me very little reason to trust you. I had to know who you are."

"And did the Raven's Claw find out my true identity?"

Houston chuckled. "He said all he could learn about you was that you were the most exciting dancer he'd ever seen and that your name is Emerada."

Her heart was warmed by the account of

Ian's praise, and she lowered her eyes so the all-knowing Houston would not see how pleased she was. "Did he tell you anything else?"

"He believes you are Santa Anna's mistress, and he confessed that you saved his life. The one seems to contradict the other."

She stood and moved to the door. "Next time he is caught, I will make certain that Santa Anna shoots him."

"Will you still help me, señorita?"

"Will you still send your claw to spy on me?"

"I can't promise not to."

She paused as she pondered her words. "Had you promised you would not spy on me, I would not have believed you. Since you have been honest with me, I will help you . . . for the time being."

Houston looked weary as he lowered his tall frame into a chair. "Thank you, señorita. I need all the help I can get."

"Be warned, Señor Houston, Santa Anna will not stop until he sees you dead. He is not a man to give up. He has an ego that must constantly be fed. Your death will be a splendid banquet for him."

"So you met him for the first time in Presidio del Rio Grande?"

"*Sí*. But I am going to meet with him when I leave here. I will contact you if I find out anything important."

"Be careful," he warned.

She worked her fingers into her gloves. "I can take care of myself. By the way, Santa Anna is on his way to San Antonio de Bexar."

Sam Houston shot up like an arrow from a bow. "Are you sure of that?"

"I am sure. He not only told me, but I have this." She handed Houston a piece of paper. "Can you read Spanish?"

"Not so well," he confessed.

She spread the paper on the table. "I will translate it for you. Although it is not a very detailed account, it contains some disturbing news."

"Please read it to me."

"It says that the first column is under the command of General Urrea and will go toward the Gulf Coast with instructions to close all ports. The force under the command of Santa Anna consists of four thousand men, fourteen cannon, nineteen hundred pack mules, forty-four wagons, and two hundred and thirty carts."

Houston gasped at the magnitude of the army. "Is this list reliable?"

"I took it from Santa Anna's pocket. I am sorry to say that I have become a thief."

"I'm not even going to ask how you got that close. Have a care, señorita. You trifle with a dangerous man. And you are so young for such a mission. There is a part of me that wants to spare you, and another part that knows I need your help."

Constance O'Banyon

She handed him the list and moved to the door. "It is you who should have a care, Houston. As I said, my bedroom looked out on your training ground. I have seen your soldiers, and I have seen Santa Anna's forces—you do not stand much of a chance against him." She opened the door. "Until next time." And she was gone.

Houston went to the window to watch her mount her horse. His eyes went to the huge man who rode at her side. Although the man had gray hair, his arms were muscled, and he looked as though he could crush a man with his bare hands. He had his claw, and the San Antonio Rose had her watchdog.

Ian came onto the porch and watched Emerada ride out of the compound. Houston emerged from the cabin to join him.

"I don't think your little señorita likes me, General."

"Perhaps not. But I need you to be my claw again. Stay close to her if you can. I have a feeling that she needs friends more than she will admit."

Ian watched her ride away, feeling somehow empty inside. "Who do you suppose she is?"

"I don't know. I have a feeling we won't learn about her until she's ready for us to—if we ever do."

"What do you suppose she's after?"

Houston shook his head. "I'm damned if I

80

know. You'd better leave now if you want to keep her in sight."

"She won't be hard to find," Ian said bitingly. "She'll hightail it back to her lover, Santa Anna."

Houston turned his eyes on his young officer. Ian's father had been one of his closest friends, and he'd promised Ian's mother that he would look after her son. *Yeah,* he thought, *I've taken care of him, all right. I've gotten him involved in a situation that might just cost Ian his life.*

"Don't always believe what your eyes see. If you do, you might miss what common sense tells you." Motioning for Ian to follow him, Houston went back inside the cabin and turned his attention to the map on his desk. "If you find out anything about the woman, send me word. Afterward, go directly to San Antonio and see what's going on. There seems to be some sort of fracas going on between Travis and Bowie. If you think it's necessary, take command yourself. Do what you can to restore order."

"Bowie and Travis are both good men. They just have different views on how this war should be fought, and therein dwells the conflict. I would not want either of them to think I was trying to take over."

"Damn it, Travis has locked his men in some broken-down old mission, and they can't move around. I gave him a direct order to blow it up and get the hell out, but apparently he disobeyed my orders. That place can't be defended, and Santa Anna's on his way there. He's probably already there. Tell them to get the hell out."

"How do you know about Santa Anna, sir?"

Houston handed Ian the document that Emerada had given him. "You can read Spanish, can't you?"

Ian quickly scanned the list. "It looks real."

"It should be. Your little dancer took it off Santa Anna himself."

Ian felt the bitter taste of disappointment gut-deep every time he heard about Emerada and the Mexican president. "I'll do what I can, sir."

"Get going then! And make Bowie and Travis see the futility of fortifying that old mission."

As Ian stepped off the porch, he gazed up at the gathering clouds. It seemed that Emerada had taken the sunlight with her when she left. The first drops of rain splattered on Ian's face as he went in the direction of his cabin to gather supplies for his journey. It didn't sit well with him that he had to settle matters with Travis and Bowie and tell them to abandon the old mission as Houston had ordered. They were both capable men and didn't need him to remind them of their duty. And he was puzzled by Houston's statement that Emerada was in danger.

Why was Houston interested in the dancer?

Chapter Six

The dust cloud that rose from hundreds of milling horses made Santa Anna's encampment easy to see from a great distance. Emerada halted her mount beside Domingo and gazed at the scene with great trepidation.

"Stay beside me. I am afraid, Domingo. If Santa Anna discovers my real intent, he will not hesitate to have me shot."

Domingo had always been a man of few words, and now was no exception. "You do not have to do this."

"*Sí*. I do. You know I do."

He merely nodded.

Emerada gathered her courage, knowing she would be safe with the fearsome but gentle giant beside her. When she had been a child, his presence had always chased away imaginary monsters. Now she needed his strength more than ever because the monster was very real—the monster had a name, and that name was Santa Anna.

She slapped her reins against the rump of her horse. "Let's go before I change my mind."

When they reached the encampment, Emerada was recognized and waved through by smiling sentries all along the way. It wasn't difficult to find Santa Anna's personal tent. Who else would dare to occupy a red and white tent made of the purest silk?

She dismounted and tossed the reins of her horse to Domingo. She was ushered into Santa Anna's tent by the man who stood guard.

Santa Anna reclined on a bed with silk coverings while a servant set out his meal on a table covered with white linen. The silver utensils and china dishes were monogrammed with gold.

Santa Anna beamed at her and rose hastily to his feet. "Señorita Emerada, you have kept your word. You have come back to me!"

She removed her hat and gripped it in her hand. "When you know me better, you will know that I always keep my word."

His eyes moved over her, taking in her beauty. "I like that in a woman, among other merits."

She hoped he could not see how she was shaking. "With your permission, *Señor Presidente*, I would like to dance for the soldiers. They must be weary and in need of entertainment."

He took her hand, raised it to his lips, and said in a deep voice, "And what about your *Presidente*? Is he not in need of entertainment?"

She withdrew her hand and moved a few steps from him. "I will dance for you as well."

"Ah, I see. You are going to be hard to win." He bowed to her. "I like a challenge. A battle too easily won soon loses its thrill." He pulled out a chair for her. "Come and dine with me. You must be famished."

Emerada sat down, realizing she was hungry. There was a chicken dish, beef, vegetables of every kind, and a bowl of exotic fruit. "Everything looks delicious."

Santa Anna filled her plate, his eyes on her every moment. "I like looking at you, Emerada. Never have I seen a woman so beautiful and graceful as you."

"You will make me blush if you continue to flatter me."

A man entered carrying a dispatch, which he handed to Santa Anna. Santa Anna excused himself while he read it, and then he wadded it in his fist. "We march on San Antonio de Bexar as planned. Those cowards in Mexico City think they can tell me how to fight a war. I am dictator, general, and president—I alone will decide where and when to fight!"

The messenger cringed visibly and hastily

departed when Santa Anna gave him permission. As if nothing unpleasant had happened, Santa Anna turned back to Emerada. "Forgive me if such matters take my attention from you. It will not happen again."

Ian flattened his body against the cliff, waiting for the sentry to turn his back. He was ready when the man moved away, and sprang forward, grasping the guard in a powerful armlock and covering his mouth. With the right amount of pressure, he snapped the man's neck. Ian felt the guard go limp and let him slide lifelessly to the ground. He hid the body behind a clump of bushes and then quickly dressed in the man's uniform.

He was pleased when the uniform fit so well that it could have been made for him. Ian had chosen a foot soldier because there was less chance of discovery. Had he chosen a cavalryman from one of the more elite units, his fellow officers would undoubtedly have noticed their companion missing from their ranks and sent up a hue and cry.

Ian shouldered his rifle and took up his sentry duty, hoping no one would notice the switch. He could hear music and laughter coming from the camp. Apparently the Mexican army was going joyously into war. He gauged the strength and number of the enemy and was astounded by the magnitude of the forces. For the first time he doubted that Houston's inferior number of volunteers—most of them farmers—could win against Santa Anna's thousands of well-trained troops, all experienced in war.

An hour later a soldier came to relieve him. The man was yawning and nodded in greeting while grumbling about having to stand night duty.

Ian made his way down the hill, his eyes sweeping the encampment, searching for the insignia of the unit he had chosen. Luck was with him again. He found the standard near the outer perimeter, located an empty bedroll, and lay down. He was sure he would not be able to sleep.

He rolled over and stared at the stars, thinking about Emerada. Houston seemed to think she was in some kind of danger, but Ian didn't agree with him. More than likely she was in the arms of the dictator right now, telling him about her conversation with Houston.

Ian was impatient to find out whether she was safe, and then he could get to the mission ahead of Santa Anna.

The Mexican army was camping on the Medina River, only twenty-five miles from San Antonio de Bexar. Ian stood on the banks of the river, wondering how much longer he could continue his disguise. So far no one had paid the slightest attention to him, and he was able to move among the soldiers with little trouble. Thus far he'd been unable to locate Emerada, although there was talk that she was traveling with Santa Anna. Since he was merely a foot soldier, he did not qualify to enter the Mexican president's inner circle, a privilege that was only available to a trusted few.

He'd often seen the president at a distance, but he had yet to see Emerada. His lips curved in distaste—she must be keeping to the dictator's tent.

The sun was sinking behind the hills, and Ian watched until it was no more than a purple splash against the horizon.

"*Amigo,*" a solder called to Ian as he walked toward the camp. "You must hurry or you will miss a wonderful thing. San Antonio Rose is going to dance for us."

Ian nodded and hurried after the man. "Why should she pay us such an honor?" he asked the soldier.

"Because, *amigo*, she is a patriot and is giving us her gift of dance."

"A patriot?" Ian said bitingly. "*Sí*, that would be her reason."

"*Sí, sí.* She is a great lady! Has she not proven that by leaving all comforts behind to travel with the president and keep his spirits up? I saw her dance once," the soldier said, pausing. "She was the most beautiful sight I have ever seen. I will take her image with me to my grave."

Ian followed the man in brooding silence. A

patriot she might be to the Mexican army, but she was a traitor to Sam Houston, and he intended to prove it. He couldn't go undetected for much longer—he would have to act soon.

A crowd of soldiers closed in around them, and it was a few moments before Ian found the soldier he'd been talking to. "Does she sleep in Santa Anna's tent?" he asked the man.

The soldier grinned. "I am told that the president is baffled by her because she keeps him dangling. I am also told that her tent is next to his. Of course, I do not know if this is so."

"I doubt she keeps him dangling," Ian muttered under his breath.

"Look, *amigo*, see where they have erected a stage for her. Hurry! hurry! We must get closer so we can see her dance."

Torchlight flickered across the hastily constructed stage while five mariachis strummed a plaintive tune on their guitars. Hundreds of soldiers of all ranks crowded into the limited space; some even perched in trees so they could watch the San Antonio Rose perform.

Ian was some distance away, leaning against a tree, his arms folded across his chest. His gaze settled on Santa Anna, who was seated next to the stage, and revulsion churned through his stomach as he thought of the man putting his hands on Emerada.

Ian elbowed his way forward while men grumbled and cursed at him. Soon he was near enough to see the stage better. He had been prepared for her appearance, but when Emerada stepped onto the stage, his breath caught in his throat.

She shimmered like a delicate jewel in an emerald green, tiered gown. At first she just stood there while the crowd went wild with adoration—they called out to her, and Ian even saw that the man next to him was crying.

She tapped one foot in time with the music. Then her arms arched gracefully above her head, weaving and intertwining. The music became more intense, and as she arched her back, the look on her face was that of a matador stepping into the bullring. She was drawing emotions from the crowd, making them fall in love with her. In that moment, any man present would have died for her—all but one, Ian McCain. His mouth twisted in scorn. She used her beauty and art like a weapon, and it angered him.

His gaze was riveted on her, and he realized that she would never betray people who worshiped her as these did. Houston was the fool if he thought she would betray Santa Anna for him. It was Houston who was her target. Ian knew that he must somehow get into her tent tonight, capture her, and find a way to spirit her away.

He would make her face Houston with the truth.

While everyone else was watching Emerada dance, Ian inched his way toward the Mexican president's headquarters. He was certain no one noticed when he slipped out of the tight circle and ducked down behind one of the silken tents.

Emerada was restless, tossing and turning on the silken sheets that had come from Santa Anna's own trunks. He had ordered that her tent be set up next to his and that it be furnished as grandly as his own.

She plumped her pillow and tried to find a comfortable position. They were within a day's march of San Antonio de Bexar, where Santa Anna had said they would engage the enemy. She knew in her heart that if her father had lived, he and her brothers would be fighting with the Americans, as were many of her people.

Emerada was uncomfortable sleeping on silk sheets and had the inclination to rip them off her bed and sleep on the bare mattress.

She heard a noise at the back of her tent and raised herself up on her elbow, staring into the darkness.

It was nothing, she told herself. *Perhaps the wind.*

Domingo had placed his own bedroll at the front of her tent, so no one, not even Santa Anna himself, could get past him.

With a sigh, she closed her eyes, wishing she could sleep. She was in the wolf's lair, and every covert action she made might mean her death. She had overplayed her hand in seeking Santa Anna's affection. He was becoming as troublesome as a lovesick youth with his first love. She didn't know how long she could keep him at arm's length. But she was committed to his destruction, and she would do whatever she must to bring that about.

Her mind turned to Ian McCain, and she resented the fact that he occupied more and more of her thoughts. Her instincts told her that Ian was an honorable man who was willing to die for Tejas, just as her family had, just as she would do if she had to.

It wasn't a sound that alerted her, but more the feeling of another presence in her tent with her. She was gripped with fear and would have cried out for Domingo if a hand hadn't clamped over her mouth.

"Do not cry out, Emerada."

She recognized Ian's voice! What in God's name was he doing in her tent?

His tone was menacing. She'd never seen him like this before. "If I remove my hand, you will not make a sound, understand?"

She nodded.

Slowly he removed his hand, but he kept a grip on her arm. "Get up and get dressed. You're coming with me," he whispered against her ear.

"Are you crazed, Ian McCain? There are soldiers everywhere. You will never make it out of camp."

"You have two choices, Emerada. You can either come with me, or die here. It's your choice."

She drew back as if he'd struck her. "You would do harm to me?"

"I will if I have to." He knew deep in his heart that he could never hurt her, but she needn't know that. "Get dressed, now!"

It was too dark to see him, but she knew he meant what he said. She stumbled out of bed and reached for her gown. "You will not get away with this, Ian McCain."

"If I don't, you will never live to tell."

A sudden ache surrounded her heart. She could not bear to think he would harm her. "Why are you doing this? Do you not know that it is you who will die?"

"If you are referring to the watchdog in front of your tent, he is snoring contentedly, and if you are referring to Santa Anna, he has his own diversion. Do you mind that he has taken another woman to bed with him?"

"If you leave now, I will not cry out. You can still get away if you are careful. It must be almost daylight."

"Hurry!" There was an urgency in his voice as he produced a rope and grabbed her wrists, wrapping it around them.

"Why are you doing this?" she asked as he pulled her forward to tie the rope.

Suddenly there was the sound of movement just outside the tent.

"Shh," he warned.

Torchlight reflected on the tent, and before Ian could react, the tent flap was drawn aside and three armed guards rushed inside. Domingo was right behind them. He looked from Emerada and back to Ian with a puzzled expression.

Santa Anna himself came in, fastening his shirt, and glared at Emerada. "What is this?" he demanded, his face red with fury.

One of the guards was holding his rifle on Ian. "I told you I saw someone sneak under the back of her tent, Excellency."

"Emerada," Santa Anna asked, his tone of voice revealing his suspicion, "who is this man, and what is he doing in your tent in the middle of the night?"

Emerada saw the jealousy reflected in Santa Anna's dark eyes. To give her time to gather her thoughts, she held up her hands to show she was tied. She had to think of something quickly or Ian would die! "This man sneaked into my tent, demanding that I go with him. He was prepared to take me away by force."

Santa Anna saw the uniform and moved to Ian, his face red with rage. "How dare you, one of my own soldiers, commit such an outrage? I demand an answer before you die, and you will die, make no mistake about that. But, should you tell me the truth, you will die quickly, instead of slowly and painfully."

Ian appeared to be unaffected by Santa

Anna's threats. He turned a cold gaze on Emerada. The giant man had cut the ropes on her wrists and had covered her with a long shawl.

One of the soldiers smashed the butt of his rifle on the back of Ian's head, and he fell to his knees. "Answer the general's question," the soldier demanded, raising his rifle again.

Ian slowly regained his feet and stared defiantly at Santa Anna, but said nothing.

Santa Anna inspected his prisoner closely, and he suddenly smiled. "You wear the uniform of one of my men, but you are an American. What do you want with this woman?"

Still, Ian said nothing.

"Take him away," the president ordered. "Tie him to a tree and use him for bayonet practice."

"Wait," Emerada spoke up. "I know who this spy is—he just told me. I waited to see how long he would try to deceive you." Emerada caught Ian's attention when she ran her fingers along the length of rope that he had brought to tie her hands. "Tell the president what you were doing in my tent."

"*Sí,*" Santa Anna demanded, his anger tightly under control. "Why are you here?"

Ian straightened his shoulders, lifted his chin, and said nothing.

Emerada twisted several loops in the rope while Ian watched. Her mouth quivered when she tried not to smile. "Why do you not answer His Excellency?"

His gaze burned into hers, and she could feel his anger like an all-consuming entity.

"Who are you?" Santa Anna demanded.

"I will tell you who he is," she said, dropping the rope down in the shape of a hangman's noose and dangling it in front of Ian's face. "He is Ian McCain."

Santa Anna's eyes widened. "The Raven's Claw?" A cruel smile played on his lips. "Can it be true? Has God smiled on me and sent me the Raven's most trusted officer?"

Ian stared dispassionately at Emerada as she dropped the rope and ground it beneath her feet. Tonight she had proved that her loyalties were with the Mexican president. It was a pity Houston would not know she was a traitor until it was too late.

Ian turned his gaze away from her and bowed to the Mexican president. "I am Colonel Ian McCain, and I have the very great honor to serve General Houston."

"Take him out now. Kill him slowly," Santa Anna said harshly.

Emerada touched Santa Anna's hand. "Wait! If you want to hit Houston where it will wound him the most, keep this man alive as your prisoner."

Santa Anna's voice was hard. "You care so much if he dies? Who is he to you?"

"I hardly know him, Antonio," she said, using Santa Anna's Christian name for the first time. "But don't you see the irony of this? Ian

McCain came here tonight to make me his prisoner and present me to Houston, just to humiliate you. Why do you not turn the tables on him? Keep this man as your prisoner and flaunt him in Houston's face. Does that not seem laughable to you? But I can assure you that Houston will not be laughing."

Santa Anna rubbed his chin thoughtfully. Finally he spoke guardedly. "I believe what you say. After all, you were tied when I entered. I was grieved when I thought he came here as your lover." He touched her face. "You are as wise as you are beautiful."

Santa Anna turned to his men. "Put him under tight security. I will decide just what will be done with him later."

Ian's arms were tied behind him, and he was hustled away. He glared icily at Emerada.

A lump crowded Emerada's throat, cutting off her breathing, but she raised her chin and stared back at him. "Your arrest will discourage others who think they can cross swords with our president and win."

Santa Anna waited for the others to leave, but when Domingo remained, staring at him disapprovingly, he spoke harshly. "Dismiss your servant. I want to be alone with you."

The big man planted his feet firmly and folded his arms across his chest, waiting for orders from Emerada.

"You may go, Domingo. I am safe with Antonio."

Reluctantly Domingo left, but he made a great noise of bedding down in front of Emerada's tent so Santa Anna would know he was near.

"At last I am alone with you," Santa Anna said silkily.

Emerada covered a yawn with her hand. "I am so weary, Antonio. The terror and excitement of this night have drained me. I am not at my best when my sleep is interrupted."

"It excites me when you use my name." His gaze slid over her disheveled hair and her soft curves visible beneath the scanty nightgown. "I want only what will make you happy."

She feigned a pout. "I was told that you have a woman with you tonight."

"She is nothing to me." His hand clamped on her shoulder. "If it is your wish, I will send her away."

"No. I do not want to be with you when you have been with someone else."

Anger flashed in his eyes, but then he relented as he always had with her. "You are a difficult woman to win. Ours will be a relationship that will last until one of us is dead. You are not like any of the others."

"Have you said this to the woman who sleeps in your tent tonight?"

"No, I have not." He smiled. "Our time will come soon, Emerada. I weary of waiting for you to make up your mind."

She moved toward her bed. "It is my hope that you will not have to wait much longer."

"You must rest," he said kindly, pressing a kiss on her lips and laughing when she pulled away. "I am grateful for your help in unmasking the Raven's Claw." Again he lowered his head and kissed her. "Take me to your dreams with you."

"You should make certain that Houston hears of his favorite's plight," she said smugly. That was the only way she had at the moment to let the general know about Ian's capture.

"I would have been in despair if he had taken you away from me." His gaze swept her body. "I will soon dispose of that rebellious rabble who have set themselves against me. When this is over, you will accompany me to back to Mexico City."

She avoided looking into his eyes lest he see the hatred she felt for him reflected there. "You do me great honor." Had she sounded convincing? she wondered.

Apparently she had, because he smiled and left.

Chapter Seven

Ian's arms and legs were bound behind him, and he was damned uncomfortable. He yanked against the ropes, but that only made them cut into his flesh. What had he gotten himself into this time?

Here he was lying facedown on the hard ground in an enemy camp. He would have preferred the firing squad to this humiliation. Many times over the last few hours he'd cursed the day he had heard of Emerada. She had been as ruthless as any man when she betrayed him to her lover.

It made him angry as hell that she would get away with this betrayal. Now, if he died, which he surely would, the dancer would go on feeding Houston false information, while reporting Houston's movements to Santa Anna.

He tugged at the ropes again. He had to escape so he could warn Houston. He glanced about him, watching the activity as the Mexicans broke camp. Tents were disassembled and loaded onto two-wheeled carts. He watched two soldiers hitching horses to cannon. The Texans were no threat to the might of this army.

Ian yanked on his ropes, no longer feeling the pain when they cut into him. He was supposed to get to San Antonio ahead of Santa Anna. Now he would arrive with the dictator, if he survived. He had walked into a situation that a child would have known to avoid. If he hadn't tried to capture the dancer, he'd now be on his way to settle the squabble between Travis and Bowie.

He'd overheard two soldiers talking, and they knew that Travis and Bowie were holed up in the Spanish mission. They had called the mission the Alamo. Dammit, how many men did Travis have, a hundred, two hundred, or less maybe?

"Damn," he swore aloud. They would all be slaughtered.

Later in the morning, the ropes were removed from Ian's legs, and he was tossed in a cart and tied to the rails. As the cart bumped along, his anger grew. What would Houston think of him if he could see him now?

A cloud of dust made him cough, and he glanced up to see Santa Anna riding by, surrounded by his usual entourage. A few moments later, Emerada rode by, and he couldn't resist the urge to call out to her.

"How's the dancer?"

Emerada slowed her mount to keep pace with the cart. She saw that Ian's lip was cut, and there was dried blood on his face. Her heart wrenched to see that he'd been treated so cruelly, but at least he was still alive.

She knew he would not welcome her pity, so she hid it from him. "The dancer is fine, señor. I wonder if you know how fortunate you are? No American during this war has stood eye-to-eye with Santa Anna and lived to tell about it. If I were you, I would be counting my blessings."

"Oh, I do, dancer—I do! I go down on my knees and bless the fate that placed me in Santa Anna's hands. That fate being you, of course."

"We see it differently. It seems to me that it was you who came to my tent, threatened me, and tried to take me away by force."

"Perhaps I just wanted to have you to myself."

"I have always observed that a person cannot be too bad off if he keeps his sense of humor— you seem to have kept yours. I hope you still have it after today. You will be going to San Antonio de Bexar. Did you know that?"

"I heard talk." Sarcasm laced his voice.

"What surprises me is that you are going along to war. Will you dance on the battlefield?"

"I have other talents besides dancing. Who knows, I may take up a rifle and join the battle."

"Well, little dancer, congratulations—it seems that Santa Anna can't do without you."

She stared straight ahead. "So it would seem." She turned to him and asked, "Are you thirsty—have they fed you?"

He looked deeply into her eyes and saw compassion reflected there. It only fueled his anger. "Oh, yes, Emerada. I dine on fine linen, have tea at three and sup fashionably late."

She nudged her horse in the flanks and joined Domingo. "That man is insufferable! I am glad he can no longer spy on me. After all, he was trying to kidnap me."

"*Sí*," Domingo replied. "And if you had not revealed his identity, he would now be dead. But he will never believe that."

"I do not care what he thinks—why should I?"

But she knew in her heart that she did care. She cared very much.

Emerada was surprised to find the streets of San Antonio deserted. The shutters on the shops and houses were closed, and there was no sign of life. This was the town where she had gone to market with her family as a child. She had once known most of the people who lived there. Where were they now?

Her mare shied and reared, spooked by the thundering sound of cannon fire. She finally managed to bring the animal under control, and glanced about in astonishment. The Alamo, the little mission where she had often gone with her mother to take delicacies to the monks, was under siege!

Had the whole world gone mad?

She heard bullets whizzing past, and a cavalry officer riding three horses ahead of her fell from his horse with a bullet wound to the head. She leaped from her horse and raced toward him. Domingo pulled her back before she reached the man.

"There is nothing you can do for him. He is dead."

This was Emerada's first bitter experience of war, and she knew in her heart that it was going to get much worse before it ended.

Later that night she dined with Santa Anna, which had become a nightly habit. This was her only way to learn about his plans, other than letting him make love to her. So far she had managed to escape his advances and still keep him interested in her. She was aware that when she left him, he'd have other women brought to him. Sometimes Emerada would see a woman leaving his tent in the early morning hours. Some of them were mere girls, and this only made her despise the dictator even more.

She glanced up and found Santa Anna watching her. "Antonio, you have enough food here to feed twenty soldiers."

"A man such as myself must keep fit. If I fall ill, who will lead my troops?"

"It seems to me, although I am but a woman and know little of such things, that it is not wise to have your foot soldiers storm the walls of the Alamo. You have already lost so many that way."

Santa Anna speared a chicken leg and held it out for her inspection. "You see this—those soldiers mean no more to me than this piece of chicken." He dropped the meat back on his plate and patted her hand. "You are right, my dear, you know little of such matters."

She had the strong urge to leap across the table and carve his heart out. Instead she forced a smile to her lips. "I know that your men are not as important as you, Antonio. No one is."

His dark gaze settled on her. "You are becoming important to me, Emerada. When will you let me make love to you?" His voice was caressing. "I want you more than I have ever wanted any woman. Surrender to me and I will never look at another woman."

She placed her napkin on the table and stood. "We will both know when the time is right." She moved quickly to the door. She had to get away from him, to breathe fresh air, to master her temper before she did something she'd regret. Now was not the time to kill the heartless dictator.

But the time was not so far away.

* * *

Emerada paced her tent, clamping her hands over her ears to shut out the continuous sound of cannon fire. She could understand why Santa Anna had taken up residence in the town—to escape the noise, and probably he was afraid his tent would be targeted by the Alamo defenders—poor brave fools. She had declined his offer to join him there, preferring to keep her distance from him for now.

Even behind the lines as she was, the ground shook and trembled every time a cannon was fired, and there seemed to be a continuous barrage. She tried not to think about the horrible carnage, the lives that were being lost on both sides.

After two days of listening to the sounds of men dying, Emerada had to do something to help. With trepidation, she made her way to the medical tent, although Domingo tried to dissuade her. There were men dying who needed help. She had lived a sheltered life until now, and she hoped she wouldn't faint at the sight of blood.

Emerada was surprised to find that two of the doctors were Americans. They were working diligently on the wounded, although she learned that they had been captured after a battle and forced into service by Santa Anna.

Silently she followed the doctors' orders, trying not to be sick at the sight of gaping wounds and so much blood. She held the hands of dying men, wrote letters to their loved ones, and held operating instruments and bandages for the doctors. Hours passed, she didn't know how many, before she finally rolled down her sleeves and left the tent of death.

Emerada was surprised to find that it was almost sundown. She breathed deeply, needing fresh air, but all she could smell was sulfur and gunpowder. She wanted to get on her horse and ride away, never looking back, but she couldn't. Nothing, not even the sight of war, the wounded and dying, could deter her from her plan.

"Hello, dancer," Ian called out as Emerada passed by. "Turned any more prisoners over to your lover today?"

Ian was tied to a live oak tree, and she considered passing him by because she was just too weary to trade insults with him. Anyway, he had a right to think Santa Anna was her lover—everyone thought they were, and they probably would be eventually. She lifted a wooden water bucket and offered him a dipperful of water.

Ian looked as if he might refuse, but he reconsidered. He drank thirstily and nodded his thanks. "You would have done better to let your lover kill me."

"He would have if I hadn't intervened. I've had to save your life twice now. Who looks after you when I am not around?"

Suddenly a bugler played the haunting

melody of the *degüello*, and Ian and Emerada stared as a red flag was raised and fluttered in the breeze—the Mexican signal that promised no mercy to the Alamo defenders. They knew that every man within those walls would be put to the sword—the defenders must know it, too.

"What you did to me was worse than any death you could imagine." Ian nodded toward the Alamo. "Men are dying in there, and I should be with them."

She dropped the dipper back in the bucket and set it on the grass. "Why? So you could die with them?"

"Yes, damn it! It's my duty." His eyes were misty, and she could see his agony. "I beg you, let me go so I can die with them."

Pity rose up inside her, and she was touched so deeply by his torment that she considered honoring his request. But she could not bear to think of those beautiful blue eyes closed in death. "No, I will not do it. You are Santa Anna's prisoner."

Ian shook his head as if to clear it and stared at the rising smoke around the Alamo. "Poor brave fools, they are all but dead now."

"I know," she said sadly. "I wish I could do something, but no one can help them now. Not even Houston. If he were here, he would be slaughtered with them. And so would you if I released you."

"Why should you care?" he asked coldly.

"You have your silk tent and your president lover."

Her dark eyes flamed with resentment. "You know nothing about me, Ian McCain. Apparently you have not yet learned that things are not always what they seem."

Her statement jarred him. Houston had said the same words to him. Ian noticed for the first time how tired she looked; there were bloodstains on her gown, and even on her hands. He realized that she'd been helping out in the field hospital. No, he didn't know her.

"Well," he said after a long silence, "perhaps Travis and Bowie can slow Santa Anna up a bit so Houston can pull his men together."

She turned to look at the bastion where the Alamo defenders were positioned and watched as a column of brave Mexican infantrymen attempted to storm the walls against a shower of bullets and cannon fire.

"It is a horrible thing to watch men die, Ian McCain. So many good men on both sides will lose their lives, and for what?" She reached down, picked up a fistful of dirt, and allowed it to sift through her fingers. "For this?"

Suddenly there was renewed urgency in Ian's voice. "Cut me loose! Let me die at the side of my fellow soldiers!"

She turned to him, wanting so badly to touch his face, to bring him comfort. "I cannot do that, Ian. There is no reason for you to die uselessly."

109

"If you have any human feelings left in you, help me escape," he implored. "I can't live with this horror! Nothing could be worse than watching men I know die and being helpless to do anything about it."

"I cannot help you."

His eyes bore into hers. "I didn't think you would, dancer. If our roles were reversed, I would show you no mercy either."

"I know." She noticed that Ian had been positioned so he was forced to watch the destruction of the Alamo. "I will see that you are given food and water."

"Do not trouble yourself. Do you think I could eat when men are dying?" His gaze went back to the Alamo, where a Mexican cannon had just blown away part of the outer wall. "Oh, God, this is my punishment," he said, lowering his head in shame. "This is what I deserve."

"Why should God punish you?"

He raised his head. His eyes were mesmerizing as he stared into hers.

"I deserve to be court-martialed for betraying my command." He slumped against the ropes. "I thought only of you when I should have been behind those walls, with Travis and Bowie," he whispered.

She reached out to him, feeling his pain in her very soul. But her hand dropped to her side. She didn't fully understand his words. He was a tormented man, and she could not help him. "Events happen for a reason, Ian. Even the outcome of war is in God's hands. It was not meant that you should die in that place."

"You don't understand. No woman could."

"I understand better than you think I do, Ian McCain." She felt the ground tremble when a twenty-pounder raked the walls of the Alamo. "You do not have to be a man to know about duty and honor."

Ian watched her walk away, and he swore under his breath. She was in his blood, behind his every action. He'd tried to convince himself that what he'd done the night he had entered her tent had been for duty's sake, but he knew better.

She was with him night and day. When he was asleep, she dominated his dreams, and when he was awake, his thoughts were all too often of her.

He watched as Mexican soldiers made another charge at the Alamo. How long could it be before they breached those walls and killed every man inside?

Chapter Eight

It was long after sundown when the continuous shelling that had lasted for twelve days suddenly ceased. Ian had been moved to a tent at the back of the Mexican lines, and he could no longer see what was happening. The silence was deafening, and he wondered if the Alamo had fallen.

If only someone would tell him what was happening. Emerada had not come near him since the day he had pleaded with her to free him. Now he wished she would come so he could learn the fate of the men at the Alamo.

He pulled and yanked on his ropes, but they would not budge. Sometime around midnight he fell into a troubled sleep.

* * *

Ian was jarred awake and wondered what had awakened him. It was still dark, but he knew it wouldn't be long until sunrise. He heard small-arms fire, but no heavy cannon. The Mexican forces must be storming the walls of the Alamo in an attempt to surprise the defenders. He sat there in the dark, feeling helpless, knowing in his heart that this was the final assault.

He now heard the rumble of a distant cannon and realized that the defenders were fighting back. It was hell, sitting there helpless while his compatriots died. It was certain that they had put up a valiant fight. They had held off superior Mexican forces for thirteen days.

After several hours the shooting stopped, and all he could hear were excited voices.

"Oh, God," he prayed, feeling shame to the very depths of his soul. "Why couldn't I die with them?"

Later in the day Ian smelled a sickening stench and he knew that it was all over, and the bodies of the valiant defenders of the Alamo were being burned. He thought of Travis and Bowie, Jim Bonham, Isaac Baker, and so many others that he hadn't even known. He'd heard rumors that David Crockett, from Tennessee, had been among the defenders. If that was so, then he would be dead, too.

How long he sat there, brooding, he didn't

know. But suddenly the tent flap was pushed aside and Emerada appeared.

"Shh," she cautioned as she removed a knife from her belt and cut through his ropes. "I have brought you a horse packed with supplies. You must leave at once. The Alamo has fallen. All are dead!"

The ropes dropped away and Ian rubbed his wrists to restore circulation. "Why are you freeing me now when it no longer matters? Why not before, when my death would mean something? I can no longer help the men at the Alamo." His throat closed, and he had to swallow several times before he could speak again. "Go away!"

"You do not have time to question me or refuse my offer. If you remain here, you will be killed. Some of the soldiers are beyond the control of their officers because they have lost brothers, uncles, fathers to the rebels. They are killing every American they find." She shuddered. "Go now, while you can."

"What will your lover think when he finds out you have released me?"

"That is not your worry. Your best chance is to skirt the town and ride north. It will soon be sundown, and then perhaps you can lose yourself in the hills."

He grabbed her arm and twisted the knife out of her hand. "We, you and I, will ride north and hide in the hills." He placed the knife at her throat. "You are coming with me."

114

"This is not necessary, Ian." There was urgency in her voice. "You don't understand—I must remain here!"

His arm tightened around her and he pulled her toward the opening, the knife still at her throat. "Don't call out," he warned.

Ian carefully looked left and right. No one was about, so he forced Emerada toward the horse and lifted her into the saddle. Sliding the knife in his belt, he mounted behind her and urged the horse into a gallop.

Emerada had chosen the animal well. The gelding carried the two of them with ease. His strides were long, and soon they left the encampment behind. Ian stopped when he got to the top of a hill and looked down at the devastating sight.

Sad and angry, he saw the crumbled walls, with fire licking at what was left of the Alamo. Where only hours ago men had fought as enemies, they were now united in death.

Emerada shifted her position so she could see Ian's face. "This is a sad day for both sides. It is my belief that this battle will be remembered by brave men everywhere. There were honorable acts, deeds of valor and heroism on both sides."

"When it is all said, they are just dead men." Ian paused as if he could not go on. Finally he said, "I should have been among their number."

"It was not meant for you to die, or you would be dead."

"You took that choice out of my hands. I'll never forgive you for that."

She turned her head forward and felt the sting of tears. "I would rather have you hate me than see you dead."

He stiffened. "Why?"

"I do not know. It just seems that our lives have become intertwined. I did not want it to be so, but it happened."

Ian had a sudden, horrible thought. "Tell me quickly, what happened to the women and children who were in the Alamo?"

"Most of them left days ago. There was one American woman and her daughter who remained with her husband. I am sorry, but I do not know her name. Santa Anna spared them and provided an escort to see them to safety."

"And I suppose, in your eyes, that makes him a compassionate man."

"I will not discuss Santa Anna with you."

He jerked on the reins and turned the horse northward, away from the burning funeral pyre, away from death and destruction.

Emerada could feel the tension in Ian. She leaned back against him, and felt his unsteady intake of breath. He was grieving for his fallen friends, and she was grieving for the dead on both sides of the war.

She rested her head against his shoulder, enveloped by his strong arms. She took a deep breath, wishing she could be absorbed into his body so she would feel no more pain.

He shoved her forward as if her touch was unwelcome. Emerada smothered a sob. Ian thought he was escaping with Santa Anna's mistress.

They had been riding for hours before Ian thought it would be safe to stop. He dismounted, holding his arms up for Emerada, and she slid into them. He quickly set her on her feet.

Ian saw Emerada stagger and catch her balance. She must be tired, but knowing her, she'd probably rather die than say so.

Ian had expected her to plead with him to release her, but she hadn't. Apparently she had accepted whatever her fate would be at his hands. He was raging inside. He could never forgive himself for neglecting his duty. Even so, there was something within him that made him want to reach out and comfort Emerada. It didn't matter that Santa Anna was her lover; she still fascinated him.

Emerada leaned against a tree and gazed back the way they'd come. "There is food in the saddlebag if you are hungry," she told him.

"Are you hungry?"

"I couldn't eat a bite." She gave a weary sigh and dropped down on the ground. "I just can't get the sight of all those men out of my mind. I see the horror of it even when I close my eyes."

"Did you betray Travis and Bowie?"

117

"You would not believe me no matter what I told you."

"No. I wouldn't."

Emerada looked into the clear sky that sparkled with stars. "It is difficult to believe that so many men died today, men who watched the sun come up this morning, but who will never see another sunrise."

"We'll camp here. It's as good a place as any," Ian said gruffly. He unstrapped the saddlebag and tossed it on the ground. She had thought of everything. There was even a rifle with a box of bullets and two canteens of water.

Emerada silently watched him.

After he'd unsaddled and hobbled the horse, he sat beside her, rummaging through the saddlebag for food. "I dare not light a fire, because someone might see it."

Still she said nothing.

He found two hard biscuits and handed one to her.

She shook her head. "Could I use enough water to wash my hands?"

"Just like a woman," he mumbled. He handed her a canteen.

"It's just that I was helping with the wounded today and the blood . . . " She shuddered. "I didn't take time to wash because I had to get you out of camp."

Ian felt as if he'd been kicked in the stomach. He took the canteen and poured the water for her. She let the water run through her fingers and onto the ground. "I feel like Pilate," she whispered, rubbing her hands together. "I will never get the blood off my hands."

"We all have blood on our hands, Emerada," Ian said, wondering what guilt had brought about such a revelation. "With the passing of time, perhaps we will both find absolution."

Emerada could feel a sob building up within her. She hadn't cried at all during the horrible attack on the Alamo. Now she couldn't seem to stop. She leaned her head against the tree, and the tears flowed freely.

She felt Ian bend down next to her and awkwardly place his hand on her shoulder. "You are so young to have witnessed such a sight. It wasn't your doing."

She shoved his hand away and stood up, glaring at him. "No, it was not my fault! I leave the killing and defacing of the land to soldiers such as you. You should look to yourself, and to men like you, for the answers."

A muscle tightened in his jaw. "Your lover won today, but at a terrible cost."

Emerada walked away from him and rested her head against the trunk of a tree, hurting terribly inside. If she had it all to do over again, would she still take the same path? Yes, she would. She hadn't been beaten yet. Of course, it might be difficult to explain to Santa Anna why she and Ian had disappeared at the same time. He would surely be suspicious.

She took in a deep breath and stared upward. To get Santa Anna to trust her again, she would have to let him make love to her. She shivered as she thought of his hands on her, his lips on hers.

How would she bear it?

Emerada was prepared to do anything to destroy Santa Anna. She would even sacrifice her beliefs, bury her conscience deep, and remember only that the man must be destroyed. She would have to become what Ian already thought she was—Santa Anna's mistress.

A short time later, she retraced her steps and found that Ian had piled up grass and was spreading a blanket over it.

"It'll be softer than the ground," he said without looking up. "I'm afraid we will have to share the blanket, since we only have the one."

"I didn't expect to be going with you, so I did not bring one for myself," she reminded him dryly.

"Make yourself comfortable. I am going to see to the horse."

"I packed oats in the leather bag."

"It seems you thought of everything," he said bitingly.

Emerada lay down on the soft bed of grass, pulled the blanket over her, and thought it felt better than a bed with Santa Anna's silk sheets on it. She turned onto her side, thinking that this had been the longest day of her life. Would she ever be able to sleep without seeing all those dead faces? She squeezed her eyes together tightly, but she trembled with fear. She needed someone to hold her, someone to assure her that this long night would pass and tomorrow would bring an end to the terrible war.

But would it?

When Ian returned, he lay down beside her. She offered him part of the blanket and moved as far away from him as she could get while still keeping her share of the blanket. He could not know that she ached for him to reach out to her, to draw her into his arms and hold her until she could stop trembling.

"Did you steal the horse?" he asked after a long, awkward silence. "Or did your lover give him to you?"

She ran her fingers through her hair, trying to remove some of the tangles. "I did not steal it. As to the other, you have already drawn your own conclusion."

He ignored her anger. He needed to talk, and it didn't matter what he said or what she answered. "He's a fine horse. Must have cost someone a hatful of gold."

"My—er . . . I once knew a family who raised blooded horses. Soledad is from their herd."

"Soledad? Why did you name a horse 'Lonely'?"

"When he was a colt, he did not want to be with the other horses. But he would follow—" She broke off for a moment. "He would follow the owner's daughter around like a faithful puppy. It was quite a sight."

121

He could tell she was troubled, and he was trying to take her mind off the battle today. He had been hard on her, and he was feeling guilty for that.

"It's a wonder the daughter could give him up, since he was so faithful to her."

"Life is full of difficulties." She turned over onto her side again and closed her eyes. "I want to sleep now."

Ian knew she would have trouble sleeping, just as he would. He had loaded the rifle earlier, and he placed it within easy reach. There were bound to be deserters spread throughout the hills, and he didn't intend to be surprised by one of them.

He heard Emerada sigh and had the strongest urge to reach out and touch her, to bring her some semblance of comfort. "If they knew my bed partner, I would be the envy of every man in Texas and Mexico tonight."

She knew him well enough by now to guess that he was going to say something insulting. "Believe me, you are just one of many," she replied, hoping to nettle him. "I am practiced at lovemaking, as you have probably guessed."

"I'm not surprised," he murmured, wondering why he was so angry. "You know too much about men not to have learned it in the bedroom."

"That does not mean that I will welcome any unwanted attention from you," she said hurriedly, hoping she hadn't given him the wrong impression. "I choose my men carefully."

"Go to sleep, San Antonio Rose; you are safe with me. I have never been one to fancy another man's leavings, especially not if that man is Santa Anna."

No one could make her as mad as Ian. "I never invited you to my bed, and I never will. I pick and choose whom I take for a lover."

He turned his back with a jerky motion, and she smiled. She had gotten under his skin at last, even if she had told a lie to do it.

Chapter Nine

In her sleep, Emerada gravitated toward the warmth of Ian's body. She fit into the curve of his arms and sighed contentedly when she snuggled tighter against him.

Her silken hair fell across his face, and he could smell some sweet, exotic scent. Carefully he reached up with the intention of removing her hair from his cheek, but when he touched the silken strand, he caressed it, loverlike.

His body came alive as if someone had lit a fire inside him. Since the first moment he'd seen her in Houston's camp, he'd wanted to kiss those defiant lips. He wanted to crush her in his arms, awaken her passion, to make her feel some of the torment she'd put him through.

Ian lowered the strand of hair from his lips,

his body trembling. She stirred something within him that burned through his whole being.

Emerada moved her face, and her lips were only inches from his. He could feel her breath on his mouth, and he sat up quickly to keep from taking her into his arms.

She merely moaned in her sleep without waking. Arranging the blanket over her so it would be a double thickness, he walked down the hill to where the horse was tethered, needing to put some distance between himself and Emerada. This dancer who admitted to being with many men had fired his passion as no other woman ever had. He stood for a long moment, trying to clear his mind.

What strange circumstance put him and Emerada on the same path? he wondered. What twist of fate made him want her so badly that it hurt?

He heard a twig snap and gazed up the hill where Emerada slept, thinking she might have awakened. She was sitting up, probably awakened by the same noise he'd heard. Perhaps it was only an animal.

Damn it, he'd left the gun behind!

Taking care to remain in the shadows, Ian climbed the hill. He couldn't be sure it was an animal, and Emerada was alone.

Emerada looked around for Ian, thinking his movement must have awakened her. She wasn't concerned. He would hardly have forced her to come with him and then abandoned her here in the wilderness.

"Well, well, Burt, lookee here at what we got us," a man remarked, stepping from behind a laurel bush and squinting at her in the half darkness. He was soon joined by his companion.

"We got ourselves a little señorita, Gip. Hey, honey, you all alone out here?"

Emerada jumped to her feet, frantically looking about for Ian. The strangers had the appearance of buffalo hunters, but they were too far south to hunt those shaggy beasts. Fear tugged at her mind as one man stepped in front of her and took her chin in his grimy hand, turning her face to the moonlight.

"You're a real beauty," Burt said, his gaze raking her delicate face. "I ain't never had me no woman as pretty as you."

"I get her after you, Gip," Burt said, dipping down and scooping up the rifle Ian had left behind. "I'm gonna have me a real good time with her."

Emerada was frozen in place. She should have run when she had the chance. The filthy man ran one hand over her breasts, pinching and kneading until she winced in pain.

"Please do not do that, señor," she said, shuddering in revulsion. She tried to back away from him, but his grip merely tightened.

"Well, now, don't she talk American all fancy like. A looker, and she's got schooling, too." His foul breath fanned her face, and when she turned her head away from him, he wheezed with laughter. "You're gonna like me, little señorita."

"I don't think so." A cold, steely voice spoke from the shadows. "Let her go," Ian warned.

Both men whirled around to see a tall man just behind them. "Who'd you be?" the man called Gip asked, noticing with satisfaction that the stranger didn't have a gun.

"I'm the man who's about to end your miserable life, you bastard. Take your hands off her!"

"Now I don't 'zackly see it like that," Burt said, displaying the rifle. "There's two of us, and only one of you, and this here must be your gun." He chuckled. "What're you gonna do, throw rocks at us, scare us to death?"

"You're wasting time," Ian said coolly. "You can either drop the guns—both of you—and ride away, or die. It is of little matter to me either way. You decide."

There was something unsettling about the calmness with which Ian spoke, and Gip laughed nervously. Still, he put on a face of bravado for his companion—after all, he was holding a gun on the stranger. He elbowed Burt in the ribs. "Tell him we done killed us five Mexicans, down to the creek this morning."

"Back-shot, no doubt," Ian said, glancing at the stars as if he were gauging time. "You have ten seconds to release her and ride away."

"I'll just shoot ya dead now and have done with it," Burt replied, cocking the rifle and aiming it at Ian's head. "Don't worry 'bout the little señorita here, 'cause when you're dead, Gip and me'll take care of her."

In that moment, Ian leaped forward so swiftly that both men were taken by surprise. He grabbed Gip's arm and slammed him into Burt with such force that both men lost their balance and tumbled to the ground, their arms and legs entangled.

Unfortunately, Emerada went down with them. Ian stepped across them, kicked their guns out of their reach, and picked up his rifle. He then extended his hand to Emerada and pulled her up, pushing her behind him, all the while keeping the rifle trained on the two men.

"While you're down there, take your boots off," Ian said.

"What! You want our boots?"

"Take them off, I said!"

Both men scrambled to comply, first one boot and then the other. They knew by the tone of his voice that he'd shoot them dead if they didn't do as he ordered.

"Get their guns and put them in the saddlebags, Emerada. Then saddle the horse and lead it up here."

After she had retrieved the guns and rushed down the hill to the horse, he spoke to Burt and Gip. "Kick your boots over here."

Again, both men did as he asked. But Gip

found his voice. "What're you gonna do with us?"

"I thought about shooting you bastards after what you tried to do to the lady, but you just aren't worth the trouble. So I've decided to take your horses, guns, and boots."

Burt glared at Ian. "Then you'd better just shoot us. Without our guns, we're as good as dead."

"That's about the way I figure it," Ian agreed. "If hostile Indians, Mexican soldiers, or wild animals don't get you, you will have a long, hard walk to civilization without boots."

"You son of a—"

"Yes, I know," Ian interrupted Gip. "I don't care that much for you either."

Burt was looking Ian over carefully, as if memorizing his face. "I'd kinda like to know your name, stranger, so I'll know who to come looking for if I live through this."

By now Emerada had ridden up, leading the two other horses.

Ian nodded. "I won't be hard to find. Name's Ian McCain."

Both men gaped at him. "The Raven's Claw!"

"Some have called me that."

"We're real sorry, Colonel. We'd never have touched your woman if'n we'd knowed it was you. Hell, we was on our way to join up with General Houston and give him a hand."

"Don't trouble about that," Ian warned them. "Houston doesn't want your cut of man in his army. If you do get out of these hills alive, I'll make certain that he hears about tonight."

"But we was just funning. We didn't really mean—"

Ian turned away and mounted one of the men's horses. "I'd walk to the west, if I were you. It's of no matter to me, but the Mexican army is swarming all over the place. They will kill any Americans they find."

He nudged the horse in the flanks, and he and Emerada rode over the hill. It was some time before distance and the wind drowned out the curses howled by Gip and Burt.

They rode until sunrise, then stopped to rest the horses.

"Ian," Emerada said, sliding off her horse. "Thank you."

"Forget it," he said.

She trembled with revulsion. "I thought they were going to . . . to . . . "

He looked at her with compassion and concern. "I know. It's over—put it behind you."

She was shivering, and her teeth chattered. "Could we have a fire to make coffee? I would love something hot to drink."

Ian looked about him to estimate the safety of their position. They were on a rise, and he could see the valley for miles around. "I think we can chance it. If you would gather wood for a fire, I'll tend to the horses. Make certain the wood is dry so it won't smoke much."

She nodded.

He placed his hand on her shoulder. "Do I have your word that you won't try to escape?"

"That is a promise I will never give." She removed the saddlebag containing the food. "You have my word that I will not try to escape until I have had something to eat and drink."

He laughed and led the horses away. Then he went through the possessions of the two men to see if there was anything they could use. They were a long way from Houston's compound, and the Indians he'd warned Gip and Burt about would also be a danger to him and Emerada. He discarded everything except foodstuff and guns. He then unsaddled one of the horses, hit it on the rump, and sent it galloping down the hill. They would be traveling fast and didn't need the extra horse.

Soon he smelled the aroma of fresh coffee and found Emerada humming as she presided over several slices of fatback that sizzled in an iron skillet. He rubbed his hands together and held them over the campfire to warm. "So you cook. I would not have numbered domestic chores among your accomplishments."

She blew a strand of dark hair out of her face and smiled at him as she turned the meat. "Perhaps it would be better if you withheld judgment until you have tasted the food."

"We had better eat fast and find shelter." He

131

nodded toward the eastern horizon. "There's a storm brewing."

Dark storm clouds were gathering to the east, and the weather fit Emerada's mood. She found Ian staring at her, and her cheeks flushed. She focused on pouring him a cup of coffee to hide her sudden shyness.

When Ian reached for the coffee, he accidentally brushed her hand. She felt as if her heart were going to jump through the wall of her chest.

She wished for her Aunt Dilena. She would know why Ian stirred all these unwelcome emotions within her.

The rain pelted down with a stinging force. Although it was the middle of the afternoon, it was almost dark as Emerada and Ian rode single-file down a steep embankment.

Emerada pulled her shawl over her head and hunched her shoulders to avoid getting wet, but nothing helped—she was soaked through. At times the rain was so hard that she couldn't see past her horse's head. They couldn't go much longer in this weather, so when she reached the bottom of the hill, she halted her mount and waited for Ian to draw even with her.

"I know a place where we can find shelter." She had to shout to be heard above the wind. "It's no more than two hours away."

Ian nodded. "Lead on."

"Stay close to me so we won't be separated.

There will be treacherous water crossings and perilous quagmires that must be avoided at all costs. They will be even worse with this rain."

"I will try to keep up," he said, nodding. "You know this country better than I do."

Chapter Ten

Because of the constant rain and the wind gusts, it took more than the two hours that Emerada had predicted to reach shelter. Both were relieved when their horses' hooves clattered over cobbled stones.

Emerada seemed to know where she was going—she guided them toward some kind of brick structure. She dismounted, shoved open the wide double doors, and led her horse into the shadowy interior.

Even though it was dark inside, she had no trouble feeling her way. She took the reins of both horses and led them into a stall. She unfastened her horse's cinch, and Ian, following her lead, unsaddled his horse.

Next she lit a lantern that hung on a rusted nail, and a ring of light encircled them.

"You seem to be familiar with this place," he said, throwing his saddle over a railing.

Emerada seemed to be struggling with her saddle, but when Ian reached out to help her, she glared at him and lifted it onto the railing herself. "I have been here before," she answered.

Ian glanced about the building. It had seen better days, but it had been well constructed. "This must have been grand in its day," he said, looking at the finished walls and the stone floors.

"I am afraid that neglect has taken its toll. But *sí*, it was grand in its day." She looked somewhat sad as she ran her hand over a rusted pitchfork that leaned against the wall. "It is as if no one ever lived here."

"What is this place?" Ian asked, noticing the rusty nails that protruded from the decaying wooden stalls.

"This is all merely a ghostly reminder of what once was a ranch where a family lived, laughed, and loved."

He looked about for a suitable place to build a fire. He saw a rusted pitchfork, a broken shovel, and a corroded curry comb. "No one had been here for some time."

"No, they have not," she answered abruptly. "The family is all gone."

135

"You have to get out of these wet clothes, or you'll catch a chill," he warned. He saw Emerada wince when he broke off some of the rotted wood to build a fire. "You don't think the owners will mind, do you?"

"No. They will not mind." She placed her hands on her hips in a defiant stance. "But I will not take my clothing off for you!"

He gave her a sideways glance. "Don't be worried about your virtue where I am concerned. I just don't want a sick woman to slow me down."

She glared at him as he removed the blanket from the saddlebags and threw it at her. "It's a little damp around the edges, but not as wet as your clothing. You can undress in one of those stalls." He nodded toward the back of the stable. "Don't worry. I won't look."

She took the blanket from him, seeing the wisdom in his suggestion. "What about you?"

"Are you worried about me?" he asked, grinning.

She stomped away, wishing him outside in the storm. "Your health is no concern of mine."

"No?"

"No!"

"Then why did you help me escape Santa Anna?"

Emerada ignored his question because she didn't really know the answer to that. Her fingers were numb from cold, and she fumbled to unhook her gown. She hung her clothing over

136

the stall and draped the blanket about her like a serape.

When she returned to Ian, he had a fire going, and she moved close to warm herself. He bent down beside her and tossed more wood on the flames, sending sparks flying.

"Ian, would you like to hear something amusing, if anything can be amusing about the deaths at the Alamo?"

"Suppose you enlighten me," he said grimly. "I found nothing humorous about it."

"You will this. Santa Anna called the battle of the Alamo a small affair, and Colonel Navarro remarked that another such victory would cost them the war."

"I doubt that would be much comfort to Travis and the others who died at the mission."

"Travis knew he was going to die; he chose death over dishonor."

Ian shivered and moved close to the fire, warming his hands. "I hope the folks who own this spread won't care that we are burning it down for firewood."

She stared into the fire as if she saw something he couldn't. "No, they would not mind."

"Do you know the family?"

"*Sí*, I knew them." She shook her head, overcome with melancholy. "I knew them very well. Talavera is the name of the ranch. The horse I ride was born and trained here."

They had both settled near the fire and stared into the flames. Finally Ian spoke. "Tell me about the family—where are they now?" He wasn't really interested in who had once lived there. He just liked listening to the sound of Emerada's voice. He had always been intrigued by her soft accent.

She shrugged. "There is not much to tell. I am hungry now."

He stood up and laughed as he reached for the saddlebags. "I wouldn't want you to be hungry. It might set off your temper," he said with irony.

"I admit that I have a temper," she said. "Josifina usually chastises me because she says a lady does not display her anger. I am afraid I have always been a disappointment to her."

"Josifina? Who is she?"

She frowned, thinking of the woman who had protected and bullied her. "She was my *niñera* when I was small; then she became my duenna. Now she is a trusted friend and servant. She must be wondering what has happened to me."

Ian smiled as he placed the coffeepot on a flat rock he'd settled among the flames and handed Emerada a piece of hard cheese.

"Why do you smile, Ian?" she wanted to know.

"I was trying to imagine you with a duenna, or for that matter, with anyone who could chastise you into submission."

"That is because you do not know Josifina. She could take you to task, Ian. You would do better tangling with those two buffalo hunters than with Josifina."

He reclined on his elbow and watched the firelight play across her midnight-colored hair which was beginning to dry and curl about her face. "Tell me more about the family who lived here. Why did they go away?"

She was silent for a moment, as if trying to think how to answer him. "You might say the members of this family were the first casualties of this war."

"In what way?"

She raised her eyes to his. "Are you really interested?"

"Yes—very."

"The people who lived here at Talavera were named Felipe and Maretta de la Rosa. When Felipe was a young man, he went to New Orleans, and there he met and fell in love with a beautiful Frenchwoman, Maretta Cloutier. They were married, and she came back to Tejas with him. Eventually they had three sons and a daughter."

"You did know them well."

"Very well. The sons grew tall and straight in the Tejas sunshine, approaching life with honor and self-respect, while the daughter was spoiled by the whole family. In her thirteenth year she was granted permission to go to New Orleans to be with her mother's sister. Later the girl sailed to France with her Aunt Dilena, who was a famous dancer and was going on a European tour."

"She is a dancer like yourself?"

"No, not like me. In Europe it is different from here. A dancer there can be admired and respected. So it was with Dilena. She was so beautiful and adored that while in France, students from the university unhitched her horses and pulled her coach. She danced for all the kings and queens of Europe, and she was worshiped wherever she traveled."

Ian was fascinated by Emerada's tale. He'd even forgotten about the coffee, and it boiled over. After he removed the pot and poured them both a cup of the hot brew, he asked, "What became of the daughter? Did she become a dancer as well?"

"That is not important. Her visit to France turned into years because her mother was stricken with typhoid fever and died. Then there was talk of war, so her father wanted her to remain safely in France with her aunt. Later, her aunt bought a home in New Orleans so the girl could be close to her father and brothers. But as much as she loved her aunt, and loved to travel, she always yearned for the time she would return to Talavera."

"Is she in France or New Orleans?"

Emerada was so caught up in her narration that she continued as if Ian hadn't spoken. "Once a year, the month of her birthday, June, her father and brothers would visit her in New Orleans. She was so proud of them, her three handsome brothers and her wonderful father."

She paused for a moment, as if she were gathering her thoughts.

Ian could sense a change in her, a heavy sadness. "You don't have to go on if it's too painful."

"I want to tell you. I have never said any of this aloud. It might help."

"Go on, then."

"The father loved Mexico, but he loved Tejas more. He taught his sons and daughter to love freedom and hate tyranny. He detested Santa Anna and what he was doing to the people and the country. Felipe de la Rosa was a friend to Stephen Austin, a good man who really cared about people—a gentle man of quiet taste and high ideals. Señor Austin swore fidelity to Mexico and considered himself a citizen. But he soon became disillusioned by the heavy hand of government. He traveled to Mexico with a petition for a separate state government for Tejas. On his way to Mexico City, he stopped to pass the night with the de la Rosa family, as was often his habit."

"I know what happened to Austin," Ian said. "But what happened to this family?"

"Señor Austin was imprisoned in Mexico City. The de la Rosa family that once lived, loved, and laughed here—the father and three sons, and any servant who tried to come to their aid that day—were murdered by Santa Anna's men. The beautiful hacienda was burned, the livestock confiscated, and the land laid to waste."

"My God! Is this true?"

She looked at him with tears in her eyes. "Sí, it is true, Ian McCain. They are all dead."

He didn't know at what point he had begun to realize that she was speaking of her own family, and she was the daughter. "Tell me about the daughter, Emerada."

"The daughter," she said, as if coming out of a trance, "selfish creature that she was, died with them that day. She is as dead as the hopes for freedom in Tejas."

"Why do you call her selfish?"

She lowered her head to her knees and began to sob. "Because she had returned from France, but she remained in New Orleans with her aunt instead of coming home to her family. She should have been with her father and brothers and shared their fate." She rolled her head from side to side, locked in total misery. "She is more dead than any one of them—she can't feel, she can't think, she can do nothing until she destroys the man who is responsible for the deaths of her family."

It all came together in Ian's mind. She wasn't with Santa Anna because she loved him—she was with him because she wanted to destroy him! She was helping Houston because she saw in him her best hope for destroying the man who had ordered the deaths of her family.

He moved forward and embraced her. At first she was stiff in his arms, but he stroked her hair and spoke softly to her, and she finally relaxed against him, sobbing all the while.

She had experienced a terrible tragedy. She was alone, but for two servants who looked after her and an aunt somewhere in France. How she must have suffered every time Santa Anna put his hands on her, hating him as she did!

"The daughter is not dead," he said softly. "You, Emerada de la Rosa, are that daughter."

"I wanted to die," she cried. "Many times I prayed to die, but God was not so merciful." She blinked the tears from her eyes, wishing she could stop crying. "They were my family. Now all that they were and all that they would ever have been is lost." She shook her head. "I am nothing without them—nothing!"

He brushed her hair out of her face and kissed her cheek. It was a chaste kiss meant only to comfort. "They are alive as long as they live in your thoughts and in your heart, Emerada. I know how you feel."

"How could you—how could anyone?"

"Emerada, look at me." He tilted her chin. "When the men at the Alamo died, and I was still alive, I wanted to throw myself on the sword of the first Mexican soldier I saw. But I know now it would have been useless. Yes, I'll always feel I should have died with them, but it was out of my hands, just as the fate of your family was out of your hands. I am not saying that my tragedy was as severe as yours, but it was a tragedy nonetheless."

"Yes, but—"

"Shh," he said, pulling her back against him. "We both have a mission, Emerada. We have Texas."

"I want my family back."

"You can't have them back, except in your memory. Keep them alive in your thoughts." He raised her head and looked into her eyes. "Lay down your sword, little warrior, and let me take it up for you."

Her eyes widened. "I do not understand."

"Let me take care of you," he repeated.

She jerked away from him. "You are asking me to be your mistress?"

He laughed and shook his head. "No, that's not my intention. I'll settle for being your friend or standing in the place of a brother."

That thought brought her no comfort. She didn't want to be Ian's sister. She wanted—she wanted—she wanted him to love her. But why? She didn't love him. She had no time for love. She had to see that Santa Anna did not destroy any more families, as he had hers. She had to get away from Ian and make her way back to Santa Anna and try to convince him that she had not run away with Ian.

"I had three brothers. I do not want any others."

"A friend then?"

She agreed with a nod of her head. She had to somehow make him think he could trust her so she could escape. "I will be your friend, for now. But the time will come when that may change."

He didn't feel like a brother or a friend. He wanted to kiss her into submission and make love to her. But that was not what she needed at the moment. She was like a crushed flower, and he wanted to see her bloom again.

"You have befriended me several times, Emerada, although I am sure it was the last thing you wanted to do. Did you know that there is an old Arabic proverb that says if you save a man's life three times, he belongs to you?"

She smiled and then laughed out loud. "Oh, no, Raven's Claw! You are not going to make me permanently responsible for your life. You are forever walking on the edge, and you might just pull me in with you the next time you fall."

He leaned back against a pile of soft hay and pulled her back with him. "You haven't told me how you came to be the San Antonio Rose."

She chewed on the end of a piece of straw pensively, as if considering how to answer him. "It was really quite simple. I knew Santa Anna had a weakness for women, but I could never just walk up to him and introduce myself. I decided to use my dancing because I am quite good at it."

"Yes. You are. But that still doesn't answer my question."

"My aunt was in Europe for a year, and she thought I was safely in New Orleans. For obvious reasons, I could not use my real name when I went to Mexico City, so I chose San Antonio Rose. I was amazed when my name grew and so many were eager to have me perform. But I still could not get near Santa Anna. So I came to Tejas. The rest you know."

"I doubt I know everything. There is much you haven't told me."

The tension that had knotted her muscles since she had came back to Talavera slowly dissolved as his soothing touch made her aware of him in a new way.

"What about your aunt, Emerada? Aren't you afraid that she will find out what you are doing?"

She looked embarrassed. "Aunt Dilena thinks I am in school in New Orleans."

"School?" He pulled away from her. "How old are you, Emerada?"

"I am nineteen—or I will be on my next birthday."

He stared at her, wondering how many other girls her age could have accomplished what Emerada had. She always seemed so fearless and capable of taking care of herself. Except for now, when he was seeing the vulnerable side of her. "Surely your aunt must be worried about you."

"She will be returning to New Orleans in early summer. I hope she will understand why I had to come to Tejas."

"She would be proud of you, Emerada. But

she has every reason to worry, too." He hugged her to him, laughing. "I was about to say you needed someone to keep you out of trouble. Let it be me."

Warmth spread through her, and she wanted him to kiss her, to touch her, to possess her whole body. She did not know that her eyes revealed much of what she was feeling when she looked at him.

Ian drew in his breath, and his grip tightened about her. He didn't know who made the first move, but their lips touched and they pressed their bodies together, needing to be even closer.

Chapter Eleven

"You do sorely tempt me, little dancer," he breathed in her ear, nestling his cheek against hers. "There is fire in you that would delight any man."

"Hold me, Ian," she said pleadingly. "Hold me very tight." Her hand went around his neck; her lips parted, inviting his kiss.

Ian gathered his thoughts and pulled back, straightening the blanket firmly about her shoulders. He hesitated, reaching for the right words to express what he was feeling and hoping he could make her understand. "Under other circumstances, I would want to make love to you. But this is not the time or place. I would only be taking unfair advantage of your vulnerability."

His rejection cut her deeply. "I am sorry if I

threw myself at you." She ducked her head and her hair fell forward, curtaining her face. "I feel so ashamed."

He moved closer to the fire and away from her. "You have done nothing to be ashamed of. I'm the one who let it go too far. I would be no better than a libertine if I took advantage of you."

Emerada assumed that Ian was trying to be kind and not hurt her feelings. He just didn't have the same feelings for her that she had for him. "I never thought to ask if there is a woman you love."

Ian was silent as he considered her question. He thought of pretty Pauline Harlandale, who was nothing like Emerada—Emerada was flame and filled with passion, while Pauline was ladylike and proper. Emerada could handle herself in dangerous situations, while Pauline would be terrified at the first sign of danger. Emerada fired his blood, and Pauline never had. He realized that Pauline had not crossed his mind in weeks—not since the first day he'd met this raven-haired beauty who was rarely out of his thoughts.

He tossed a stick of wood on the fire and watched the sparks fly, deciding to answer Emerada's question as honestly as he could.

"There is someone I have known most of my life. Her name is Pauline Harlandale. We have an understanding . . . of sorts. At least, her family and my mother expect us to marry."

149

Emerada just looked at him, her eyes luminous in the firelight. He held himself stiff, fighting the urge to take her in his arms again. He tried to recall how he'd planned to send for Pauline when this war was over so they could be married and settle down in Texas. At the moment, he was having trouble remembering Pauline's face. His blood had never burned when he was with her, as it did now with Emerada.

"It must be a great comfort to know where your life is going," she said.

At the moment, all Ian could think about was the wild sensations that were coursing through his body. He was thinking how softly her skin glowed in the firelight, and how he wanted to reach out and touch her. "What about you, Emerada?" he asked. "Do you have someone you care about?"

"When I left Tejas to live with my aunt, I was too young to think about love. When we are in residence in New Orleans, my aunt is always reclusive and we do not socialize. I believe it is her time to rest in mind and body and to learn new dances."

"And when you are in France?"

"There my aunt protects me, and Domingo and Josifina keep all men away from me." She flexed her tired muscles and sighed. "So I have had little chance to meet any man, much less lose my heart to one."

She tossed her long hair and fixed him with a hard glare. "The only man in my life at the moment is Santa Anna. I find that I am much more consumed by hatred than I ever could be by that trivial feeling called love."

Ian spoke with amazement. "You have never imagined yourself in love?"

"I know about the love I had for my family, but I know nothing of the love you speak of. Since returning to Tejas, I have had men say they loved me, while I knew that all they felt was lust for the dancer in me."

He felt his heart ache for her, and he resisted the urge to comfort her again. "I believe many men love you."

She turned to stare at him. "I do not even know what love is. Can you explain to me about the love that happens between a man and a woman?"

"That is a question you should ask a woman. I am not sure I can explain it to you, or if I really know."

"Josifina is the only woman I could ask, and she never married, so I am not sure she knows. Of course, Aunt Dilena knows about love— many men have loved her."

"Wouldn't your aunt disapprove of your . . . enticing Santa Anna to . . . " He rolled to his feet. "Damn it, don't answer that. It's none of my business what you do."

She stood up beside him. "Then why did you make me come with you?"

"I thought you were spying for Santa Anna. I wanted to make you admit it to Houston."

"And now?"

"I no longer believe that you are on Santa Anna's side in this war."

"Then you will let me go?"

He shook his head and moved to a wooden tub that was turned upside down, where he seated himself. "No, I can't do that either. You would be in danger if you went back now."

She dropped down beside him and arranged the blanket about her, knowing she would escape the first chance she got. He had taken her away from her mission, and she had to find a way to get back. "Tell me about yourself—what was your life like before you came to Tejas?" she asked, attempting to lure him into trusting her.

He removed his wet boots and placed them by the fire. "What was my life like before I met you?" he mused aloud.

"Why did you come to Tejas?"

"I was born in Virginia. My father was a member of the House of Burgesses and later became Thomas Jefferson's ambassador to some obscure South Sea island. He died before I was born." He paused as if he were having trouble with his voice. Then he said in an explosion of honesty. "If I am going to be honest, I will have to admit that my father never married my mother. I am what is known as a bastard."

She gasped, curling her fingers to keep from reaching out to him. "I . . . am sorry."

He glared at her. "Are you?"

"Not for the reason you think—I am sorry because it obviously brings you pain. It is of little matter to me."

"The pain has passed long ago. I don't know why I am telling you about this. I never told anyone else." He smiled at her. "It seems we are baring our souls tonight, little dancer."

"Was your life so bad?"

"Not at all. You see, my father was on his way back to America to marry my mother when his ship went down in a storm. I missed being legitimate by one week."

"It must have been a tragedy for your mother."

"Yes, it was. Sam Houston had received a letter from my father, telling him of his plans to marry my mother, who waited for him in Georgia. She took my father's name, and no one questioned the marriage or my birth. I suppose Houston's presence suppressed any doubt that might have occurred in anyone's mind. My mother went to Virginia, and the McCain family embraced her as my father's wife. My grandparents were very happy when I was born. They had no children but my father. And I was their only grandchild."

"Surely your mother did not tell you the facts of your birth."

"Of course not. It wasn't until six years ago when I overheard my mother and Houston talking. It was late one night, when they thought I was asleep. I never told either of them that I'd overheard their conversation."

"Why did General Houston help your mother?"

"Since he was my father's friend, I suppose he took it upon himself to rectify the happenstance of my birth." His gaze locked with hers. "Are you repulsed by my background?"

"Why should I be? You are the same person you were before I knew about your birth."

He avoided her eyes, not wanting Emerada to know that her acceptance of his circumstances moved him deeply. He had often wondered what Pauline would do if she knew the secret of his birth. "You are more generous than most people would be. I'm sure if my background were made public, I would find myself alone and friendless."

"You underestimate the impact you have on people. Knowing you, how could anyone care about such a triviality as the circumstance of your birth?"

His head swung around, and he looked at her for a moment before speaking. "For six years I have lived with the ghost of my parents' mistakes, and you just reduced it to a triviality." He laughed, feeling strangely lighthearted. "You are an uncommon woman, Emerada de la Rosa."

"You are fortunate to have General Houston," she said, deliberately changing the subject.

"In many ways, he has been my symbolic father through the years. Perhaps one day we will speak of my birth, but it never seems to be the right time."

"Can you not let the past go? It has little to do with the man you are today." She stared into the flickering firelight. "Houston is a man of great honor. I have felt that about him, and now that I have heard your story, I believe it even more." Unaware that she was doing so, she wound a lock of hair around her finger. "What about your mother—did she ever marry?"

"No. I don't believe she ever got over my father's death."

"So Houston brought you to Tejas with him?"

"No, he didn't bring me to Texas right away. To please my grandparents, I went to William and Mary College as my father had. Much to their dismay, in my third year I decided I wanted to attend West Point. Then, quite suddenly, last year the general sent for me." Ian smiled to himself. "My mother must have written to him that I needed guidance. She is a Southern lady who believes nothing good can be gained by going to a 'Yankee' military school."

Emerada was puzzled. "I did not know there was a division between the states in America."

"Only in some people's minds. Some people in the South talk about a country separate from the United States. Houston thinks nothing will ever come of it—he calls it mere saber rattling."

He watched her move back to the fire, settling herself close to its warmth. "This has been a night for confessions, little dancer."

"Please do not call me that. I detest it when you do."

He moved closer to the fire. His clothing was still wet, and he felt very uncomfortable. "Then I shall never call you that name again." His voice was strangely gentle. "I would not want to hurt you."

She dipped her head. Hurt her? For some reason, her heart felt as if it had been shattered into slivers of broken glass. She tried to think of the woman who waited for him back in Virginia. Did she know how fortunate she was to have the love of this extraordinary man?

"Did you learn to dance from your aunt?" Ian asked, taking up the thread of their conversation.

"Not at first. She hired dance instructors for me. She is often very indulgent with me, and I adore her. She and my mother were very close, and she tried to do for me what my mother would have liked."

"Do you miss France?"

"I miss my aunt—but France, no. Tejas is my home; this is where my family died, and this is where I want to die." She glanced up at him. "What about you? Do you miss Virginia?"

"Something happens to a man or a woman when they come to Texas. They either love it or they hate it. Those who hate it leave, and those who love it seem willing to die for it."

"Under which group do you fall—hate and leave, or love and die?" It seemed to her that his eyes became even bluer as he gazed back at her in astonishment.

"I took an oath to defend Texas with my life. So far I have done little to honor that oath."

"But you will. The main battle has not yet been fought. That one will be fought between Santa Anna and Houston, and truthfully, I do not know what the outcome will be. Surely Santa Anna has might on his side. And if you think about it the way he does, he also has right on his side. Tejas is the territory of Mexico. He is merely trying to keep what is his."

"Under other circumstances, Emerada, and with another ruler who represented all the people, Texas would have basked in Mexico's glory. But look what happened to your family merely because they welcomed a friend into their home. No man should have to live in fear because of who his friends are—or for that matter, what his beliefs are. There are many people who have suffered the same fate as your family. The time to say no to the dictator is past—war is the only way to achieve justice and remove him from power. Many people simply talk about this, Emerada, but you have done something about it."

"My mission will not be finished until he is either dead or out of power."

Ian could almost see her with a flaming sword in her hand. In the beginning he'd had very little respect for her, thinking she was nothing more than a saloon entertainer, although a better dancer than most. Now he realized she walked a dangerous line as a spy. If her true purpose was uncovered by Santa Anna, she would be put to death. "Emerada, go back to your aunt in New Orleans, or France, or wherever she is. Seek a safe haven until this is all over."

"I shall do just that, on the day you leave Tejas and return to Virginia."

"You know I can't do that."

"And I cannot abandon my principles any more than you can. The day the dictator is defeated is the day I ride away, and not before."

Tenderly he ran his hand down her silken hair. "Has anyone told you that you are a stubborn woman?"

"*Sí*. Many times."

Suddenly Emerada was overcome with a feeling of desperation. She knew in her heart that she was going to have to give herself to Santa Anna. There was no avoiding it. If she went back now, she would have to use her body to convince Santa Anna that he could trust her.

She turned away from Ian so he would not see the tears gathering in her eyes. To have that monster's hands on her made her feel sick inside. To have him be the first man to take her body made her want to cry. If only Ian could be the first man to make love to her, perhaps it wouldn't be so bad when she gave herself to Santa Anna.

She turned back to Ian, moistened her dry lips with her tongue, and raised her gaze to his. She moved closer to him and touched her lips to his.

She was surprised by the emotions she unleashed in him. His arms slid around her, holding her like a vise. She could feel his intake of breath, the hardness of his chest, the feel of his lips on hers.

He was drawing all her strength and stirring wild emotions she had never before experienced.

His mouth moved from hers to her cheek, and he whispered harshly in her ear, "If only you knew the restraint I have been keeping on myself. If only . . ."

He grabbed her to him and just held her for a moment. Then he lowered his mouth to hers and whispered against them, "I want you more than I have ever wanted a woman."

With joy singing in her heart, she wound her arms around his neck. "Then make love to me, Ian. I want you to."

With an unsuppressed groan, he eased her backward, his body moving against her. "God help me," he murmured, "because I can't help myself." He held her for a moment, breathing deeply. "I can't think or reason when you look at me with those soft brown eyes. Whenever I'm near you, I want you so damned bad it feels like my body's on fire. You feel it, too—this attraction between us." He pulled back and looked into her eyes. "Don't deny it."

"Sí," she admitted. "I feel it, too."

She tilted her head back and offered him her lips. "I feel it now."

His mouth plundered hers, and she felt a thrill of satisfaction when he groaned and whispered her name.

"Emerada, what are you doing to me?" He shoved her away roughly. "I won't do to a woman what my father did to my mother."

Her eyes were wide with confusion. "You have never been with a woman?"

He stood up and moved away from the firelight, trying to think how to answer her. "I am a man with a . . . healthy appetite. But I have never been with a woman who wasn't . . . experienced. It isn't my habit to deflower virgins. Even I have a code of honor."

"What makes you think I am a virgin?"

"Because I know now that you have been keeping Santa Anna's lust under control."

"I have up until now," she admitted. She glanced at him. "Did you mean that you have bedded only women who—"

He turned back to her, shaking his head. "We

shouldn't be having this conversation. It's late, and you should get some rest."

Emerada's heart was pounding so hard that it seemed louder than the rain that pattered on the roof. He wanted her; he'd admitted it. She stood up and walked over to him, dropping the blanket.

"Look at me and tell me you do not want me."

He dropped his gaze, refusing to look at her. "Go to sleep, Emerada."

"I will if you tell me you do not want me."

Ian's gaze lifted, and he stared at the most beautiful sight he'd ever seen. The shadows of the flickering firelight seemed like fingers caressing every curve. Her breasts were uplifted, her head thrown back, defying him to touch her.

With a strangled cry, he pulled her to him. "My lips can't deny what my body craves more than life."

Chapter Twelve

Ian's hands moved over Emerada's skin, and she trembled against him. He had never been so aware of a woman as he was of her. Her fingers slid into his hair, and she brought his mouth closer to hers. He heard every sigh, felt every tremor that shook her body, and knew that she was treading new ground and was confused by it. He also knew that he had awakened feelings that she had never before experienced.

With each practiced touch, he knew how to make her want him more. She was his for the taking, and yet he hesitated, drawing back and gazing into her misty eyes. "Are you sure?"

Her voice was barely audible. "*Sí.* I am very sure."

His groin ached and throbbed. He wanted

her so badly he could hardly hold himself back. "Emerada, you will regret this later."

"No. I will not."

He took the blanket and led her to one of the stalls, where he gently laid her down. He still had the feeling that he shouldn't do this to her. Emerada was not the kind of woman he could make love to and then walk away. Kneeling down beside her, he touched her cheek, and she turned her head to kiss his hand.

"Emerada, Emerada, there is so much inside of me, so much I want to say, and yet . . . "

She unbuttoned the top button of his shirt, then the second, and slipped her hand inside to touch the mat of black hair on his chest. "The time for talking is over, Ian."

He tightened his lips to keep from gasping when she moved his hand to her bare breast. "Emerada . . . "

She suddenly laughed, and it was like music to his ears. "It would seem I am seducing you, Ian."

Moving back, he ripped his shirt off and tossed it aside. She could feel the tension in him as he stripped off his wet trousers and came back to her.

The fire had died down, throwing only flickering light across Ian's body. Emerada had never seen a naked man before, and she had never imagined that Ian was so strong and muscled or possessed such raw power. His body was hard and lean, his waist narrow, his shoulders wide, and he was beautiful to look upon.

Gently he took her in his arms, holding her away from contact with his body. "You should never look at me like that," he said, nuzzling her ear. "It drives me out of my mind."

Emerada pressed her body against his, and when their flesh touched, she was breathless from the contact. The intensity of her feelings made her quake inside, and she wondered if Ian could feel it, too. Warmth and pleasure spread through her, and she never wanted to lose the essence of those feelings.

He spoke to her softly as he glided his hand through her hair. He put his lips to a strand that curled around his finger. "I have always been fascinated by your hair. It's beyond description. Did you know that?"

Their faces were so close she could see dark blue flecks in his light blue eyes. "How is that?"

"Tonight your hair is like a cloud of black silk. But in the sunlight it sparkles with red. I have never seen a more beautiful sight, except when you dance."

She was so swept away by his praise that she could almost have purred. So this was what it felt like to have a man make love with words.

Emerada was having a difficult time concentrating on what Ian was saying because his virile body was issuing its own command, and her body was answering. "My black hair comes from my Mexican father. The red is from my French mother."

He smiled and lifted her chin. "Oh, that explains it." He traced the outline of her face with his thumb. "Emerada, do you know what is going to happen between us?"

She nodded. "I can imagine it."

"You do understand that when I make love to you, you will no longer be considered a maiden?"

"I know." Her voice was breathless, because his head dipped and his lips touched the pulse at her throat. When he raised his head, a lock of dark hair fell across his forehead, and she pushed it aside.

"And still you want me to make love to you?"

She tossed her head back, and her breasts brushed against his cheek. She watched passion flame in his eyes, and when he groaned in pleasure, she knew he was feeling the same intensity of passion as she. Why, then, did he hesitate?

"But . . . " She was confused. "Do you not want me?" she asked, aching for him to master her body, to satisfy the yearning she felt deep inside.

His answer was breathed against her breast just before he kissed the rosy nipple. Then he ran his mouth hotly across her other breast. "Yes, my sweet—yes, I do."

Emerada was taken on a passionate journey

that left her quaking. He was an expert on where to touch her and what would bring her the most pleasure. Already her insides were a quivering mass, her head was spinning, and he had only touched and kissed her. How much more wonderful it would be when he entered her body. She felt heat rush through her veins at the thought. She knew he was going slowly because of her inexperience. She remembered once overhearing two of her aunt's French maids discussing how much it hurt the first time a man made love to a woman. Pain? Yes, the feel of his hands on her bare breasts, his mouth on hers, his whispered words in her ear, they were all beautifully painful. Now his mouth started a downward trail, and she arched her back to get closer to him.

Finally, when she thought she could stand it no longer, he placed his hands on both sides of her face.

"Emerada."

She saw the veins standing out in his neck from the tight control he was keeping over his emotions.

"I can't stop now."

"I do not want you to stop." She wanted desperately to know what it felt like to be one with him, even if it was only for this one night. Her arms slid around his shoulders, and she gloried in the feel of his muscled back. Her eyes welcomed him, her lips invited him, and she opened her heart and body to him.

Ian's wonderful hands seemed to worship her with each touch. So slowly did he part her legs and move into position that she didn't realize what was happening until she felt his velvet hardness glide into her. He did not penetrate far, not at first.

Hot wave after hot wave rocked her body, and she arched forward to receive him.

His hand went to her back to still her. "Easy, sweetheart," he warned. "There is no hurry. I don't want to hurt you."

She turned her head from side to side, trying not to cry out in ecstasy when he eased farther inside her. Whoever said it would hurt had not known Ian's lovemaking. He was so gentle, pulling back slowly, and then with the same slowness sliding forward. Oh, so sweetly did she respond to him. For a while it was enough for her. Ian's lovemaking was like nothing she could have imagined. She wanted to be with him, like this, forever.

Then it changed!

Ian's lips covered hers, and he pushed deeper inside her. Her fingers slid into his hair, and she pressed her lips tightly against his. She was shocked when his tongue slid into her mouth, making her tingle all the way to her toes.

His hands guided her forward to meet his thrust, and he slowly drew her back, instructing her with gentleness that soon turned to raw passion.

Emerada moved her hips of her own accord, meeting him, then releasing him, only to take him deeper inside her again. She could hardly breathe for the beating of her heart. He was her, and she was him—there was no beginning and no end. Like earth meeting sky, their flesh was joined and they became one.

Emerada knew that no matter what happened after tonight, she was no longer the same. Her body would forever belong to Ian.

As for her heart, that was another matter. She had something she must do, and she could not think about love—she just couldn't.

But what were these powerful feelings she had for him?

"Sweet, sweet Emerada," he murmured against her mouth. "I never knew I could feel like this."

"I know," she said, catching her breath just as he slid deeper into her. Now she had all of him—she possessed him as no other woman ever would—she knew that in the deepest recesses of her mind.

A gasp caught in her throat, and she was amazed to hear her own voice begging him not to stop.

He was giving her a gift; she knew that, too. He was giving her more than he'd ever given another woman. She whimpered and her body tightened, trembled, and seemed to unleash an explosion of ecstasy that they shared.

She felt Ian tremble; then they both lay quietly, saying nothing, only feeling, experiencing the calmness that came with finding the perfect mate.

Ian's touch conveyed more than words ever could. He kissed her lips, ran his hand over her breast, and then pulled her tightly against him, almost possessively.

Emerada's hand glided up his back, and she buried her lips against his neck and pressed tighter against him. She didn't know how long this strange and wonderful ritual went on, but she soon became aware of the rain hitting the roof. A horse whinnied from one of the stalls.

He took her face and turned her head to him. "Are you all right?"

She looked deeply into his eyes, feeling as if she could drown in them. "I have never been so all right."

His hand went to her stomach. "You felt no pain?"

"Not the kind you mean." She bit her lip, suddenly feeling shy. "I am glad it happened."

He rested his chin on the top of her head. "So am I. Something wonderful happened between us, Emerada. I don't know if you realize that, since you have not had a man touch you before me. I suspected it would be so for us, but now I know for sure."

"I . . . " She could not meet his gaze. "Even though I have never been with a man before, I know what happened to me surpassed any feeling I have ever had."

He hugged her to him, pressing her head against his heart. "I will want you for the rest of my life."

She smiled and glanced up at him. "That long?"

"And then beyond. How could I know that night you danced into my life that I would—"

She placed her hand over his mouth. "Do not say anything tonight that you may want to retract tomorrow." She gave him her most seductive glance. "Of course, once the San Antonio Rose captures a man in her web, he is caught for life."

He laughed and kissed her soundly. "Vixen."

"Seducer of women," she teased back.

Ian suddenly grabbed her, and before she could protest, he lifted her in his arms and laughingly carried her toward the front of the stable. He kicked the door open with his foot.

When she realized what he was doing, she clung to his neck. "No, Ian! It is raining outside, and we are not wearing anything!"

"Who will see us—the frogs?"

He stepped outside, and they were hit by a deluge of rain. He swung her around laughingly, and her joyous laughter joined his.

The cool, cleansing rain washed over them, but she didn't feel it because Ian's lips were on hers. After a long, drugging kiss, he carried her back inside the stable. Draping her in the blanket, he pulled on his trousers and built up the campfire. He sat down before it and drew her onto his lap.

His expression was serious as he looked into her eyes. "Do you really feel as I do, Emerada?"

The cold rain had cooled her passion, and she stared at him, trying not to think about their lovemaking. "What do you feel?"

"That life is suddenly sweeter, that the world is a better place, and that tomorrow will only be better."

She considered his words for a moment. She did not think tomorrow would be better, because she must leave him. "Ian, tomorrow there will still be a war to fight, people will die, and women will weep. But," she said pensively, "life will be sweeter after tonight."

"Damned right," he said, tasting her lips. Then, cocking his head to the side, he arched an eyebrow and gave her an inquiring look.

She threw her arms around him, surrendering to him once more.

For now Emerada could forget the terrible war that raged across Tejas, and the lives that had been lost. For now she was gripped by something magnificent, and she knew that Ian was finding forgetfulness in her arms—if only for tonight.

It was in the early hours of the morning and still dark when Emerada slipped out of Ian's arms while he still slept. Silently she dressed and saddled her horse. She then bent down to Ian, wanting to curl up beside him once more, but she dared not. If she didn't leave now, she never would.

His dark hair was swept across his forehead, and his long lashes lay softly against his cheeks. At that moment, she wanted him to open his eyes so she could look into their shimmering depths for the last time.

But she dared not kiss his lips as she wanted, because if he should awaken, he wouldn't allow her to leave.

"Please understand that I must continue on the path I have chosen, and you must go your way," she whispered.

He murmured in his sleep, but didn't awaken.

When Emerada grasped her horse's reins and walked toward the door, she turned back to Ian. With a resigned sigh, she went back to him, bent down, and kissed his lips.

"I do not think we will ever meet again," she said softly. With Ian, she had become a different person, someone she didn't recognize. He made her reach deep within herself and discover emotions she'd never known she possessed. He brought out the best and worst in her.

With a heavy heart, she turned and walked away.

She mounted her horse and rode off into the predawn shadows, heading in the direction where she knew she would find Santa Anna.

When she was a safe distance from Ian, she halted and glanced back, her heart aching. She allowed her eyes to move over the charred remains of what had once been a happy home.

She nudged her horse in the flanks and rode away, leaving the past and its ghosts behind. Even Ian belonged to the past, but she would never forget the one glorious night she had spent in his arms.

When she gave herself to Santa Anna, she would close her eyes and imagine it was Ian touching her.

Chapter Thirteen

Ian awoke when sunlight beamed through a crack in the door and hit his face. He gazed around the stable, looking for Emerada, but she wasn't there. She must have gone outside, he reasoned.

He smiled, remembering last night. He was a man who had found his lady, and he wasn't about to let her get away from him. Not that she'd try. He was sure that Emerada had felt the same as he had last night.

He was glad the storm had moved away so they could make better time reaching General Houston. They should leave right away, though.

Ian shoved the door open and squinted in the bright sunlight. It was going to be a hot day, not unusual for this part of Texas, even in the winter.

He drew in a deep breath, feeling revived and reborn. Emerada had done that for him. Excitement stirred within him as he called to her. "Emerada, where are you?"

When she didn't answer, he walked toward the charred ruins of the hacienda, thinking he'd find her there. As he walked along the overgrown path, he saw several ancient gravestones in a fenced area. None of the graves looked new enough to be those of her father or brothers. He wondered why their bodies would be buried in a different place from other family members.

He could only imagine how difficult it had been for Emerada to return to Talavera. She had probably needed to be alone this morning and was walking somewhere.

Ian edged along the rough walls of the house that had been gutted by fire. Most of the interior was nothing but charred and crumbling ruins, but it must have been magnificent at one time. Now it was only a skeletal reminder of the home it had once been. Still not worried, he made his way through a breezeway that had miraculously not been touched by the fire. He found the back of the house still intact, and he leaned against the cool, thick walls, his gaze sweeping the pastureland, hoping to see Emerada.

There was nothing there but sadness. He had to get her away as quickly as possible.

He would convince her to stay in Nacog-doches, where he could see her more often. He smiled, and then laughed out loud. Perhaps they would be married right away. He didn't want the least bit of scandal to touch Emerada's life.

Married! Was he thinking of marriage?

His mind had been taking him in that direction without his being aware of it. He hurriedly retraced his steps, anxious to tell Emerada—or to ask her—to marry him. He supposed that would be the proper approach.

As he reached the barn, he saw something he had missed earlier. Emerada had carved a sentiment for him in the mud, using a stick, no doubt.

The smile left his face as he read her message: *Ian, I had to go.*

Ian raised his face upward, crying out in agony, but his voice only echoed among the ruins. "No, Emerada! No!"

Emerada rode her horse hard. She had to get to Presidio del Rio Grande so she could be certain Josifina was all right, and then she must lose no time in locating Santa Anna. Josifina was surely out of her mind with worry by now, and she could only imagine what Domingo must be thinking about her disappearance. Possibly he was with Josifina, knowing that was the first place she would go if she were able.

It was after nightfall on the third day that Emerada reached the village. The streets were strangely quiet, the square empty. She rode to the hotel and dismounted, looping the reins over the hitching post.

When she entered the lobby, the man behind the desk looked startled for a moment. "Ah, señorita, you are sadly too late for the burial rites."

She was confused. "What? Who died?"

He shook his head. "I am sorry to tell you that your maid was found dead in your room—three . . . no, four days ago."

Sudden pain surrounded her heart, and she bounded up the stairs. It couldn't be true—not her Josifina!

Emerada opened the door and was immediately clutched in Domingo's tight hug. "I knew you would come," he said, leading her to a chair and guiding her down.

She buried her face in her hands and sobbed, overwhelmed by the loss of her dear Josifina. "It is my fault. I should have been with her." She moaned. "I should have taken better care of her."

"It was not your fault. Josifina was eighty-three years old, and her heart gave out. If she was here, she would tell you not to blame yourself."

"It *is* my fault."

"You were Josifina's life," Domingo said kindly. "Just to be with you was her happiness."

"Were you with her . . . when it happened?"

"No. After I took your message to General Houston, I went back to San Antonio de Bexar, only to find no one knew where you were. It was said you left with the American prisoner, but I knew you did not go with him of your own free will. I also knew that if you could escape from him, you would come here, so I waited for you."

"I do not know what to do now, Domingo. Everything has gone wrong."

The big man nodded. "We should go back to France to be with your aunt."

She raised her head and brushed her tears away. "I cannot do that—you know what I must do."

He sighed and looked resigned. "I was certain you would not give up now. When do we catch up with Santa Anna?"

She stumbled toward the bed, feeling so weary. "I must sleep until morning. Tomorrow I will want to go to Josifina's grave. Then we will leave."

"Rest for now," he said softly, wondering what hell she'd lived through.

She turned onto her side and closed her eyes, immediately falling asleep, but Domingo saw that she trembled from crying so hard. He covered her with a shawl, then moved to the window and sat in a chair. He would watch over her as he always had.

Emerada faced many dangers, but she was

not a coward, and that was why Domingo had to take better care of her. She always rushed into trouble before devising a plan to escape. She had no one but him now to look after her and keep her from harm.

Ian was astonished by the pitiful sight he saw along the road. Fear had spread through the settlements after the fall of the Alamo, and American families were fleeing for the border. The rains had come again, making it even more miserable for the continuous exodus from Texas.

He passed barefoot women and children looking bedraggled and frightened. They kept glancing over their shoulders, as if they expected Santa Anna to come bearing down on them at any moment. They had every right to be afraid, because the Mexican army was at their backs and moving toward them at a fast pace.

It was a gloomy afternoon when Ian entered San Felipe de Austin. A sentry shouted out to him, "Colonel McCain, have you heard the news? Texas has done gone and declared independence, and we have us a president! President David Burnet!"

Ian smiled and waved, too weary to consider what that would mean to the men who would be called upon to defend the newly declared country.

With a heavy heart, he located General

Houston's headquarters. He had dreaded the moment he'd have to tell Houston that he'd failed in his mission to save the situation in San Antonio.

When he entered the cabin, Houston looked up from his paperwork with a grim expression. "What's kept you?"

"I was Santa Anna's prisoner. I had to fight the rain and mud, and this morning I had a skirmish with three enemy soldiers."

"Hell, boy, is that all?" Houston chuckled. "I already heard about your capture. I thought you were too smart to get yourself caught, but I knew you'd escape somehow."

"I'm not feeling too good about getting myself captured." He lowered his gaze and stared at his muddy boots. "I let you down in San Antonio. I should have been with Travis, Bowie, and the others."

"I'm glad you weren't, because you'd be dead now. How do you think I'd explain that to your ma?"

"There is no excusing what I did."

Houston shook his head in annoyance. "You're the best man I've got, and I'll stack you up against any of Santa Anna's men—any day, anytime. But don't come whining to me about failing. This war isn't over yet, and I need you."

Ian knew he should feel relieved by the general's confidence in him, but he felt worse. "I'm ashamed that I didn't get the men out of the Alamo, sir. You have reason to court-martial—"

Houston interrupted him. "I'm not going to let you off that easily. No one could feel sorrier than I do about the brave men who died at that mission. But we don't have time to lament. Santa Anna is regrouping and ready to take us on. We've got ourselves an all-out war, and we still don't have an army." Houston glanced back at his paper. "If I could only be sure of Santa Anna's movements."

"Do you want me to find out, sir?"

"No, I don't. From now on I want you at my right hand. Even though we're undermanned and untrained, those men out there have got the taste of freedom in their gullets, and that's the best reason I know to get a man to fight." Houston rolled up the parchment and shoved it in a leather satchel. "By the way, what do you think about our independence and our new president?"

Ian wearily ran his hand through his hair. "I'm reserving judgment until I find out if we can keep the new country and the new president," he answered impassively.

"Tell me, what did you find out about the woman, Ian?"

"I discovered that Emerada de la Rosa is her real name." He drew in a deep breath that expanded his chest. "She claims she's willing to die to bring Santa Anna to his knees. She's braver than most men I know, and she'll probably get herself killed."

"I see she got under your skin."

"You can't imagine."

Houston scratched his chin. "I had a feeling she might be genuine. She can still be of help to us if she keeps us informed of Santa Anna's movements. Is that her intention?"

"I believe so, sir." Ian walked toward the door. "I need to wash the dust off."

"Catch yourself some sleep. Looks like you haven't seen a bed in days."

Ian walked through the camp, where husbands, fathers, and old men were being trained in the finer points of war. Most of them couldn't even march in step. One man looked to be in his eighties and shouldered a battered old flintlock musket. Ian had seen Santa Anna's power up close, and he wondered how in the hell this slovenly force could hope to win against the well-trained, battle-hardened Mexican army.

He found an empty cot in the officers' tent. Not even bothering to remove his mud-splattered clothing, he lay down and immediately fell asleep.

His sleep was dreamless; even Emerada didn't visit him in the shadowy, peaceful world where—for a time—he found forgetfulness.

Chapter Fourteen

A warm breeze swept the high-flying clouds across an azure sky as Emerada and Domingo reached the outskirts of San Antonio de Bexar. She had learned that Santa Anna still lingered there.

Emerada had decided not to approach Santa Anna, but to allow him to find her.

She felt sickened by the gruesome sight that greeted them as they entered the town, or what was left of it. She avoided looking at the ruins of the Alamo, where vivid memories of death still haunted her. She saw the remnants of houses that had been destroyed; those that were still standing had either been blown apart by cannons or had been burned. Where there had once been orchards and vegetable gardens, there were now toppled fences, trampled gardens, and uprooted trees.

Emerada stared straight ahead, no longer able to look at the devastation all around her.

"What kind of a world is it, Domingo, when the simple people are made to suffer the most?" She felt a sorrow so infinite, so deep, it tore at her heart. "Why must it be this way?"

"Give the people time and they will rebuild," the big man assured her. "Life goes on—it always has; it always will."

"This was once a lovely market town with vendors selling their wares. People laughed, and children played in the shadow of the mission."

"It will be again."

"I hope so. Oh, I do hope so!"

Emerada had been asked by Juan Seguin's aide to dance at La Villita where most of the run-down huts had been burned by the Alamo defenders during the siege. She had readily agreed, wanting to help the people. All she could give them was the gift of her dance.

Emerada had another reason for agreeing to dance. Santa Anna would surely hear about it and seek her out.

She wondered if he'd be angry and shoot her on sight, or if she could make him believe that she'd been taken away against her will and had managed to escape. After all, as far as it went, it was the truth.

* * *

A bright moon seemed to be suspended in the sky, and its light blended with the many lanterns that had been placed in a circle in the courtyard, where the San Antonio Rose was to dance.

People pressed forward to get a glimpse of the legendary beauty. Children sat cross-legged upon the cobbles under the watchful eyes of their mothers. Soldiers, officers and enlisted men, stood shoulder-to-shoulder in a wide circle—many were battle-worn, some wounded, but still they came to witness the dance of the adored one.

A guitar strummed and a trumpet blared, drawing everyone's attention to the circle of light where the dancer appeared. Emerada did not come among the poor people dressed in splendor, but barefoot, and wearing a plain black ruffled skirt and a white peasant blouse—and they loved her for it. Across her head, and covering the lower half of her face, she was swathed in a black silk shawl decorated with velvet roses and long silk fringe.

She rose to the balls of her feet with the grace of a ballerina, then spun around with her arms weaving artfully upward. With a loud strum of the guitar, she allowed the shawl to fall away from her face, and the audience gasped at the sight of her beauty.

With wild abandon, she waved the shawl about her, like the movements of a matador advancing into a bullring.

185

The crowd followed her every move adoringly. Young girls imagined they could grow into a beauty like the San Antonio Rose, and every man wondered what it would feel like just to touch her soft skin, or have her look at him with those brilliant eyes.

Her movements were pure, like poetry of the body, and many cried as they watched her. She was offering them a moment of forgetfulness in this time of war and death, a moment she shared with them alone.

The moment Emerada had dreaded came halfway through her dance. Santa Anna's aide-de-camp was shoving people aside and making a path for the president general.

His hands on his hips, Santa Anna showed his displeasure at Emerada's dance by his stiff stance.

Emerada gathered her gown to her knees and moved toward Santa Anna, her eyes staring into his. She tossed her long hair and snapped her fingers.

When she was almost even with Santa Anna, she saw movement beside him, and she looked into the wistful eyes of a small girl who could be no more than ten years old.

Laughing, Emerada bent and draped the shawl across the child's shoulder and was rewarded by the girl throwing her arms around her neck and placing a kiss on her cheek.

The crowd cheered and nodded their approval—all but one. Santa Anna stood ramrod-straight, his arms now folded across his chest, his gaze hard and unyielding.

Emerada knew she had to act fast. She sauntered up to him, her gaze unwavering, her smile seductive as she reached forward and withdrew his sword from its scabbard.

Santa Anna did not blink.

Emerada swashed the sword several times near his face, but Santa Anna still didn't blink. And when his aide stepped forward to protect him from what looked like an attack, the dictator waved him aside.

The audience tingled with excitement when Emerada leaped with effortless grace and landed, slicing the sword artfully through the air.

She put everything she had into the dance. In a fluid motion, she was airborne. Bringing in her training as a ballerina, she spun on the balls of her feet, then charged like a warrior.

At last she stood in front of Santa Anna, extending his sword to him across her arm, and when he took it, she knelt before him and bowed her head. If he was going to take her life, let it be now.

Santa Anna took her arm and pulled her to her feet, while the crowd remained silent. When the dictator finally smiled and cried out *"Bravísima,"* the audience joined in a deafening chorus of approval.

Emerada looked at him inquiringly, and he drew her into the circle of his arms and cried in a loud voice, "Let us celebrate, my people. The San Antonio Rose has returned to us."

There was music and dancing in the streets as Santa Anna led Emerada away from the crowd. She had to steel herself to keep from drawing away from the touch of his hand. This man with personal magnetism and great power could draw other people to him, but not her. There had been a moment while she had been dancing with his sword that she'd been tempted to bury it in his black heart.

Santa Anna's aides fell back a few paces as he approached his living quarters, and when he led Emerada inside, he closed the door, and they were alone for the first time since her return.

She tried not to show her fear, but he must have sensed it, because he seated her on a folding chair with a cushion of green velvet and smiled kindly. "I know what happened to you. Some of my men saw the Raven's Claw take you away by force. They tried to follow you, but lost your trail in the darkness." He touched her cheek. "Did that man hurt you?"

She shook her head, unable to speak for a moment. She knew Santa Anna, and she knew that he was testing her in some way. "I must be honest with you. I cut his ropes and set him free. Our soldiers were killing every American they could find. I did not think you wanted that man to die. Nor did I expect him to take me as his prisoner."

Santa Anna's eyes closed, and when he

opened them, she could see relief in the dark depths. "We saw that Ian McCain's ropes had been cut, and I suspected that you had freed him. If you had not told me the truth, it would have gone hard with you tonight. As much as I admire you, I would not hesitate to condemn a traitor to death—not even you."

She almost shouted that she knew how ruthless he could be, but she averted her glance. "If I had betrayed you, would I have returned?"

He went down on his knees before her and raised her head, forcing her to meet his gaze. "He did not hurt you, did he?"

"No. He did not harm me."

"I do not like to think about what could have happened to you while you were in that man's hands. How did you escape?"

"I waited until he was asleep and slipped away. I do not think he was happy when he awoke and found me gone."

"What man would want to lose you?"

"He did not want me for himself. He was taking me to General Houston. I do not know why."

"I believe it is as you first suspected—to humiliate me."

He sat across from her and watched her closely, and from the gleam in his eyes, she knew he was still not through testing her.

"When you escaped from Ian McCain, did you come straight here?"

"No, I did not. I knew my maid, Josifina,

would be worried about me. So I rode to Presidio del Rio Grande to comfort her."

"Why did you not bring your maid here with you, if she was so worried about you?"

He watched her with the expression of a marauding hawk, and Emerada knew that he was waiting for her to make a mistake. She suspected he already knew about her movements in Presidio del Rio Grande.

A sudden rush of tears took her by surprise and startled Santa Anna.

"I was too late. I am always too late to help those I love. Josifina was dead when I reached Presidio del Rio Grande."

Santa Anna was beside her, tucking her into his arms to console her. "I am so sorry. I knew about this, of course, but I did not know that she meant so much to you. After all, she was only a servant."

Emerada ground her teeth at his graceless attempt to soothe her, and she wanted to fling his arms away from her. Instead she bit her lip and laid her head against his shoulder, while his stiff epaulets cut into her cheek.

"Josifina was more than a servant."

His hand moved up and down her arm as he pressed her closer. "I understand, beautiful one. But these are difficult times for everyone."

She wanted to cry out in protest when she felt his hot lips on her neck, but she suffered in silence. He mistook the shudder that racked her body for one of ecstasy, not knowing that it was from revulsion.

"I will take care of you, Emerada. After tonight, you will dance only for me. I was jealous of all the eyes that watched you tonight. I was even jealous of the small girl who embraced you."

Emerada wondered how she would ever be able to let him make love to her when the time came. She couldn't even endure his hands on her. She shoved him away and stood on shaky legs. "No, I cannot do this."

He looked puzzled. Women seldom repelled his amorous advances. He imagined that Emerada was still grieving over the death of her maid.

"There is no rush." He patted her hand. "There is always tomorrow."

Suddenly there was the sound of heavy footsteps, and someone pounded on the door. "*Señor Presidente!* Our glorious men have killed the foreigners at Goliad. Fort Defiance is in our hands!"

Santa Anna's eyes gleamed with pleasure, and he opened the door to a weary courier, who must have ridden hard to bring him the news.

"Then my orders have been carried out," Santa Anna said with a satisfied nod of his head. "*Bueno! Bueno!* One by one, step by step, I will drive the Americans out of my country.

Their blood will mix with the soil that they strive to steal from Mexico."

Emerada paled. The death and destruction continued. For all she knew, Ian could be among the dead. Houston had sent him to the Alamo; he might very well have sent him to Goliad.

She had to find out!

Chapter Fifteen

The sun had just reached its zenith when Emerada halted her horse and turned to Domingo. "Houston is camped below. Ride back to Santa Anna as fast as you can, and do whatever you must to keep him from becoming suspicious. If he asks where I am, tell him you do not know. I will think up something convincing to tell him by the time I get back."

"I do not like leaving you." He gazed down at the tents that dotted the grounds of the Groce plantation. "It is no longer safe for you to travel alone."

She placed her gloved hand over his. "I must do this, Domingo. If I were a man, you would not question me for doing my duty."

He nodded, turned his horse, and rode away.

Emerada nudged her mount forward and rode in the direction of the plantation. When she saw two men near one of the tents, she wondered whether they would know if Ian was safe. Something like a physical pain stabbed at her heart. She had never intended to see Ian again, and now she was afraid he was dead.

The soldiers knew Emerada on sight and waved her through. One of them, with straw-colored hair and long, lanky arms, respectfully removed his hat and pointed toward the house. "The general ain't here right now, but Colonel McCain's over to the creek, ma'am."

Her heart stopped, and she couldn't speak past the tightening in her throat. She swallowed twice and asked, "When do you expect General Houston to return?"

The second man wiped the sweat from his face on his sleeve. "Can't rightly say. The general don't tell me his business, and I don't ask."

With dread in her heart, Emerada followed the man's directions to the creek, knowing she would have to face Ian after all. With Houston away, she'd have to tell someone her news, and Ian was the only one who knew about her arrangement with Houston.

When Emerada reached the creek, she saw Ian talking to several other men. He was so engrossed in their conversation that he didn't even know she was there. She dismounted and looped the reins over the narrow branch of a wild pecan tree. She waited for him to acknowledge her, wishing she could mount her horse and ride away.

She hadn't expected it to be so painful to see him again.

It was a hot day, and a dry wind stirred through Ian's dark hair—she knew the feel of his hair, since she'd run her fingers through it when he'd held her in his arms. Ian's voice was suddenly raised in anger, and she remembered how softly he had spoken to her the night they had made love.

Her gaze moved over him lovingly. He wore his uniform trousers, but his jacket was tossed aside, and his white shirt was open at the neck with the sleeves rolled up to his elbows. One muscled leg was propped on a fallen log, and her gaze went to the hand that rested on his knee. She was overwhelmed with weakness as she remembered those hands touching her. She could almost feel them on her now.

Dear God, she thought in a panic, her heart thundering inside her. *Don't let me feel, don't let me remember how it was between us, not now!*

Anger laced Ian's words as he spoke to the men. "I'm only going to say this once, so listen well. If you don't like the way General Houston commands this army, then get on your horse and leave now! I'd rather have one reliable man at my side than twelve malcontents."

"Now, Ian, we aren't complaining, we just

don't understand why the general's giving the appearance of running from Santa Anna. We want to fight that son of a—"

The man broke off and stared at Emerada. He then hurriedly whispered to Ian. Coldly, Ian looked over his shoulder at her.

Emerada could feel the chill of Ian's stare, but she forced herself to walk toward him.

"We'll take this up later," Ian told the men, and dismissed them with a nod.

When the men passed by Emerada, they smiled and tipped their hats. She waited for them to be out of earshot before she turned her attention to Ian. She had to face him now, before she lost her nerve. "I hoped to speak to General Houston, but I was told he is away."

Ian studied her silently. Emerada was the last person he'd expected to see there. "I'm always at your service," he said. "How can I help you, Señorita de la Rosa?"

He was stiff and reserved, and it hurt to see him that way, but there was nothing she could say to satisfy his anger. "I have ill tidings, Ian. I am sorry to be the bearer of such grave news."

He glanced at her lathered mount. "It seems you didn't spare your horse getting here. What can be so important that you would ride that poor animal into the ground? Dare I hope you want to replay the little performance you gave me that night at Talavera?"

She wanted to strike out at him, to answer

his cruelty with the same ruthlessness he displayed, but she held her temper and stared into his eyes.

"I rode all night to get here, and I am weary, Ian. I do not have time to spar with you or answer such absurd questions."

His voice was suddenly silky smooth. "What I have in mind won't take all that long."

She curled her hand into a fist, and her rebellious spirit took over. "There are more important things to discuss than what happened between us, Ian."

"What could be more important?"

"Men dying." Emerada went to the creek and cupped her hands, drinking thirstily, giving herself time to regain her composure. At last she stood up and turned back to him.

"What I have to tell you is important." The heat was so intense that she felt light-headed, and she almost stumbled, but caught herself in time. "I would have preferred to tell General Houston, but you will have to do."

He put out his hand, indicating she should precede him to stand beneath the shade of a pecan tree.

Emerada leaned against the rough bark and swallowed several times. She really did feel sick to her stomach. Her hands were trembling, but she didn't know if it was from weariness or from being so near Ian.

He let out a long breath. "What is your news, Emerada?"

She met his gaze. "Do you know a man called Fannin?"

The expression of arrogance left his face, and his eyes took on a look of concern. "Yes, I know him. Why?"

She brushed a curl from her face and wished she had another sip of water. "There is no easy way to tell you. Fannin and his men were killed at Goliad," she whispered.

Ian gazed upward at the branches, and she would have thought he was unaffected by her words if it hadn't been for the tightening of his jaw. "Are you certain of this information?"

"I was with Santa Anna when the messenger arrived from Goliad with the news."

He dipped his head and looked at her for a long, poignant moment. "Can you possibly be telling the truth? If I believed you, would I be courting disaster?" He clamped his hands on her shoulders and brought her closer to him. "I know Houston has decided to trust you, Emerada, but I don't. I no longer believe the fable you wove about Santa Anna having your family murdered. You used your story to gain my sympathy and to earn my trust. Well, it didn't work."

"You are a fool," she spat out. "I will not squander my time on such as you, Ian McCain."

"I've had time to think and weigh the story you told me that night, Emerada. You were in the dictator's pocket then, and you still are." He glanced at her and shook his head. "I have to admit that you are the best weapon Santa Anna has."

She was losing her patience. She knew Ian was speaking from hurt pride and nothing more. "What could I possibly have to gain by contriving such a story?"

"Damn it! Houston ordered Fannin to abandon Fort Defiance. He would not disobey orders. I don't believe you."

"Just like he ordered Travis to leave the Alamo? There seems to be wide insubordination in the ranks, Ian McCain."

"Why would Fannin disobey Houston?"

"I do not know about such things. But here is more information you might want to pass on to Houston. Santa Anna has ordered that every foreigner with a gun in his hand is to be executed."

Ian seemed to have a hard time finding his voice. "If you know that much, perhaps you can tell me how Fannin died?"

"I heard the courier tell Santa Anna about his death." She shuddered, thinking she was going to be sick, right there in front of Ian. "Do not make me tell you."

"The general will want to know," he insisted.

She drew in a deep breath. "Very well. Fannin and his men were held captive for a week, having surrendered with the agreement that they would be taken prisoner and not shot." She lowered her gaze, feeling shame for the unchivalrous manner in which Fannin and his men had died. "They were executed without mercy."

Ian closed his eyes for a moment, and when he opened them, Emerada saw the unleashed anger reflected there.

"There is something more, Ian."

"Yes?"

"Santa Anna believes the war is all but over. Soon he will come at you with everything he has."

He walked away from her and stood at the edge of the creek. "Let him come. We're ready for him."

"No," she said, walking over to him. "I do not know what Houston is doing, but it appears to me, and to Santa Anna, that he is running away. And, from the conversation I overheard when I came up, it would appear some of your men believe it also."

"The general will fight on his own terms. When he is ready, he will engage your Santa Anna, but not before."

"He is not my Santa Anna!"

"Is he not?" In a sudden move, Ian pulled her into his arms. "Has he made love to you? Has he tasted the sweetness of your lips, as I once did?"

She shoved against him, and he dropped his arms.

"What happens between me and Santa Anna is none of your affair," she replied in reprisal.

"One night with you does not give you any right to question what I do."

"Perhaps not," he whispered, "but it was certainly a pleasant diversion for a few hours." He saw her face whiten, and he wondered why he was deliberately trying to humiliate her. With forced composure, he changed the subject. "Just think about this, Emerada. The next time we meet Santa Anna, it will be on our terms and in a place Houston chooses."

She walked to her horse and turned back to him. "Tell Houston to choose soon, or all his men will desert him and Santa Anna will sweep over you like he did the walls of the Alamo."

Neither of them saw the man walking toward them until he drew even with Emerada.

"The lady makes a lot of sense, Ian," Houston said, giving her an encouraging smile.

"Sir," Ian said. "Your little spy has been telling me a concocted story about Fannin."

Houston seemed to age before their eyes, and he gave Ian a disapproving glance. "If this gracious lady told you that Fannin and all his men are dead, believe her—it's true."

Ian turned his head toward the creek and stared at the rushing water, feeling like an utter fool. He'd allowed his jealousy of Emerada to rule his thinking. She had ridden all night to bring them the news. He had offered her neither food nor a place to rest. He staggered under the weight of his guilt. Emerada was valuable to Houston, and he had treated her like a whore.

"Señor Houston," Emerada said, looking at him in desperation. "I have come to plead with you to do something soon, or all will be lost."

"Emerada, do you trust me?" he asked her kindly.

"It is not a matter of trust. I am trying to decide if you are a man of greatness or a coward."

Houston chuckled. Few people ever spoke to him so candidly, and he found it refreshing. "So you have heard the stories that call me a coward, Emerada? History is every man's judge—let it be mine as well."

"Everyone is talking about your running away," she said with honesty. "I believe you are misguided, but you are not a coward. You are giving Santa Anna the advantage when you run, and he is laughing at you."

Houston nodded. "I've heard that my actions are being referred to as the 'Runaway Scrape.'"

"I have heard that, too," Emerada admitted.

"Come," Houston said, offering her his arm. "You will eat with me and then rest before you return to Santa Anna."

"I don't think she should go back to him, sir," Ian said quickly. "It's getting too dangerous for her."

"That's why you will escort her most of the way back," Houston said with irony. "I do trust that you can keep her safe, Colonel McCain?"

He smiled down at Emerada. "So far, she's always had to save your skin."

Emerada was not pleased that Ian was to be her escort, and from the dark look on his face, he was none too pleased either.

Houston led Emerada away. "You'll leave early in the morning, Ian."

Emerada stopped, her gaze searching Houston's eyes. "What if I could end Santa Anna's life? I can easily arrange to be alone with him. It would be a simple thing to kill him."

Houston shook his head. "Have you ever killed a man, Emerada?"

"No. But he is not a man. The people of Mexico would be better off without him."

"I pray you will not attempt such an act. They would only send someone else to take his place, probably his brother-in-law, General Cos, who is every bit as ruthless as Santa Anna."

She nodded. "I suppose you are right. I can wait."

Houston guided her forward. "I want you to come out of this war alive, Emerada. I have grown fond of you."

She looked at him with an earnest expression on her face. "And I of you, General."

Chapter Sixteen

It was still dark when Emerada emerged on the porch. She had felt ill all night and hadn't slept very well. At times she'd felt feverish and would kick the covers off; then she'd suffer from chills and pull the covers high.

She could not be ill. There was too much she had to accomplish. Everything was beginning to come together, and she had to help Houston.

She half hoped that Ian would not be there and she could just ride away alone. But he was waiting for her, and when she came down the steps, he sat forward in his saddle and nodded stiffly. She didn't acknowledge him in any way after the things he'd said to her the day before. Besides, he didn't want to be with her any more than she wanted him there.

She slipped her booted foot into the stirrup and mounted the horse. Without a backward glance, she started her horse off at a gallop.

Ian and Emerada rode for over an hour in silence. Finally she halted her mount and looked out over a bluff at the rising sun as it spread color across the land.

"It's beautiful, isn't it?" Ian remarked next to her.

Her eyes swept over the deep valley to a distant river that reflected the sunlight like a golden prism. "It's breathtaking. It is difficult to believe there is a war raging when it looks so peaceful."

Ian turned to her, his gaze tracing her face. "Yes, breathtaking."

She took in a deep breath and guided her horse forward. "There is no need for you to come with me any farther. If Santa Anna sees you again, I will not be able to save you."

"Houston wanted me to accompany you to Santa Anna's encampment—I suppose you know where it is?"

"*Sí.* I know where to find him."

"No doubt you do," he said under his breath.

For the second time in two days, Emerada felt light-headed and lethargic. She gripped the reins of her horse and hugged its flanks with her knees, praying she would not be unseated.

When they stopped to rest the horses, she felt so cold that she couldn't stop trembling. She couldn't give in to weakness—she had to keep moving. She led her horse down a steep incline, counting each step, putting one foot in front of the other. The churning nausea came in waves, and she willed herself not to give in to it.

Suddenly blackness hovered over her, and she clutched her horse's mane to support herself, but she could not stop the blackness from encroaching. Emerada felt herself falling downward. She was unconscious by the time she hit the ground.

Ian saw Emerada fall, and he leaped to catch her, but he couldn't reach her in time. Helplessly he watched as she rolled downward and struck her head against a boulder at the bottom of the hill.

He lifted her head and examined her carefully. There was a wide gash on her forehead that was bleeding. He was puzzled as to why she had fallen. He didn't see her lose her footing; she just seemed to pitch forward.

When he touched her face, he discovered that she was burning up with fever.

How long had she been ill, and why hadn't she said something to him about it?

"Emerada de la Rosa, you're the damnedest woman I've ever known. Were you too proud to ask me for help?" Ian knew she couldn't hear him, but it helped allay some of his fear to hear his own voice. He couldn't tell how badly she was hurt, or how ill she was.

He removed his coat and placed it under her

head and then went back up the hill and led the horses down to where Emerada lay. Taking his canteen, he wet his neckerchief and placed it on her head wound.

"Don't worry," he said, softly touching her cheek. "I won't let anything happen to you."

When he'd examined her for broken bones and found none, he gently lifted her and carried her to the other side of the boulder, where the ground was reasonably level. He opened his bedroll and placed her on it, then built a fire to keep her warm, unmindful that there might be hostile Indians or Mexican patrols in the area who would see the fire.

After he had applied ointment and bandaged her head, he saw that her body was still trembling from chills. He put his own blanket over her and sat beside her, his rifle across his lap. Emerada was in no condition to go on, so for the moment there was nothing more he could do for her. He tried to control the panic that rose inside him.

She had to be all right—she just had to!

Emerada groaned, and her eyes fluttered, but she didn't open them.

Ian placed his hand on her arm and said softly, "Don't worry, dearest one; no one will harm you tonight—I won't let them."

She hadn't regained consciousness, and he knew that wasn't a good sign. She was so pale!

Ian raised his head to the now dark sky, with an earnest prayer on his lips. "God, don't let anything happen to her. If you have to take one of us, let it be me. Take me—not her."

Emerada regained consciousness with an excruciating headache. When she turned her head, pain shot through her temple. She reached up and found a makeshift bandage across her forehead. It took her a moment to remember what had happened to her. The last thing she remembered was falling into darkness.

Although she was underneath two woolen blankets, and there was a welcome campfire blazing next to her, she was still cold. She glanced to her left and found Ian sleeping.

He jerked awake and looked at her. "How do you feel?" His touch was gentle, and concern was etched on his face.

"I do not know what happened to me." Her hand went to her head. "Why is my head bandaged?"

He moved closer to her and tucked the blanket about her shoulders. "You hit your head when you fell. Try not to move more than necessary."

Her teeth were chattering. "I am so cold."

He placed his hand on her head. "How long have you had a fever?"

"I am not sure. I did not feel well all day yesterday, but I thought it would pass."

"You push yourself too hard, Emerada. Why

can't you stay home and knit socks like other women?"

She tried to sit up, but he pushed her back down, and she didn't object. "Is that the kind of woman you prefer, Ian—one who will knit your socks and answer to your every command?"

A smile curved his lips. "I seem to prefer a spirited dancer who has more courage than good sense, and more stubbornness than ten men."

She was not amused by his assessment of her. "If that was a compliment, Ian McCain, it was not flattering. But whatever could I have done to earn such high praise?"

He stood up and placed more wood on the fire, then listened to the night sounds before turning his attention back to her. "Go to sleep. We have already lost half a day. I hope you are able to ride in the morning."

She wished her head would stop throbbing and the world would right itself. "Who appointed you my protector, Ian?"

"God only knows."

She suddenly gave him a weak smile. "I believe it was Houston."

He raised an eyebrow and gave her a disgruntled glance. "If I'd known the trouble you were going to cost me, I'd never have spoken to you that first day. And I would have refused Houston's orders to find out who you were."

209

She turned her head away and closed her eyes. "Go away. I do not want to talk to you."

Ian watched her for a moment and then settled down beside her. It was a good sign that she had regained consciousness. "You are strong of body and spirit and will never allow a little thing like illness to slow you down for long."

"I want to sleep," she muttered.

And she did.

It was almost daylight when Ian heard riders in the distance. He quickly threw dirt on the fire and gripped his rifle, grateful that a heavy fog blanketed the countryside.

Emerada sat up, her eyes wide. "Is something wrong?"

"Shh."

She edged closer to him when she heard Mexican voices. "Do you see them?"

"No," he whispered. "But that is to our advantage because they can't see us either. I only hope they didn't see our fire."

"You must leave," she urged Ian, getting to her knees and touching his shoulder. "They will not hurt me."

"You can't be sure of that." He placed his finger to his lips. "Shh. They're just below."

Emerada could hear her heartbeat pounding in her head. She was frightened, but not for herself. If Santa Anna's men caught Ian, they would kill him. "Please go. I do not want them to find you here."

He pushed her back down on the bedroll and positioned his body between her and the riders. For a long moment neither of them moved.

Just when Emerada thought they were safe, one of their horses whinnied, and she knew the riders must have heard it. "Ian, what shall we do?"

He grabbed her by the arm and pulled her to her feet. Before she knew what he was about, he lifted her in his arms and moved back up the incline. When they reached the top, he set her on her feet and paused to catch his breath.

"We have to hide, Emerada. They will come looking for us. Can you walk if I support your weight?"

"*Sí.* Let us hurry! It sounds like they've found our camp."

Ian gripped her about the waist and helped her over the rough terrain until he found a place where time and weather had carved a depression into the limestone cliff. It was large enough for only one person to hide, so he quickly shoved Emerada inside and placed bushes in front of her.

"What are you doing?" she asked frantically when she realized that he wasn't coming in with her.

"I'm going to draw them away from you. Keep quiet until I come back for you."

She would have protested, but he'd already moved away. She pressed her back against the rough stone wall and prayed for his safety. He was deliberately drawing attention to himself so the men wouldn't find her hiding place.

There was nothing for Emerada to do but remain quiet. She knew Ian well enough to realize that he would put himself in danger to rescue her. A chill caused her to shake uncontrollably, and her head hurt so. But her main concern was for Ian. Nothing must happen to him.

Time passed slowly, and soon the bright sunlight burned away the fog. Emerada saw a flash of blue uniform and knew it was Mexican soldiers coming back down the hill. She held her breath when they stopped near her hiding place.

From her vantage point Emerada could see five men. One of them spoke. "We will never find them. We have wasted enough time. Let us rejoin General Cos." Emerada recognized one of the soldiers. He was usually near Santa Anna, but she didn't know his name.

It seemed like an eternity before the men moved on down the hill. A short time later she heard them mount their horses and ride away. But she did not move, afraid they might be trying to trick her into believing they had left.

Suddenly Ian was there, removing the branches and helping her to stand. "Are you all right?" he asked, looking her over.

She nodded. "They have probably taken our horses, leaving us to walk."

"They did. I saw them leading our mounts away. No doubt they took everything else, too."

"Why did you not ride away when you had the chance? I told you they would not harm me."

He gave her a disbelieving glance. "You have a short memory, Emerada. Have you forgotten those two men who attacked you the last time we were together?"

"But they were Americans. These were Santa Anna's soldiers. They would not have harmed me, for fear of reprisal from him."

"It's of little matter now." He squinted toward the horizon. "We have no food, water, blankets, or horses. And we're probably lost. So if you have any idea where we are, you must guide us." He looked doubtful. "We can't stay here. Do you feel like going on?"

She nodded. "I know where we are. We are on land that belonged to my father before Santa Anna confiscated it. If we walk in a westerly direction, we will come to Talavera."

Ian turned to her and smiled. "I have fond memories of the stable there."

She gave him an angry glance, and he held up his hand in surrender. "I was merely remembering. You can't blame a man for that."

Chapter Seventeen

Emerada was still feverish, and her head throbbed every time she took a step. She knew they must go on. They had to find shelter before dark.

Once she stumbled and fell, and Ian picked her up and carried her. When she tried to protest, he silenced her with a glance.

She laid her head against his shoulder, feeling as if it belonged there. She had been right the first day when some sixth sense told her that her life would be interlocked with Ian's. Every time she left him, fate seemed to pull her back.

She delighted in the feel of his muscled arms about her. Turning her face against his neck, she felt his pulse throb against her lips. Warmth flowed through her body like a flooding river. No man would ever make her feel the emotions that Ian did.

He shifted her weight and looked down at her with a passionate glance. "If you don't stop that, Emerada, I can't promise not to retaliate," he said in a deep voice.

She felt the blush on her cheeks and hid her face. With the fever raging through her, she wasn't sure what was real and what was imagination. But she knew that he wanted her as much as she wanted him, and she would have to fight against those feelings.

"You can put me down now. I can walk."

He placed her on firm ground and dabbed at his forehead with his neckerchief. "Do you feel like you can go a little farther?"

"It is not much farther now. Talavera is just over that next rise."

"Lean on me," he said. "When you need to rest, let me know."

Emerada didn't think she could take another step as they made their way down the hill. It was almost dark, and the stable was a welcome sight.

Ian saw her stumble and lifted her in his arms once again. "I'll carry you the last few steps, Emerada. You shouldn't even be out of bed in your condition, let alone hiking through the countryside."

"It's good to be home," she said, too weary to protest.

"Do you still think of Talavera as home?"

"No matter where I go, or what I do in the future, this will always be my home. Even though the Mexican government confiscated it, my family paid for this land in blood, and so will I, if I have to."

He carried her as easily as if she were a child. "I wonder why you haven't asked Santa Anna to restore the land to you."

She glared at him and wriggled to get out of his arms. "I would not ask anything of him. I want no favors from that cowardly president general who remains well behind the lines while his men die."

"Be still or I'll drop you, Emerada. Anything can set off that Mexican temper of yours."

"You can, Ian. Especially when you think I should ask Santa Anna for a favor."

He entered the stable and placed her on her feet. "Emerada, I never know what's in your mind. What makes you think you have to take on Santa Anna all by yourself? You might consider allowing the Texas army to get him for you."

"I have cast my lot with Houston, but I am no longer sure he is the man to confront Santa Anna."

Emerada moved into the cool interior, realizing she no longer had a fever. It had been hot today, but as the sun began to set, there was a chill in the air.

"Houston knows what he's doing," Ian said curtly.

"I pray you are right."

She glanced at him, and he noticed that her lips trembled. "One way or another, it will be all over soon, Emerada. Then we can create a new life here in this wonderful land."

"A new life for you, and the woman you are betrothed to. I will not stay in Tejas when the war has ended."

He couldn't deny that he was betrothed to Pauline, and he wasn't really free to ask anything of Emerada. But he couldn't let her go either. "You know I will help you, Emerada. I want to take care of you."

"I do not want your help any more than I want Santa Anna's. I want to owe no one."

"You are setting yourself up for a very lonely life, Emerada."

She raised her shoulders and shrugged. "My life has been too crowded of late. I would welcome loneliness."

In frustration, he blurted out, "I can't talk to you when you're like this!"

She struck a flint and lit the lantern that illuminated the darkened corners of the stable. "I just want to rest."

Ian looked about him in total amazement. The stable had been swept, and there was fresh hay in the stalls and supplies on a shelf.

Emerada picked up a bucket and thrust it at

him. "The well still has fresh water." She smiled at the bemused expression on his face. "Domingo cleaned and laid in fresh supplies—canned goods and blankets—on the chance that I might need to hide out here later, should circumstances go against me."

Ian gripped the bucket handle and walked toward the door. "Everything we need but a horse."

After he left, she dropped to her knees, too ill to move. It wouldn't be safe to lay a fire, since there were so many soldiers about, but she should get the blankets and make the beds. Wearily she made her way to the tack room and gathered several blankets in her arms. Moving to one of the stalls, she spread a blanket over the fresh straw and lay down, rolling up in it to keep warm.

When Ian returned, she was already asleep. He quietly opened a can of beans he found with the supplies and ate them in the near dark. Afterward he put another blanket on Emerada and went to the next stall to make his bed.

Although he was tired and every muscle ached, it was a long time before he fell asleep. He had visions of the last night he'd spent there with Emerada, visions that turned to dreams when he at last fell asleep.

Ian awoke and rolled to his feet. He went directly to the stall where Emerada had slept and found it empty. In a panic, he quickly searched the stable, but she wasn't anywhere to be seen.

Had she left him in the middle of the night, just as she did before?

She was ill and had no horse. He hurried to the door—he had to find her!

A bright moon poured its light across the grotesque, unnatural shape of the burned-out house, and he saw her standing before it, her head lowered, her hands clasped in front of her. He could only imagine what horrors were eating at her mind.

When he approached her, she turned into his arms and laid her head against his chest. "Ian, I can't get their deaths out of my mind. It was the despicable act of a monster."

He clasped her to him, feeling her anguish as if it were his own. "I understand how you feel. And for the first time I understand why you feel it your duty to avenge your family."

She blinked back her tears. "I need to know how they died, but no one can tell me." Her body trembled. "I pray it was quick and merciful." She grasped his shirtfront and looked into his face. "I am so afraid that they were burned alive. I must know—I must!"

Ian kissed the top of her head. "Don't think about it, Emerada. If it is humanly possible, I will find out for you."

She allowed Ian to lead her back to the stable and wrap her in a blanket. "I believe we can

Constance O'Banyon

risk a fire now." He placed his hand on her forehead. "You don't have fever."

"The sickness of the body has passed, but the sickness of the soul still rages inside me." She watched him lay a fire, and her eyes focused on the flames when they licked hungrily at the dry wood. "It must be very painful to die by fire."

Ian went on his knees before her and tilted her face to him. "Stop thinking about it, Emerada."

"If only I could."

He scooped her into his arms, his hands moving up and down her back. "Think of something else, sweet one," he whispered against her ear. "Think about the good times you had with your family. Remember their smiles, their laughter, and how grieved they would be if they knew how sad you are."

She nodded, as his hands, which had been comforting only moments before, now evoked a yearning within her. She pulled back enough so she could place her hands on both sides of his face. With a boldness that came from need, she moved forward, her lips lightly touching his.

Ian stiffened at first, but he could not deny the passion that flowed through his body. He had wanted to comfort her; now all he could think about was taking possession of her body.

"Emerada, my sweet, sweet love," he said as he picked her up in his arms and carried her to the closest stall. He placed her gently on the blanket and went down beside her, molding her shape to his, swelling against her, kissing her until she moaned with the same burning longing that consumed him.

Emerada wanted to tear her clothes off, to remove all barriers between her and heaven.

Ian's hand slid beneath her blouse and swept over her breasts, teasing the nipples between his fingers and rekindling the passion she'd felt for him the first time he had made love to her. But this time her yearning was deeper and more profound, because she knew what it felt like in that perfect moment when their bodies melded.

"I wasn't going to do this again," he said in a deep voice, his hands impatiently pushing her skirt over her hips. "I can't stop myself."

She boldly slid her hand down his chest and across his stomach. "I do not want you to stop, Ian. Make love to me. Make me forget everything else."

"Emerada, I have never before given so much of myself to a woman. I want you to know that."

"Oh, Ian," she said, placing a kiss on his lips, feeling sorrow cut into her like a knife. "Do not give so much of yourself to me. Save it for the woman you will marry."

Then his hand swept downward, parting her legs and gently caressing her. Her arms tightened about his neck, and her lips welcomed his kiss. His mouth ravished hers, drawing a moan of unrestrained pleasure.

"My own, my heart," he said, twining his hands in her hair and raising it to his lips.

He had been systematically undressing her, kissing her, touching her, and soon his own clothing lay in a heap with hers.

Emerada felt his swollen arousal hot between her legs and groaned in pleasure. She gripped his shoulders as he glided inside her, holding him tightly to her, wishing she could be absorbed into him.

His smooth strokes reached deep inside her, and she thought she would scream from the feelings that washed over her. Wave after wave of pleasure went through her like a ravishing tidal wave.

He spoke softly to her, teaching her, prodding her, instructing, and she was his apt pupil. Each new experience brought her a deeper joy. There was no part of her body his hands and lips did not touch.

The shabby stable was awash in golden light and became a paradise in their shared passion.

When Ian's rhythm changed, she rode to a higher plane of passion with him.

"Making love to you is like a magical potion." He groaned. "I can never have enough, and I never want to stop."

"Yes," she answered in a whisper and then a gasp, because his lips had just settled on her breast. "Never enough."

With each powerful stroke, her body rocked against his. The pain was in the beauty of it and knowing that they would probably never be together like this again.

She spread her legs, giving him easier access, and he took advantage, giving her all of him. Her stomach seemed to tighten, and then her whole body quaked with fulfillment. Emerada gripped Ian's shoulders when he rapidly thrust forward, bringing her even more pleasure.

She cried out his name and went limp against him as both their bodies reached for that final pleasurable climax.

Her lips moved over his face until she found his mouth. His arms tightened about her so lovingly that she wanted to cry. Theirs had been a perfect joining. They both knew it, but neither one admitted it aloud.

"Are you all right?" he asked, releasing her and laying the palm of his hand against her stomach.

She shook her head, unable to say what was in her heart. How dear of him to worry that he'd hurt her.

"No. I felt no pain."

He sat up, suddenly overcome with shame. "I never meant to do this to you again, Emerada. You have enough troubles without my adding to them."

She laughed and coaxed him back down to her. "Perhaps it was my design to seduce you again, Ian McCain. I think perhaps I did the first time."

"You make me feel so alive," he said, running

his hand over her breasts, knowing that he wanted her again.

She swung over on top of him, and he gasped at her bold move. "I am the dancer that steals men's hearts—did you not know?"

He went hard again and slid into her. "Yes," he said, closing his eyes when she moved back and forth on him, "I know you've stolen mine."

Ian lay back, watching Emerada as the morning shadows played across her beautiful face. She was like a different person now. Moments ago she had been warm and loving in his arms. Now she was in that secret place in her mind where she went in her torment. He knew she was thinking about her family.

"Have you a plan for getting us out of here?" he asked. "You seem to manage everything else."

Her gaze melted into his. "As it happens, I do have a plan. I have learned never to leave anything to chance."

"And what would that be?"

"When I did not return to Santa Anna's camp, Domingo must have guessed that I would come here, if I possibly could. If I know him, he will be here soon."

He sat up and looked at her in amazement. "You have a plan for everything, don't you?"

"I have to, Ian."

"There is still no way of talking you out of this crazy scheme with Santa Anna, is there?"

"No."

"I thought not. I should save my breath." He rolled to his feet, drawing an admiring glance from her. "I wouldn't want Domingo to find me with no clothes on, would I?"

Emerada folded her arms behind her head, allowing her gaze to sweep up his muscled body. "He would kill you, I think."

He pushed his leg into his trousers and said, "If you look at me like that, I'll throw caution to the wind and take my chances with Domingo. Or," he said, watching her carefully, "we could tell him that we are going to be married."

She searched his face to see if he was serious. He seemed to be anticipating her answer. Oh, how she would love to be his wife, to wake up every morning in his arms. But that was never to be. The untimely death of her family haunted her, and their voices seemed to cry out to her inner soul. She would see them avenged. And Ian had his Pauline.

She gracefully stood and shrugged her shoulders with pretended indifference. "You do not want a wife like me, Ian. I merely used you. I had to."

He gripped her shoulders and spun her around. "What is that supposed to mean?"

"I had to know how to please Santa Anna." She moved away from him and began to dress. "What is your opinion, Ian McCain, will he be pleased with me now? Have you taught me well?"

He felt as though someone had just slammed a fist into his stomach. "Oh, yes," he said, with the intention of trading hurt for hurt. He swept her an exaggerated bow. "I was glad to play your stud, little dancer. You can now feel confident that you can service the dictator as well as any woman of the streets."

She willed herself not to cry, but, oh, how deeply he had wounded her. Well, she deserved his scorn, didn't she?

The sound of horses kept her from having to reply.

"That will be Domingo," she said, going out the door and stepping into the sunshine.

Faithful Domingo looked her over carefully. "I was worried when you did not return. Then when some of the soldiers came into camp leading Soledad, I came to look for you."

Emerada turned to Ian. "You can take my horse, and I will ride with Domingo."

The big man reached down and lifted her up behind him, eyeing Ian all the while.

Ian pushed his boot into the stirrup and mounted. "I will inform Houston that I did my duty to you," he said coldly, kicking the horse into a gallop.

"That man is never very polite," Domingo observed.

Emerada leaned her head forward against her faithful Domingo's back. "I hurt him badly. I doubt he will ever look at me again."

"And this matters to you?"

"It matters very much."

Domingo silently urged the horse forward. There was something different about Emerada, and he didn't yet know what it was. Whatever it was, it involved Colonel Ian McCain, of that he was certain.

Chapter Eighteen

When Emerada rode through Santa Anna's camp, most of the men were having their siesta. There were only a few sentries on duty, and they passed her through with the usual friendly greeting.

Moments later she entered Santa Anna's tent and stood before him with a forced smile. He had been writing at his folding desk and glanced up at her, his face etched with anger.

"Excellency," she said, feigning excitement. "Each day you move closer to General Houston. Soon you will have him cornered, and he will have nowhere to run. Then you can crush him!"

Santa Anna made a gesture dismissing his aide and waited for him to leave before he spoke. "Why do you speak to me so formally, Emerada?"

She lowered her gaze. "Sometimes I am overwhelmed by your magnificence and it is difficult to do otherwise."

He picked up a penknife and ran his finger down the sharp blade. "Emerada, have you seen what happens to those who deceive me?" His dark gaze pierced hers. "It is not a pleasant sight. Just because you are a woman that will not stay my hand from your punishment."

She rushed to him, going down on her knees, thinking what a great actress she had become—rather than humble herself before him, she would like to grab that penknife and shove it into his murderous heart.

"Antonio, you cannot think I would deceive you." She took the hand that held the knife and pressed it against her breast. "If you believe this, end my suffering now."

He dropped the knife and gathered her to him. "Beautiful one, why do you torment me so? I want you—you know I do." His lips pressed against her cheek. "Where do you go when you leave me? And why have you not yet come to my bed?"

She closed her eyes to hide her disgust. The man who had murdered her family was about to make love to her. She prayed she could get through it without clawing his eyes out.

"Antonio, I am here now."

She saw passion in his eyes, but she also saw

doubt. She would have to go through with it this time if she was going to allay his suspicions.

"Where do you go when you are away?" he asked in a commanding voice, suddenly shoving her away. "I want you to stay with me."

"I thought you knew that a dancer must practice every day. I cannot practice with so many men around, so I go off by myself."

"This is what your man, Domingo, told me."

Emerada felt no regret about lying to this man. "It is true. A good dancer will never neglect her duty to her art." Her arms slid around his shoulders. "And I am a good dancer, Antonio."

Excitement showed in his dark eyes. "Dance for me now."

She licked her lips and parted them. "If that is your wish. But we have no music."

His hand moved over her breast, and his lips covered hers. She had every reason to believe this was a man who knew how to seduce and please a woman, but not her—never her!

Emerada playfully pushed him away and stood, releasing her hair so it flowed about her shoulders. She was amazed at how easily she had manipulated the dictator.

"I need no music to dance for the Napoleon of the West."

His gaze raked over her, and she could see that he was excited. She prayed she could make it a long dance.

"General," his aide called out, rushing into the tent.

Santa Anna jumped to his feet, a murderous glint in his eyes. "How dare you come into my tent without permission? I will have you stripped of rank for this!"

Emerada could not believe her good fortune. She'd been rescued from giving herself to Santa Anna. With pity, she watched the aide explain his outburst. But the man seemed undaunted, so she suspected he must be accustomed to Santa Anna's unpredictable temperament.

"But, Excellency, you told me to let you know the moment the Americans are on the move again. Houston has broken camp."

Santa Anna turned to Emerada regretfully. "I am sorry, my dear. But I must attend to my duty. You will forgive me?"

"Of course." She moved to the opening and turned back to him, smiling. "Until later, Antonio." Then she hurried out of the tent, happy to have escaped his impassioned advances yet again.

Emerada lingered near Santa Anna's tent with the pretense of lacing her boots. A guard approached her and spoke apologetically. "I am sorry, señorita, but you must move away from the president's tent."

She looked at the man and raised her skirt to her knees. "You would not want me to trip on the laces, would you, Captain?"

231

The man swallowed hard and shook his head, his eyes on her shapely legs. "No, señorita."

Santa Anna's angry voice could be plainly heard by her and the captain. "Imbecile! You dare to interrupt me when I am entertaining the San Antonio Rose!"

"Excellency, I had to! It is believed that Houston intends to use the ferry at the San Jacinto River to elude our army. I suggest that we move at once to intercept the enemy forces."

"We have him!" Santa Anna shouted. "The coward will not stop running until he reaches the border. But we will be there to stop his retreat."

Emerada could imagine Santa Anna bent over his map, and she heard him speak to his aide. "Order the camp struck at once. We rendezvous at the San Jacinto River. I will have Houston trapped between the river, here—and Buffalo Bayou, here. There will be nowhere for him to run!"

Emerada dropped her skirt and gave the captain another smile. Then she walked away with her hips swaying, trying to impart a casual demeanor. When she was out of sight, she hurried to find Domingo.

Houston must be warned at once!

Ian's uniform was splattered with mud. He unfastened his buckle and removed his saber. The skirmish with the Mexican patrol on the road to Harrisburg had felt good. He and the five men under his command had left seven of the enemy dead and taken five more prisoners, while none of his men had even a scratch.

Ian had just unbuttoned his shirt when his tent flap was pushed open and Emerada entered.

"Where is Houston?" she asked hurriedly, trying not to look at his bare chest or remember what it felt like to run her fingers over the dark hair there.

His glance locked with hers. "He is out with a patrol."

"I must see him at once. Take me to him."

He sat down on the edge of his cot and began removing his muddy boots. "Can't. I don't know which way he went."

"Send someone to find him."

He dropped his boots and stood. "You'll just have to tell me or wait for the general to return."

She stalked toward him and tapped her finger angrily against his chest. "Then you had better find out where he is and get him back here. Santa Anna is on the move, and he knows where you are!"

"Is that supposed to scare me?"

"You had better be scared. He has twenty-five hundred men at his disposal. How many do you have, Ian McCain?"

He captured her hand and held it in a tight

grip. "You know something I've noticed about you, Emerada? When you are angry with me, you use my whole name."

"I am angry. I have waited a long time for Santa Anna to come up against Houston's forces." She jerked her hand free. "I will just have to find Houston myself." She moved to the opening and was about to leave, when he took her by the shoulder and spun her around.

"You have us all dancing to your tune, don't you, little dancer? Me, Houston, and Santa Anna."

"This is no time to argue, Ian. Santa Anna is coming, and you have to stop him!"

His hand dropped away. "Tell me about it," he said at last.

"Do you have a map?"

He went to the camp table, found his map, and unrolled it.

She studied it for a moment and then jabbed her finger on a point. "Mark this well so you can relate it to Houston—Santa Anna intends to trap the Texas army between the San Jacinto River here, and Buffalo Bayou, here."

Ian nodded. "A good plan. No one ever said Santa Anna didn't have the heart of a general."

"You would do well not to underestimate Santa Anna." She walked away from him and turned before she left. "Tell Houston I will do everything I can to keep Santa Anna occupied."

"If anyone can do it, you can," he said almost too casually.

She could tell by his expression that he'd like to say more, but she didn't have time to listen—she had to get back. "Tell Houston I will not be able to contact him again. It's too dangerous. Already Santa Anna is suspicious." She pushed the flap aside. "Good luck, Ian McCain. Take care of yourself." She felt ripped apart by sadness, just thinking about him going into battle. "Do not let anything happen to you."

She rushed outside, half hoping that Ian would come after her, but he didn't.

Ian was in torment, thinking of Emerada in the hands of a man like Santa Anna. If any of them were in danger, it was she, and there was nothing he could do to help her. He reached for one of his boots and shoved his foot into it.

"God keep you safe, my darling," he whispered, knowing they could all be dead by tomorrow.

Emerada rode away swiftly, knowing that this time she had only a three-hour ride to reach Santa Anna's camp.

The two forces were coming closer together, and she didn't hold much hope that Houston could beat Santa Anna.

Chapter Nineteen

Covered by a long black cape, Emerada moved through the Mexican camp on her way to Santa Anna's tent. She could feel the apprehension running through the camp; the soldiers were alert and preparing for a final engagement with the Texas army.

She felt great sorrow in her heart, knowing the fate of Tejas would be decided in a matter of hours, on this very spot. She was still not certain that Houston could win when Santa Anna's force outnumbered him two to one. But she was going to do everything she could to give Houston the advantage.

When she reached Santa Anna's tent, she told the guard she wanted to see the president. He disappeared inside, and moments later Santa Anna himself greeted her and led her inside.

"My dear, you must have sensed I needed you on this eve of battle. Come and comfort me."

There were five officers present, and each one bowed gallantly to her, while their bold eyes appreciated her beauty.

"If you are occupied, I could come back later," she said, turning as though to leave.

Santa Anna took her hand and raised it to his lips, his eyes lingering on hers. "No, stay. We are all but finished here."

Santa Anna seated her on a stool and turned to the others. "Keep the men alert and double the guard. I want no surprises."

Emerada laughed in delight—or she hoped it sounded that way. "Is there really any reason to double the guards? It is not likely that Houston, with his ragtag lot, will attack us. Even he could not be so foolish."

Her voice held a challenge, and Santa Anna examined her eyes to see if there was any mockery there. Sometimes he wasn't sure whether she was goading him, or if she just had a playful nature. "What do you suggest?" he asked.

"It is not for me to say, Excellency," Emerada answered. "But if the men are to be prepared for a battle tomorrow, should they not rest now?" Her laughter was infectious, and his officers joined in. "Houston would have to stop running from you before he could attack, Antonio."

"She is right," one of the officers agreed. "It is unlikely that we will be set upon by a coward."

Santa Anna considered for a moment, and then he nodded. "Houston has displayed his cowardice for all to laugh at him." He turned to his officer. "Have the men stand down, rest, and prepare for tomorrow. Go to it, now. All of you, out!"

After the officers saluted and departed, Santa Anna turned to Emerada. "And how shall I prepare for tomorrow?"

Emerada realized that Houston and Santa Anna were on their final collision course, and Houston needed her help. This was her day of reckoning, and she knew what she must do. She smiled up at Santa Anna. "I am here to see to your pleasure. Would you like that, Antonio?"

His eyes gleamed. "Is this the day I have waited for, Emerada?"

She sauntered up to him and tossed her head, giving him a seductive look. "This is the day I promised I would give you, *Señor Presidente*. This will be a day you will never forget."

He trembled with pleasure. "Why do you wear that heavy cape? Take it off and come into my arms."

"Not just yet," she said, going to the opening and speaking to someone just outside. "Play softly the songs I told you to play, and do not stop until I tell you to. And," she said, raising her voice so it would carry, "*el Presidente* does not want to be disturbed for any reason—do you understand?"

Santa Anna looked quizzical when he heard the strains of a plaintive tune strummed on a guitar. He watched Emerada drop her cape, and he lost his breath when he saw her skimpy costume. Her gown was made of gauzy yellow material that he could see through, and she was wearing almost nothing underneath and wore no shoes upon her feet.

She snapped her fingers, threw back her head so her midnight-colored hair swung to her waist. She inched toward him, then danced just out of reach.

"I have never danced this dance for anyone else," she said as she moved her hips. "It was taught to me by a Gypsy woman from the Romany tribe. It is said that this very dance was performed before Napoleon himself. How fitting that I should dance the dance for you, since you are the Napoleon of the West."

Santa Anna could not tear his eyes away from the beautiful woman he'd so long desired. With his heart leaping in his chest, he sucked air into his lungs. He was so overcome by the sensuous way she moved her hips that he could not speak.

Emerada's hands arched over her head, weaving, hypnotizing, enticing. She wondered how long it would take Santa Anna to tire of her dance and insist on more from her.

Emerada forced a smile to her lips while she circled, almost touching him and then pulling back.

In Emerada's mind, she was dancing for Ian. She did not see the dictator's dark gaze, but Ian's blue eyes. She would probably never see him again, but that was the way it had to be. Ian would never want to touch her after she gave Santa Anna everything he wanted in order to keep him distracted.

Santa Anna moved to the bed and began to unbutton his tunic. "Dance, Emerada, dance," he said in a husky voice. "Dance only for me."

The Texas army came soundlessly across the prairie, under the cover of tall grass. They were so near the Mexican encampment that they could hear an occasional voice.

Ian led a group of cavalrymen, and he, like everyone else, expected to be met by strong resistance, but so far there was none. When they were within two hundred yards, they were discovered and a warning cry went up—but it was too late for the unfortunate Mexicans, who had been caught resting, with only a few guards on duty.

With a vengeance, the Texas army swooped down upon them, slashing and cutting their way through the camp.

Santa Anna had just pulled Emerada onto the bed with him when the first shots rang out.

"What is happening?" he cried, jumping to his feet and running to the tent opening.

Emerada reached for her cape and draped it about her shoulders. "I would think, *Señor Presidente*, that would be General Houston."

"This was not supposed to happen. Is Houston crazy?" His eyes darted about the tent as he looked for a weapon.

"*Sí*," Emerada replied, with joy singing in her heart. "Houston is *loco* like a fox."

Santa Anna was too distracted to notice the sarcasm in Emerada's voice. The gunfire intensified, and he slid his feet into red Moroccan slippers and moved toward his pistol. "I must flee at once! I cannot fall into Houston's hands. He will kill me!"

Emerada moved slowly toward Santa Anna; her hand reached for the dagger that had been concealed in a secret pocket inside her cape. "No, he will not kill you." She had almost reached him, and was prepared to bury her dagger in his heart, when one of his officers burst in.

"*Presidente*, I must get you away quickly," the man said, his eyes wide with horror. "The Americans have overrun the camp, and they will come straight for you. I have brought you something to wear so if they do see you, they will not know who you are."

"There is no time to change. Let us go now!" Santa Anna mumbled, grabbing up the clothes. "Come, Emerada, you must come with us."

She tried not to smile. Houston had done it! Now it would be Santa Anna who was running!

Santa Anna ran from the tent, and Emerada watched him mount a horse and ride in the opposite direction from the fighting. "You will not get far," she called out, but he didn't hear her. He was heading toward the swamps.

Emerada gazed about her while bullets whizzed past her head. This was not what she wanted, to see all those brave Mexican soldiers being cut down while their *presidente* ran like the coward he was.

Domingo rode up, leading her mount. "It is time to leave, Emerada," he said, his eyes filled with sadness.

She swung onto the horse, and they rode away from the scene of death and destruction. There was no happiness in her heart, only a heaviness that invaded her mind. She had helped set this in motion when she'd first pitted her wit against Santa Anna's, and now she must live with the consequences.

The Texans—as most of them now insisted on being called—had won in the most one-sided battle ever fought. They had killed or captured a force twice their size, with only two casualties and seventeen wounded.

One of the wounded was General Sam Houston.

* * *

With Domingo at her side, Emerada pushed her way through the throng of prisoners, searching for Santa Anna.

"He has to be here," she said frantically. "This can't all have been for nothing. He will be dressed as a peasant."

One of the soldiers fell to his knees and looked up at her. "San Antonio Rose, are the Americans going to kill us?"

Pity swelled in her heart for the poor unfortunate men who had done no more than their duty to their country. She knew that many of Houston's troops had attacked the enemy without mercy, taking vengeance for the men who had died at the Alamo and Goliad, but she also knew that Houston would not allow these prisoners to suffer the same fate.

"General Houston is not a butcher like Santa Anna. Now that the fighting is over, you will be treated fairly."

"You will speak to the American general for us, señorita."

"*Sí*, I will speak to him on your behalf. I have little doubt that you will soon be allowed to return to your homes."

"*Gracias*, beautiful one. I will remember you in my prayers from this day forward."

She smiled and moved away. It was heartbreaking to see the proud Mexican soldiers reduced to begging for their lives. They had fought a valiant fight and lost. Texas would soon be a free and independent country. Although her father would have been proud of that, she could find no reason to rejoice. All she wanted to do was find Santa Anna. Then her duty would be finished and she could leave.

When the sun set on that first horrible day, Santa Anna had still not been found. Domingo found Emerada standing on the riverbank, gazing forlornly across the water.

"Knowing it was a worry of yours, I found out that Ian McCain came through the battle unharmed."

Relief ripped through her like a cleansing tide, and she drew in a long breath. "I knew he had to be safe. What about General Houston? I heard he was wounded. How bad is it?"

"General Houston has a minor, but painful, leg wound. Not so bad, considering he had three horses shot from under him during the battle."

She closed her eyes and gathered her thoughts. "And they still have not found Santa Anna?"

"No. But General Houston begs you to come to him. He wants to tell everyone what you did for Tejas."

"Go to him and tell him one of the favors I ask of him is to keep my part in all this a secret." She thrust a note into his huge hand. "Deliver this to Houston. Tell him I will call in my debt when Santa Anna is in his custody. Remind him of his promise to me."

Chapter Twenty

Emerada wandered aimlessly around the small space afforded by the cone-shaped tent where she had been staying since the battle ended the day before. She had no intention of leaving until Santa Anna had been found.

Domingo was quietly watching her as she threw up her hands in disgust.

"Domingo, can you tell me what good Houston accomplished in defeating Santa Anna's army but letting the dictator slip through his hands?"

He shrugged. "A man accustomed to every comfort cannot hide for long, Emerada."

The sound of cheering erupted, and Emerada rushed outside to see what had caused the jubilee. Men were darting about, clapping each other on the back, obviously happy about something.

"What has happened?" she asked one of the men closest to her.

"Haven't you heard, ma'am? They've caught Santa Anna! He was dressed like a peasant and was hiding in the swamp. Our men brought him back as a prisoner, not knowing who he was. Santa Anna must've felt he'd made fools of us even though he was in our custody."

"How did they discover his identity?"

"It happened when they were putting him with the other prisoners, ma'am. His own men recognized him and commenced to bow and scrape, calling out '*Presidente.*' Wish I could've seen that devil's face when he was taken straightaway to Houston."

Emerada walked hurriedly toward Houston's tent. This was the day she'd waited for. Now was the time to ask Houston to honor his debt to her.

When she was within fifty yards of her goal, a guard, tall and slender, with shoulder-length hair and an apologetic look on his face, pointed his rifle in front of her, not threateningly, just to get her attention. "No one goes past this point, ma'am," he told her. "Houston's interrogating the Mexican president."

She shoved his gun aside and walked past him. "If you are going to stop me, señor, you will have to shoot me in the back."

The frantic guard hurried after her. "But, ma'am, I have my orders."

She paid no attention to him. Her gaze was on the men who were crowded around Houston's headquarters. She elbowed her way through and pushed the guard aside at the entrance.

Houston lay upon a cot, his foot bandaged and elevated on a folded blanket. He smiled at Emerada as she approached him.

"Well, Señorita de la Rosa, it seems Texas owes you a great debt."

"I have no time for your accolades, Houston. Where is Santa Anna? I want to see him."

Houston rose up on his elbow. "Now, Emerada, you know I can't let you see him. Ask anything else of me, but not that."

She went down on her knees to him, not to beg, but so that she would be on his eye level. "I told you I would help you in your war, Houston, and I have kept my word, have I not?"

He nodded. "You did, Emerada. For all I know, we might have lost the war but for the information you supplied us. We would have many dead, and possibly would have been beaten soundly if you hadn't kept Santa Anna occupied so we could surprise him."

"You cannot know what it cost me to keep him occupied." She lowered her gaze and gathered her courage before looking back at him. "If you are a man of your word, Houston, I have come to collect my debt."

"And what would that be?"

"I want to be alone with Santa Anna for five minutes. That is all I ask."

"You want to kill him, don't you, Emerada?"

"I will kill him, Houston—make no mistake about that!"

He shook his head and laid his hand gently on her shoulder. "You know I can't allow that to happen."

"Then you will not keep your word?" She looked at him with contempt. "I sometimes thought you a coward, Houston, and at times I thought you a little pompous, but I never thought you dishonorable. I always believed you were a man of your word."

Sam Houston was silent for a moment. "Take her to Santa Anna, Ian. But see she doesn't harm him. I have given my word that he can go free, and I will keep my word."

Emerada had not known that Ian was in the tent with them. When she felt his hand on her shoulder, she shook it off and stood on her own. "General Houston, have you lost your mind? You allowed your own men to die at the Alamo, and yet you let their murderer go free. What kind of justice is that? Do you not know that if you allow Santa Anna his freedom, he will be back? You will only have to fight him again, and next time he may win!"

"War makes strange demands on us, Emerada."

"You will honor your word to the man who

248

murdered your countrymen, but you will not keep your word to me. I spit on your honor, Houston."

Without a backward look, she left the tent and took a big gulp of air when she was outside. She turned to Ian, who had followed her.

"So this is what we can expect from the man we both served, the man we trusted to free Tejas?" Angry tears welled in her eyes and ran down her cheeks before she brushed them away angrily. "Take me to the dictator. I want him to know what a fool he was to trust me—just like I was a fool to trust Houston."

"You're wrong, Emerada. General Houston instructed me to take you to see Santa Anna. But I have to remain with you the whole time. And I can't allow you to harm him in any way."

She looked upward. "Then everything I have done has been for nothing."

He gazed into the distance, his eyes narrowing. "What did you do to keep him distracted?"

She jabbed her finger into his chest. "You do not want to know."

Ian and Houston were the only ones who knew the part Emerada had played in bringing about the downfall of Santa Anna, and he realized that she was feeling betrayed.

He guided her toward the tent where Santa Anna was being held. "Emerada, you aren't the only one who thinks Santa Anna deserves to be executed. But Houston feels that the Mexican president will be punished severely by his own government for signing away Texas. We are free, Emerada, and that's what this war was all about. It wasn't about personal hurts or even revenge. It was about freedom!"

She paused and glared at him. "That might mean something to you, but not to me. I want Santa Anna's death!"

Ian wanted to kill the dictator himself because Emerada must have been forced to give in to his lustful urges to keep him distracted. It hadn't escaped his notice that she had avoided looking directly into his eyes. It must mean that Santa Anna had made love to her. "Santa Anna must have left his tent in a hurry when we attacked," Ian said, changing the subject. "When he was found, he was wearing red leather slippers."

"When the firing started, you never saw such a coward. He was out and gone before I could stop him."

Ian nodded to a tent that was under heavy guard. "He's there. It would seem Santa Anna has many vices, among which is an opium habit. He asked Houston for his opium box, which had been confiscated along with his other belongings."

"And Houston gave it to him?"

"He did."

Ian saw her shoulders straighten and her chin quiver. "You do not have to come with me, Ian."

"Oh, but I do, Emerada. I don't trust you to be alone with him."

"As you wish." She moved forward, and when the guards would have stopped her, Ian nodded for them to let her pass. But he stayed right next to her.

Santa Anna was sitting at a writing desk when they entered. On seeing Emerada, he smiled and put down the pen. "Emerada! My dear, who would have thought you would come to me in my time of need, just as you did the night of the battle?" He stepped toward her and reached for her hands. She did not pull away.

"How did you know I needed you?"

Ian watched as she stiffened and pulled her hands out of his grasp. "You are a fool, Antonio! You still do not know what happened that night, do you?"

"*Sí*." He gripped her hand and raised it to his lips. "You knew that I was on the eve of my darkest hour and you came to comfort me."

Ian wanted to rip the Mexican general's heart out, but he knew he could not take his eyes off Emerada or she would do just that.

She shoved Santa Anna away. "I did not go to comfort you, fool. I was there to distract you so General Houston could sneak up on you."

Santa Anna's face drained of color, and he dropped down on a stool. "I see it all now. That is why you convinced me I did not need double guards."

"It was easy to make you believe anything I wanted you to," she said. Hatred curled through her mind and dominated her thoughts. "And now you are a beaten man with nowhere to go. You lost Tejas to the Americans, and that will not make you a popular man in Mexico."

Santa Anna buried his face in his hands. "I thought you cared for me. When you—" He glanced up at Ian. "Many things are clear now. It was you who persuaded me not to shoot that man because you were working with him and Houston. What a fool I was."

"None of that is important," Emerada said, moving closer to him, her hand going to her waist, where she had hidden her dagger. "Do you really want to know why I helped bring about your downfall, *Señor Presidente?*"

His eyes were dark and searching. "What have I ever done to you but love you—yes, I could have loved you more than any other woman I have ever known. Why did you do this to me?"

She wanted to strike him, to smash his face, to make it so he wouldn't be able to seduce innocent young girls so easily. She took a deep breath and asked in a steady voice, "Do you remember Felipe de la Rosa and his three sons, who lived on Talavera Ranch?"

Santa Anna nodded. "I always recall the names of traitors. They housed Stephen Austin, whom I imprisoned. I should have had him put to death, as I did the de la Rosa family."

Before Ian realized what she was going to do, Emerada whipped out her dagger and pressed it against Santa Anna's throat. "You demon from hell, on your feet!"

Santa Anna stood up slowly, licking his lips in fear.

"I never told you my full name, did I, *Señor Presidente?*" She pressed so hard on the dagger that a drop of blood ran down the blade. "My name is Emerada de la Rosa, and you had my father and brothers murdered. They never did anything disloyal to you, but I have. I have deceived you at every turn, and I have helped bring you to your present state."

"Don't do it, Emerada," Ian cautioned, slowly moving closer to her. "He's not worth it. Think about it."

"Stand back, Ian, or I promise you, I'll spill every drop of blood he has in his body. Why should he live when better men than he have died for his glory?"

Emerada looked into Santa Anna's eyes, which were glazed with terror. "Can you think of any reason that I should let you live?"

He nodded. "I am sorry about your family. Had I known they were—"

"I do not want to hear anything you have to say, dictator."

"Emerada," Ian said, as he moved ever closer

to her. "I don't believe you are capable of killing anyone—not even him."

She turned to Ian, and he saw hatred burning in the depths of her eyes. "I could kill this man, and the world would be a better place for it."

Ian knew that if he moved any closer she might just drive the dagger into Santa Anna's throat. He decided to trust his instinct; if he was wrong, Houston could have his head afterward. "Go ahead, Emerada, kill him. If you really believe it will bring you peace of mind, drive the knife into his throat. If you think your father and brothers would expect it of you and would be proud of such a deed, do it!"

"Are you crazed, Colonel McCain?" Santa Anna said, his gaze never leaving Emerada's. "Have you forgotten that I spared your life?"

"Do not speak to him, Antonio," Emerada warned. "Speak to me. I am the one who holds your life at the tip of my blade."

"What do you want from me?" he asked, his glance now darting to Ian for help. "Say what you want, and I will do it."

"You had your soldiers burn Talavera—what I want to know is . . . " She faltered for a moment, trying to put her worst fears into words. "Did my family burn in the house? Did you have them burned . . . alive?"

"No, no, beautiful one. They died mercifully. I'm sure they did."

The knife in her hand wavered. "You do not even know how they died, do you? You ordered their deaths, but you did not even bother to ask the men who murdered them how it happened."

"I do not burn people," he said, his voice trembling with fear.

"What about the defenders of the Alamo?" she reminded him.

"They were already dead when I had their bodies burned." His eyes went again to Ian. "For God's sake, Raven's Claw, help me!"

"Are you going to kill him," Ian asked casually, "or are you going to talk him to death?"

Emerada's eyes bore into Santa Anna's, and the dagger in her hand wavered. She saw sweat appear on the dictator's face. She wanted to drive the knife into him, but when the moment came, she cried out and dropped the knife.

"I cannot do it!" She shook her head. "I lived for this day, and I cannot kill him."

She covered her face with her trembling hands and turned away, while Santa Anna dropped to his knees because he could no longer stand.

Ian slipped his arms around her, and she looked at him, stunned. "Why could I not kill him?"

"If you had, you would be no better than he is. I believe your family can rest in peace now. You have done many brave deeds, Emerada, but the most heroic of them all was what you did just now. You could have killed him, and yet you spared his life."

She pushed Ian away and ran outside, calling for Domingo.

Ian picked up her dagger where she'd dropped it and looked at Santa Anna. "You don't know how close you came to death. She would have been justified if she had killed you. And I have little doubt that if Houston knew her story, he'd have let her do it."

"So," Santa Anna said, feeling braver now, "will you tell Houston?"

"The story is not mine to tell." He wanted to ask the man if he'd laid his hands on Emerada, if he'd made love to her, but of course he couldn't do that. He was afraid to know the truth.

"Let us hope you sleep lightly," Ian taunted. "One never knows with Emerada. She might change her mind and pay you another visit."

"It is your duty to see that I am protected."

"Yes, you sniveling coward. I'd like to give you the same chance you gave Travis and Bowie, and so would many others." He shrugged. "Yes, if I were you, I'd sleep lightly."

Ian went outside in time to see Emerada riding out of camp, with her ever faithful Domingo at her side. He knew where she was going. When Houston could spare him, he would ride to Talavera.

He walked in the direction of Houston's headquarters. Emerada had been ill-used by all of them. He could only guess what unspeakable acts she'd been forced to perform to keep Santa Anna occupied.

Emerada was in a pensive mood as she rode away from the encampment. Her work for Houston was over. He had won, and Tejas was free. But she found little gratification in that. Perhaps one day she would, but not now. She'd had Santa Anna under the blade, yet allowed him to live. She had made terrible sacrifices, and for what?

She felt every mile that stretched between her and Ian. She loved him, and probably always would. In the deepest recesses of her mind, she must have known it from the beginning.

"Where do we go, Emerada?" Domingo asked.

"We go to Talavera. I will remain there for a while. Then we will go to New Orleans and possibly France. I want to see my aunt."

"We will not rebuild the ranch?"

"It is not mine, Domingo. If you recall, Santa Anna confiscated it."

"I feel sure Señor Houston will give it back to you if you ask him."

"No. I will never ask Houston for anything else—I will never see him again."

"Or Ian McCain?"

"I will not see him either. He told me that he has a woman waiting for him in America."

Domingo said nothing more. Emerada had

lost her heart to the tall American. And it seemed to him that her affection was returned. Why, then, was she running from Ian McCain, and why had Ian McCain allowed her to leave?

Chapter Twenty-one

Emerada moved through the charred ruins of Talavera, pausing beside the fireplace and chimney which were still standing. It seemed to her that she could hear the echo of laughter from the past, but, of course, it was only the wind whistling through the chimney.

She shook her head and moved away. When she left this time, she would never return. The past was dead, and she had to deal with the living. Her aunt would soon be returning to New Orleans; she had to be there when Aunt Dilena arrived. There were many things she had to confess to her aunt, and none of them would make the woman happy.

Her hand went down to rest on her stomach. She was carrying Ian's child. She had first begun to suspect it several weeks ago, when she awoke every morning feeling sick to her stomach. Ian had impregnated her the first night they had made love. Already her stomach was slightly rounded, and her clothing was tight at the waist. The time would come when she would no longer be able to hide her condition, and she must leave Tejas before that happened.

She had not yet told Domingo that she was with child, but he was shrewd and had probably guessed it already.

She glanced up at the gathering darkness, her thoughts tumbling over each other. "Domingo," she called, as she hurried to the stable. "Domingo. We must be ready to leave before dawn tomorrow."

Domingo paused at his sweeping and leaned on the broom. "Where do we go?"

"New Orleans."

"To see your aunt?"

"*Sí*. I will never return to Tejas." She shook her head. "I am not even certain that I will remain in New Orleans for long."

He nodded, feeling sad inside. For four weeks he had watched the road leading to Talavera, expecting Ian McCain to come for Emerada, but he had not come.

He leaned the broom against the wall and laid wood for a fire. Perhaps he should have found a way to tell McCain that he had fathered Emerada's child. But it was not for him to tell. "I will make ready to leave," he said simply.

* * *

Ian knew before he arrived at the stable that Emerada had gone. He dismounted, cursing the duty that had kept him at Houston's side for so long.

He shoved against the door, and the rusty hinges creaked open. The only sound that could be heard was the calling of a mourning dove and the beating of his heart.

She was gone!

He gazed around the walls and across the floor. It was apparent from the cleanly swept floor and the evidence of a recent fire that someone had been here.

He bent down and examined the ashes. The fire was still warm, perhaps three hours old. He saw no blankets or foodstuffs. Emerada had been there very recently, but from all indications, she would not be returning.

Desperation gnawed at his mind, and his shoulders slumped under the heavy feeling of loss.

Where could she have gone? How would he ever find her? She could be anywhere. Hell, she could even have gone to France.

He tried to remember all that Emerada had told him about her aunt. What was her name?

He walked outside and examined two sets of footprints. The larger set of prints would be Domingo's, and the smaller, Emerada's. He traced the outline of her small footprint, feeling as if his heart had just been ripped out of his chest.

A despondent Ian mounted his horse and followed the trail long enough to discover that Emerada and Domingo had ridden in an easterly direction. They could be heading for Galveston to take a ship for France.

He suddenly smiled. No! She hadn't gone to France. She'd told him about her aunt's home in New Orleans. That was where she was heading. If she wasn't there, surely someone could tell him where to find her.

He nudged his horse into a gallop. He could not desert Houston now to follow her, but he would never give up until he found her. He tried not to think what his life would be like without her. He tried to ignore the panic that ate at his mind.

He tried . . . but he didn't succeed.

September

Emerada walked across the wide veranda of the stately old house on Rampart Street that was a remarkable testimony to the French Colonial style. She stepped into the walled garden that her aunt had always taken pride in, keeping two gardeners to care for it. Now it was so overgrown with weeds that Emerada could barely make out the pathway.

She stood very still, breathing in the wonderful perfumed mixture of flowers blending with the musty aroma that was purely New Orleans.

She and her Aunt Dilena had rarely been in residence at this house, since her aunt's dancing kept them mostly in Europe. It wasn't until four years ago that she had been separated from her aunt for the first time. Emerada had attended the Palitier's School for Young Ladies here in New Orleans. She had been at the school when she'd learned about the deaths of her father and brothers.

Emerada wished for the peacefulness that she'd once known in this garden. Now all she could feel was the deep sorrow that washed through her, the torment that tore at her heart, and the loneliness that was so deep and tragic that it haunted her day and night.

She glanced back at the huge house, which was in desperate need of paint. It was there that she had learned to dance from a dance master her Aunt Dilena had employed for her. When her talent had exceeded that of the master, her aunt had taken over her training, insisting that Emerada polish her skills.

Emerada stooped to smell a red rose, plucked it, and ran her finger over the velvet-soft petals. There were sad memories here, too. Her beloved Aunt Dilena was dead.

She bowed under the weight of her sorrow. Now she had lost the last member of her family, and she was so terribly alone. Sadly, she hadn't been with her aunt when she died, just as she hadn't been with her father and brothers when they had died.

Emerada raised her head as a mild breeze dried her tears. How could she have known that while she was in Tejas, her Aunt Dilena would contract yellow fever? Molly, her aunt's maid, explained to Emerada that her Aunt Dilena had come home early from France and found Emerada gone. She had taken ill the day before she was going to set out to look for Emerada. Her beautiful, kind aunt, who had been her world for so long, had died alone, without Emerada to comfort her. Had her aunt known how much she loved her? She must have.

Even beyond the grave, her aunt had reached out and touched her life. She had left her this house, but there was little money for its up-keep—she had been forced to dismiss all the servants but Molly, who'd been with her aunt for thirty years. Her aunt had also left her the town house in Paris, which seemed more like home than this New Orleans residence. Emerada had decided that when the baby came she would sell this house and move to France.

She pressed the palm of her hand against her swollen stomach, trying to think of something happy. There was the promise of a new life growing within her. This child, Ian's child, was a great comfort to her in her sadness. With this baby, a part of Ian would always be with her.

She had thought a great deal about how she would present the baby to the world, and she had finally decided that she would give the child Ian's last name. Ian need never know. He wasn't going to find her in New Orleans, and certainly not when she moved to France.

Emerada knew that she and Ian had touched each other in a special way—with her it was love, with him, probably something quite different. Even so, she knew that the memory of her would be stamped on Ian's mind, just as his was on hers. Their lovemaking had been beautiful and exciting. She wasn't wrong about that. He'd even admitted it to her.

She crushed the flower in her hand and remembered the feel of his lips on hers. Yes, thoughts of her might pass fleetingly through his mind when he first took a wife to his bed. But that was all she'd ever be to him—a fleeting thought.

Perhaps, with the passing of time, when he had fathered children by his wife, Ian wouldn't even remember her at all.

But she would always remember him. She would have his child to remind her.

Emerada was asleep and came awake with a start. She gasped and ran her hand over her stomach. She felt a fluttering like butterfly wings inside her. With the moon streaming through her window, she reached over and lit the oil lamp.

Plumping her pillow, she propped herself up

and waited for a repeat of the wonderful sensation. The baby had moved—that had to be what she'd felt. It was alive and growing inside her, taking nourishment from her body.

"I love you," she whispered. "Whether you are a son or a daughter, I promise you that if it is in my power, you will never know a sad day. I will dry your tears, kiss away your hurts, and be with you as you grow strong and honorable, like your father."

The fluttering stirred within her again, and her eyes widened with wonder. Now she truly felt like a mother.

She turned onto her side and slid down on her pillow. What little money she had would soon dwindle. The well-being of her baby was suddenly foremost in her thoughts. She would have to do something soon to ensure the child's future.

When she went to France, she would dance, as her aunt had. Many of her aunt's friends would help her in that. She was talented. She knew that. Of course, she would have to dance under another name in Paris. She would never again be the San Antonio Rose.

She was thoughtful for a moment. Her Aunt Dilena had used only her first name as her stage name.

Emerada? Yes, that was what she would do.

Of course, after the baby was born, she would have to practice long, hard hours. But she'd worry about that when the time came.

She thought of a little boy she'd seen in the market the day before. He must have been about two years old. The father had gripped the child's hand, stopping to introduce his son to everyone he met. She thought of her own father and how he had influenced her life.

A child needed a father, and hers would have only her.

She pounded her pillow, making a hollow for her head. "I will love this baby enough for two parents," she vowed.

She blew out the lamp and settled into the soft bed. She wondered if the child would have its father's wonderful eyes.

Oh, please, she thought, feeling warmth surround her heart, *let this child have Ian's beautiful blue eyes.*

Chapter Twenty-two

October

Emerada was restless. It had been raining for five days straight, making it impossible for her to get out of the house. The rain pelted relentlessly against the roof, and she stood at the window, watching wide runnels streak down the glass, making it difficult to see past the front gate.

She knew no one in the town. Her aunt had cultivated no friendships in New Orleans, using this house only when she was weary of the adoring crowds and wanted to be alone. Those quiet times Emerada had spent with her aunt were among her most treasured memories.

She moved away from the window and

stared up at her Aunt Dilena's portrait, which hung above the mantel. Her aunt wore a frilly white ballerina costume, with her red hair spilling down her back and a half smile on her face.

Many of her aunt's friends had remarked upon how alike the two of them looked, but Emerada knew she would never be the beauty her Aunt Dilena had been. As she stared at the portrait, wishing she could will her aunt back to life, a tear trailed down her cheek.

Loneliness ripped at her heart, and she glanced upward, trying to control her raw emotions. Molly had explained to Emerada after one of her bouts with crying that when a woman was going to have a baby, her emotions would often spill over. But didn't she have good cause to cry? She had no one except Domingo, and she couldn't share her deepest thoughts with him. If only Josifina had lived. She would have helped her get through this trying time in her life.

For so long now she had been exposed to death and sadness—the death of her family, her aunt, Josifina, and all the people who'd died in the war. She embraced the thought of the life that stirred within her body. She needed this baby. It would be someone to love, someone who would need her.

Emerada wrapped her red woolen shawl tightly about herself and took up her vigil at the window once more. Lonely hours stretched ahead of her, with no companion to brighten the shadowy corners of her life.

She wondered what Ian was doing at that moment. Could he be thinking of her as she was of him?

There was a knock on the front door, and she heard Molly's footsteps pass the morning room on her way to the door. Emerada was sure it must be the farmer delivering milk and cheese. But why would he come out on a day such as this? she wondered.

She heard a man's deep voice but could not hear what was being said.

Moments later she heard Molly's light footsteps approaching. She poked her head through the doorway, her plump face etched into a concerned frown.

"There's a gentleman to see you, ma'am. He said his name is Ian McCain."

Emerada didn't know whether to laugh or cry. He had come!

Then panic set in, and she wondered if she should see him at all. If he found out about the baby, he would feel obligated to marry her.

"Shall I tell him you are indisposed?" the maid asked, seeing how pale Emerada's cheeks were.

"No," Emerada said, draping her shawl about her in such a way that it concealed her rounded stomach. "Show him in, Molly. And prepare a light lunch. He may be hungry. Make coffee for later. I'll ring if I want you to serve lunch."

When Molly withdrew, Emerada clasped her hands nervously. Had she made a mistake in seeing Ian?

Oh, why has he come?

There was no mistaking Ian's heavy boot steps against the parquet floor. She looked up just as he appeared at the door, his tall frame filling the doorway. He wore a blue cutaway coat over tight-fitting black pantaloons tucked inside knee boots. His stiff white shirt collar rested against his tanned cheeks, and he carried a small leather pouch. His dark hair glistened from the rain, and she was reminded of the time he had held her in his arms, standing in the rain at Talavera.

He had never looked so handsome, and Emerada's heart felt as if it had slammed against her chest. She clutched her shawl tightly to keep her hands from shaking.

"Ian. What a surprise! How ever did you find me?" She hoped her voice didn't tremble—she knew she was talking too fast, but she always did when she was nervous. "What brings you to New Orleans?"

Ian said simply, "You."

If he had displayed any emotion, showed the slightest bit of happiness at seeing her, she would have been in his arms. But he merely looked at her with an air of detachment.

"You came all this way when a letter would have sufficed?"

He moved farther into the room, reminding her of her manners. "Please be seated. You must be chilled. Let me offer you something warm to drink, or brandy if you like. Perhaps you are hungry?"

He waited for her to be seated before he took a seat across from her and placed the leather pouch beside him. "No, thank you. I dined earlier."

"Of course."

They were like two polite strangers meeting for the first time. She sat on the edge of her seat as if she might take flight at the least provocation, while he was stiff and formal.

"I trust you left General Houston in good health?"

He leaned back, placed his arm across the back of the sofa, and looked at her for a long moment before answering. "He is well and sends you his regards."

Again they lapsed into silence. Hers wasn't so much that she didn't know what to say; it was because she cared so deeply for Ian that she felt vulnerable and unsure of herself. She was afraid that at any moment her emotions would spill out and she wouldn't be able to control what she said.

She clasped her hands in her lap. "Our newspapers are filled with the wondrous things taking place in Tejas, or should I say Texas.

Imagine, a country unto itself. My father would have been proud."

"He would have been proud of you, Emerada."

She made sure not to look directly into his eyes, because they were too unsettling and had the power to make her melt inside. "I do not think he would be proud of some of the things I did to accomplish my goals, Ian."

Again, silence.

After a while Ian stood up and walked over to the mantel, studying the portrait that hung there.

He glanced back at Emerada. "Your aunt?"

"*Sí.* That was done three years ago in Paris by an artist, I believe, of some renown."

"I can see where you get your beauty. You are very like her."

"You are too kind. I am nothing like her, although I will always strive to have her goodness."

"Am I to be allowed to meet her? I have heard you speak so kindly of her that I would be honored to make her acquaintance."

She lowered her head. "I am sorry that will not be possible."

"Of course, she must be in Europe."

"No. My aunt . . . died while I was in Tejas."

He came to her, bending down on his knees and taking her hands in a warm clasp. "Emerada, what can I say to comfort you? I am so sorry!"

She felt the heat of his hands, and she wanted to lay her head on his shoulder, seeking what comfort it would bring. Instead, she forced herself to stay where she was.

"Thank you for your sympathy, Ian. Now, if there is nothing further to discuss, I am very weary."

"Nothing further!" He turned her to face him. "Have you any idea what I had to go through to find you? Nothing further, you say! You can't suppose that I came all this way to pass pleasantries with you?"

She raised her gaze to his and saw anger in his blue eyes. "Why did you come, Ian?"

"I'm damned if I know!"

He moved to the sofa and retrieved the pouch, opened the flap, and withdrew a parchment, displaying it for her inspection. "You will notice that this bears the new, but not yet official, seal of Texas. I was empowered by President Houston to present this to you with his heartfelt gratitude."

"I do not understand," she said. "Houston is president?"

"I believe that comes as no surprise to anyone."

"Of course. Many people believe Tejas will benefit from his leadership."

He arched an eyebrow at her. "There was a time when you would have thought him the right man for the office."

"I still do. But I have not quite forgiven him for his lenient treatment of Santa Anna."

Ian stood before her in a proud military stance. She wondered what he was thinking and what emotions warred within him. He looked at her coldly, like some disinterested stranger.

"I will read the document to you," he said in a dispassionate voice. " 'In gratitude, the great Republic of Texas wishes to acknowledge and reward Emerada de la Rosa for her acts of heroism during our fight for independence. Therefore, Texas returns and conveys to her and her heirs the property known as the Talavera Ranch, which was previously awarded to the de la Rosa family by a Spanish land grant dated 1786.' "

Emerada covered her eyes as he continued to read the legal document that restored Talavera to her. She willed herself not to cry, but tears swam in her eyes. She hardly heard his words until the last sentence.

" 'Please accept our heartfelt appreciation for the bravery you displayed in defense of your country.' "

Ian folded the parchment and handed it to her. "You will see that it's signed by Sam Houston himself."

He placed the document in her hand, and she looked up at him. "I do not know what to say."

"Say nothing. If anyone deserves to be honored, it's you."

"I do not want anyone to know about what I did."

He nodded. "Houston was sensitive to your feelings. It seems he made you a promise that he would never tell anyone unless you gave him leave to. Regardless what you may think, Houston keeps his word."

"I will never give him permission to make my part in the war public knowledge."

"Then history will never hear about the valuable service that the San Antonio Rose rendered Texas. There will be rumors, of course, but Houston will never break faith with you."

"You know all about me, Ian. Will you keep my secret?"

"I will never speak of it to anyone. It is your secret, and yours alone." He sat back down and studied her face. "Pity, though. You did so much for our cause."

"But I did not do it for any noble reason."

"Yes, you did. You did it out of love for your family."

She smiled at him. "Thank you. And when you see Houston . . . never mind. I will write to him. I am grateful that Talavera has been returned to me."

He watched her closely. "Will you return to Texas?"

She wanted to go home to Tejas more than

anything, to rebuild the ranch house and to live again in her childhood home. But she could never do that now. She had to think about her baby.

"No. I suppose I will engage a solicitor to find a buyer for the ranch. It is prime land and should be easy to dispose of."

He stood up and nodded toward the rest of the room. "So this is what you want out of life? I had thought you loved the ranch. Why are you so determined to be rid of it when it meant so much to you before?"

"You would not understand."

There was anger in his voice. "Try me." His gaze fell on the shawl she had carefully arranged to hide her pregnancy.

He reached out to touch the edge of it. "I believe this is how you first came into my life. How well I remember the first time I retrieved your shawl."

"And this is how we will part," she said, snatching the shawl out of his fingers.

"I am going to be in New Orleans on business for a week to ten days. May I see you again?"

She knew she should sever all ties with Ian. There was danger in seeing him again. But she was not ready to dismiss him from her life just yet. She would see him once more.

"Yes, if you would like."

He bowed to her. "Until later, then."

"*Sí.* Until the next time."

After Ian left, a battle waged inside Emerada's head—a battle between tears and pride. Pride won.

That night when she went to bed, she had trouble sleeping. All she could think about was Ian's cold indifference to her.

Through her window, she watched the moon rise, and she was still awake to see it set.

Chapter Twenty-three

For three days Emerada kept a vigil at the front window. Every time a carriage approached, her heart would leap to her throat. When it didn't stop, she would be crushed with disappointment.

On the fourth day Emerada paced the length of the veranda, knowing she could not go on this way. If she remained in New Orleans, she would always have that small hope in the back of her mind that Ian would come for her. Also, there would always be the fear that he would find out about the baby.

She hurried into the house, calling Domingo. She found him in the workroom, shining her black leather boots.

"I have come to a decision," she told him.

"Tomorrow I want you to go to the dock and make arrangements for us to sail for France."

He was accustomed to Emerada's impulsiveness, so, undaunted, he asked the practical question. "Have we money?"

"I have decided to sell some of my aunt's jewels. Then, when this house sells, we will have enough money to last until I can dance."

Domingo nodded, knowing she had it all worked out in her mind. Emerada was the most capable woman he'd ever known. What worried him was that she had no fear. She was unaware of the times he'd had to protect her from trouble of her own making. She didn't know about all the men he'd had to keep away from her. He'd broken a few arms and cracked a few heads to keep her safe. But he was getting old, and the time might come when he could no longer protect her. What would happen to her then?

"I will see to it tomorrow. Will I need a ticket for Molly?"

"No, Domingo. Molly will not want to leave New Orleans. I will have to make other arrangements for her." She looked wistful. "Although I would like to have her with me when the baby comes."

He nodded and went back to polishing her boots—this was the first time she'd mentioned the baby to him. He hummed at his work, thinking he could live in France as well as anywhere, as long as he was near Emerada. After all, he'd promised her father that he would always take care of her. It seemed she was going to need him more than ever now that there was a little one on the way.

Ian waited for the maid to answer his knock. Business for Houston had kept him occupied for the last week. Now he was ready to return to Texas, but he couldn't go without seeing Emerada once more.

Domingo opened the door and nodded for him to enter. "Señorita Emerada is not in, Señor McCain. You may wait for her, but she will be gone for most of the day."

"I had planned on leaving later today. Could you tell me where I can find her?"

The big man was silent for a moment. "*Sí.* Do you know where the cemetery is located?"

"I can find it."

"She went there to place flowers on her aunt's grave."

Ian thanked him and retraced his steps to the carriage. When he thought about Emerada, it was with such a deep ache. She had been so young and innocent, and he sometimes felt guilty that he'd taken advantage of her. There was so much left unsaid between them. It would probably never be said now.

The carriage moved down the street, and he leaned back, wondering what his life would be like if he could never see Emerada again.

* * *

A midmorning shower had left pools of water on the uneven walkway, and Emerada stepped cautiously around them. When she reached her aunt's tomb, she stared silently up at the monument that rose like a sentinel above the grave. It was a white marble angel with spread wings, its gaze looking toward heaven. She placed the roses on the monument and dropped to her knees, bowing her head in prayer.

And that was the way Ian found her.

Not wanting to intrude on her mourning, he waited for her to finish her prayer. He was glad for the chance to observe Emerada without her being aware of it. A warm breeze lifted the curls from her shoulders, and he could almost feel the texture of her hair. Since the cobblestones were rough, she had used her shawl to kneel upon. He wondered if she might be cold. She easily became ill when she was chilled. He exhaled a tortured breath. Would he ever stop worrying about her?

Emerada made the sign of the cross and stood, her face once more turned upward to the winged angle. Ian's loving gaze began at her slender neck and worked downward. Her bodice was loose, but he could still see the outline of her firm breasts. He liked her in yellow; it made her skin glow. Yes, there was definitely a glow about her. As his gaze moved to her waist, he froze.

Emerada heard someone beside her, and turned to meet Ian's gaze. He looked confused, and she wondered why.

"I did not expect you here, Ian McCain," she said, reaching for her shawl. That was when she realized her mistake; she should have kept the shawl in place to conceal her rounded stomach!

She could tell from his stricken expression that Ian knew about the baby.

"My God, Emerada, why didn't you let me know? You could have written me, and I would have come right away."

Her hand trembled, and she knotted her shawl, twisting the delicate fringe around her finger so tightly it turned blue. "If you are referring to my baby, it is none of your concern, Ian. There was no reason for me to tell you."

He came closer to her, and she quickly stepped back.

"Is it mine?"

The fact that he could ask such an insulting question made it easy to speak the lie that was forming in her mind. She certainly didn't want him to feel any responsibility toward her or the baby.

"This baby is not yours."

Emerada saw him flinch at her words.

"Then it has to be Santa Anna's baby."

She let her silence confirm his suspicion.

Emerada saw his outraged expression, but he quickly pushed his anger aside. "It doesn't matter who the father is; you need a husband.

There are too many children without fathers. This one will have a name—mine."

"You take too much for granted, Ian. Do you feel it is your duty to offer me marriage as gratitude from the great Republic of Texas, for services rendered?"

The muscles in his neck tightened from the obvious restraint he was exercising over his anger. "How could you think that? I know you don't want to marry Santa Anna, even if he were free to marry you—that leaves only me."

Her heart was crying, *Say you love me, say you love me, and I will be in your arms—I will tell you that you are my baby's true father.*

"You owe me nothing, Ian, just as I owe you nothing. Why would you think I want your name for my child? What makes you think I want a husband—any husband?" She moved down the walkway, and he followed her. "I will admit that your offer is magnanimous, Ian. However, I would never have thought you so charitable as to offer marriage."

"Then you don't know me at all. Do you think I care who the father is? I will be a father to your child."

She paused and looked up at him, hoping the misery she felt didn't reflect in her eyes. "I believe I have something to say about that. And, as I recall, you are already betrothed to a woman in Virginia."

"That is not a concern." He studied her face closely. "I am beginning to understand. You don't want to marry me because I was also born without benefit of a father. Is that your reason, Emerada?"

Anguish seemed carved into his face. Ian turned away from her and glanced back at the marble angel that loomed above her aunt's tomb. "Would she have approved of your having this child without marriage?"

"I do not know." She shook her head, realizing how deeply she had hurt him. She should have remembered how troubled he was over the manner of his own birth. He was offering to help her, even though he believed the baby was Santa Anna's.

"I appreciate how you feel, Ian." She placed her hand on his arm. "This child will not suffer as you have. I will make certain of that. You see, this baby will be born in France, and someday I will tell my baby how heroic his father was."

He spun around, his eyes searching hers. "Then you will lie to the child. Will you tell the child that his father was willing to let his men die while he hid in the swamps like a sniveling coward? Or will you tell the child that his real father had his grandfather and uncles put to death?"

She felt hot tears gather behind her lashes. "My baby will know everything when the time comes."

"I can't accept the fact that you are so callous about the baby's future. I know what it feels like to have no father. Would you condemn your baby to that fate?"

"My child will not know who Santa Anna is, Ian. France is a long way away. You lived with your father's name, although it was not legally yours. So will this child."

She could tell Ian was struggling with his next words. "So you allowed that butcher to put his hands on you, just so you could destroy him. You risked having his child so you could have your revenge. I don't understand that kind of reasoning, and I don't believe your family would have thanked you for allowing the dictator to impregnate you!"

Her sadness turned to anger at his accusations. "Yet you think it was perfectly all right for me to let *you* make love to me?" She curled her hands into fists. Nothing would ever induce her to tell him the truth now. Not after he'd hurled insults at her head. "Do not forget that I kept Santa Anna distracted so your army could overpower him. Surely that was worth a little sacrifice?"

They glared at each other for a long moment; then she spoke. "I have nothing more to say to you, Ian McCain."

She watched his features harden, as if he was trying to comprehend all she'd told him. He shrugged. "Perhaps I'm wrong. You may have liked that man's hands on you. I have heard that many women do."

She turned and hurried toward her carriage,

unmindful of the puddles of water. She had nothing more to say to Ian, ever!

Suddenly Ian gripped her arm and spun her around. "I was not finished talking to you."

"Do you expect to force me to listen to you? For that is what you will have to do—force me. I never want to see you again."

He didn't loosen his grip on her for fear she would take flight. He could feel the rise and fall of her breasts as he gripped her tighter against him. "This baby will have my name, Emerada. Think about it—I give the child my name, you go back to Texas with me and remain until the child is born, and then you are free to go where you will. I will make no demands on you, and you will make none on me. The final result will be that your child will have a name. Is the baby not worth a small sacrifice?"

She was astonished by his offer. "You are saying if I marry you, neither of us will be tied to the other?"

He stepped away from her, cramming his hands in his pockets because he didn't know what else to do with them. He stared at a branch that swayed in the wind, just above Emerada's head. "I merely want to make it clear that if you marry me, you will be free to leave after the baby arrives."

She knew she was going to agree to marry him because of the baby. He would never have to know that the child she bore was indeed his.

She would go with him to Tejas, have the baby, and then return to France.

She remembered him telling her about the woman that he was betrothed to in Virginia. She couldn't say he had ever kept his feelings for the woman a secret. He must love Pauline very much, although he had shared beautiful, intimate moments with Emerada. Emerada would steal only a little from the woman for her baby's sake. Then Ian would be free to go to his Pauline.

"If I marry you, Ian, will you promise to give me my freedom after the baby is born?"

"You have my word that the day you give birth, you will be free of me forever."

"Is that a promise?"

"I gave you my word, and I never go back on my word."

She straightened her shoulders and looked into his eyes. "I have always found you to be trustworthy. I will marry you, have this child, and then take up my life again."

He nodded and held out his arm to her. "It's a bargain."

A sudden clap of thunder shook the ground, and it started raining hard. Ian hurried Emerada to his carriage and told her to wait while he dismissed her driver.

Emerada leaned back, dabbing rain from her face with her lace handkerchief, wondering if she'd lost her mind. She had just agreed to marry Ian, knowing he loved someone else.

She must be begging for heartache. She'd tried to convince herself that she was marrying Ian only for the baby, but she couldn't lie to herself. She loved Ian, and the thought of never seeing him again had been so painful she could hardly endure it.

Her face burned with shame for allowing Ian to believe that she had been intimate with Santa Anna. It made her sick inside that Ian would always believe she had allowed Santa Anna to touch her. She'd found out the day of the battle that she would have killed either Santa Anna or herself before she would have allowed that monster to make love to her. Why didn't Ian know that about her?

Ian climbed into the coach and sat opposite her. "You are soaked. We had better get you home."

"Where will we live in Tejas, Ian?"

"I have been assigned the sad duty of helping rebuild San Antonio. I believe there is a boardinghouse where you'll be quite comfortable until I can find something more suitable."

Emerada was glad for the opportunity to talk of something other than her and the baby. "What a sad task you have ahead of you, Ian. There will be so many people who will need help, and so much destroyed that must be rebuilt."

"So it would seem. I'm still in the Texas army and must fulfill my duties, Emerada. I believe I can safely say that you will not have to endure my presence, except on rare occasions." He wiped the raindrops on his forehead with his coatsleeve. "Is this arrangement to your satisfaction?"

She searched his face for evidence of the gentleness she'd seen in him at Talavera when he had planted his seed in her. This Ian was more like the man she'd first met, a cold, impersonal stranger.

It was on the tip of her tongue to tell him the truth, but she caught herself just in time. "I have no objections to the arrangement."

"Have you any objections to leaving New Orleans?"

Emerada shook her head. "No, none."

The carriage hit a bump, and he grabbed her to steady her, and then released her. "For the baby's sake, we must sometimes give the appearance of a happily married couple."

"I understand," she said, turning away from him to stare out the window. "For the baby's sake."

Chapter Twenty-four

The wedding took place in the rectory of St. Louis Cathedral, with Domingo and Molly as witnesses. Emerada wore a soft blue gown with a matching mantilla. Ian wore a black coat and trousers, his hair neatly combed, his manner curt and dispassionate. He was solemn throughout the whole ceremony, and Emerada noticed that he didn't once look at her, not even when he slid the gold band on her finger. His detached attitude wounded her deeply, and she supposed he was thinking of the woman back in Virginia.

On the carriage ride back to the house, continuous rain pelted the carriage, contributing to Emerada's gloomy mood. She had just been married to the man she loved, but she didn't feel like a happy bride.

As the dancer, San Antonio Rose, Emerada had been adored and loved by many men, but not by the one who really mattered—not by her new husband.

"We have not spoken about our life together, Ian. What do you expect of me?"

His glance settled on her, but she could read nothing in those piercing blue eyes. "I expect nothing from you, Emerada. Your life will be your own. All I ask is that you do nothing to endanger yourself or the child. I know how impulsive you can be at times."

She felt her anger rise, but she managed to control it. She turned her head away and stared out into the rain. "As you wish."

The carriage came to a halt, but Ian made no attempt to disembark, and she looked at him inquiringly.

"You have not said what you will expect from me, Emerada."

She wanted to throw her arms around him and beg him to hold her. She was frightened by the unknown future that yawned before her. While she had pursued Santa Anna, she'd had a purpose. Now she had none.

"I want nothing from you, Ian. I am grateful to you for marrying me—not many men would have been so thoughtful. But this is a marriage that neither of us wanted. Under those circumstances, I do not think we should try to pretend with each other."

Ian glanced at her quickly. "What do you mean?"

"Just that we should not pretend to have emotions that we do not feel for each other."

"I see." He shoved the door open and stepped out into the rain, offering her his hand.

Domingo was waiting with an umbrella to usher them inside the house, where the delicious aroma of food wafted through the air.

"Evidently Molly has prepared one of her exceptional meals. She prepares excellent French cuisine, Ian. I will be sorry to leave her."

"I believe we can accommodate her if you want to take her with you."

She stood near the doorway while he advanced into the parlor. "Molly is getting on in years, and she has told me that she does not want to leave New Orleans." Emerada looked up at him, undecided, finding it unpleasant to have to ask her new husband for money. "If you could lend me enough money to pension Molly off, I would repay you just as soon I sell this house." Her expression was troubled. "You see, she served my aunt for many years, and Aunt Dilena would expect me to provide for her old age." She ducked her head. "Aunt Dilena was so young, she never considered that she might . . . die; therefore, she made no provision for poor Molly."

Suddenly her eyes opened in dismay. "Forgive me, Ian. I was so thoughtless. You may not have the money for Molly's pension. And you have already done so much for me."

"I have the means, Emerada. You have but to tell me the amount you need."

"Thank you. But there is more, Ian. Domingo goes with me. I will not leave him behind—not that he would let me go anywhere without him."

He noticed how pale she was. "Sit down, Emerada. We need to discuss a few things."

She eased down on a chair and waited for him to continue.

"I once told you a little about myself. Perhaps I should explain more at this time."

"It is not necessary."

He moved to the fireplace and rested his arm on the mantel. "I believe it is, Emerada." He paused briefly, as if choosing his words carefully. "I told you that my mother and father were never married."

"Ian," she said softly. "That makes no difference to me. If not for our marriage, my baby would know the same fate. I thought a lot about that when you asked me to marry you." She looked at him earnestly. "I will save you some time. The baby is the only reason I agreed to marry you, and that is the only reason you asked me to marry you. There. I have saved us both the trouble of explaining our feelings."

He took the poker and moved the logs

around until rekindled flames warmed the room. Then he turned back to her. "I want you to understand about my circumstances—I believe it's important."

"If you wish."

"My grandfather, my father's father, was a wealthy landowner. When he died, he left everything to me."

Emerada considered his words. "You are telling me that you have money?"

"I am telling you that I am considered wealthy, Emerada. It will be no hardship for me to pension off Molly or to see that Domingo has suitable lodgings."

Shame stained her cheeks. She wished there had been another way to help Molly. She was being drawn further and further into Ian's debt. "I thank you, and I will repay you one day—you have my word on that."

He drew in an agitated breath. "Damn it!" he said in a growl. "I don't want you to repay me, Emerada."

She gathered her shawl about her, feeling suddenly cold. "But I will. It is important to me that I own no one, not even you." She shook her head. "Aunt Dilena was quite wealthy, but she lived lavishly. When I paid off her debts, there was little left—just this house and the one in France."

He frowned and glanced at the flickering flames. "Obviously my wealth has made no impression on you."

295

"Did you think it would? Surely you cannot believe I married you for money. My father had wealth, and I was raised having everything I wanted. I would rather have my family back than all the wealth in the world."

"I sensed you would feel that way," Ian said tolerantly. "The point I'm trying to make in my own clumsy fashion is that I can and will take care of you financially."

Molly appeared at the door, smiling brightly, increasing the tiny, weblike wrinkles that fanned out about her eyes. "If you please, luncheon is ready."

Ian walked to the door and held his arm out to Emerada. "Shall we dine, Mrs. McCain?"

Emerada placed her hand on his arm, thinking their behavior was proper and formal enough for two strangers, but stilted and awkward for a man and woman who had just become husband and wife.

The meal was as strained as the earlier part of the day had been. Emerada sat at one end of her aunt's dark pine table, which shone so brightly she could see her reflection in it, and Ian sat at the other end. She hardly tasted a bit of the food that Molly had prepared for them.

Emerada stared down at her plate, pushing a puffy tart around with her fork. When she looked up, she found Ian staring at her with the strangest expression on his face. She knew in that moment that he was remembering their time together at Talavera, and she blushed.

"You hardly ate anything," he said, standing and moving around the table to sit beside her. "Shouldn't you eat for the baby's sake?"

"I have no appetite," was the only reply she was capable of making under the scrutiny of his brilliant blue eyes.

"I have business to conduct this afternoon. Will you mind if I leave you for a while?"

Mind! Of course she minded—it was her wedding day. "Not at all," she managed to say. "It will give me a chance to go over some details with my attorney."

"I should return by the dinner hour. If I'm not back by seven, eat without me." He took out his pocket watch and checked the time. "Yes, I can just about make it."

Emerada wondered where he was going, but she would rather cut out her tongue than ask. "After I see my attorney, I have errands of my own," she said matter-of-factly. "If I am not here when you return, make yourself at home."

He smiled and bowed. "You're too kind."

When Ian had almost reached the door, she called out to him. "I saw your traveling bag in the entryway. I will have Domingo see to it for you. Do you prefer a bedroom with a view of the front of the house, or would you rather overlook the garden?"

He walked back to her and drew in a deep breath. "Emerada, I prefer to share your room."

Her breath quickened, and she looked down at her clasped hands. "We have not discussed this. I thought that—"

He held up his hand to silence her and glanced at the door to make certain that Molly and Domingo could not overhear. "I believe we should begin our marriage with the appearance of harmony, beginning with the servants."

"But—"

"Emerada, don't concern yourself that I will trouble you with unwanted attention—I won't bother you at all."

Before she could answer, he moved to the door. "I'll tell Domingo to place my belongings in your bedroom."

When he disappeared down the hallway, she sank back against her chair. Ian was very clever. She could hardly go to Domingo and tell him to move Ian to another room—not after her new husband instructed him to put his belongings in her bedroom.

"Insufferable man," she muttered, standing up and throwing her napkin on the table. "Headstrong, manipulative man!"

She had been a wife less than a day, and already she regretted her decision to marry Ian.

The sun had gone down long before, and still Ian hadn't returned. Emerada lay in bed, listening to every carriage that rattled down the street.

She turned up the wick on the lamp and stared at the page of the book she was reading, or rather attempting to read. Her eyes went across the room to Ian's traveling bag, and she glared at it as if it were Ian himself.

A tear rolled down her cheek, and she angrily brushed it away. This was not the dream she'd always had of her wedding night. She didn't even know where her husband was, and when he did return, there would be no loving arms to hold her.

She must never forget, not even for a moment, that Ian had married her for only the sake of the child.

It was only moments later when Emerada heard a carriage stop at the front of the house. She gripped her book so tightly that her knuckles whitened; then she took a deep breath. She had faced far worse than an uninterested husband in the last year. She could surely handle Ian with little trouble.

She heard his footsteps coming down the hall, and the light rap on the door.

"Come in."

Ian entered the room, his glance settling on her. Emerada's hair spilled across her shoulders like shimmering black satin. Her white nightgown was modest, with a high neck and long sleeves with lace that fell across her wrists. She glanced up at him and smiled tightly, then went back to reading her book.

"I'm sorry to be so late. I'm glad you didn't wait to eat dinner with me."

Emerada felt as if she couldn't draw her

breath. When Ian was in a room, he seemed to fill it with his very essence. He looked so handsome—so magnificent. He was all male, and he knew it.

"Molly kept your dinner warm for you," she said.

"She needn't have bothered. I already ate."

She wondered what kind of business had kept him in town, and with whom he'd dined, but she would never ask. "I put you on the daybed," she said, nodding across the room. "I hope you will find it comfortable."

Ian moved to the fireplace and held his hands out to the flames. "I'm sure I will."

Emerada glanced back at her book, determined to ignore him. He had, after all, left her alone most of the day. Even if theirs wasn't a real marriage, he should have been more considerate of her feelings.

She was so absorbed in her thoughts that she didn't realized that Ian had come up beside her until he spoke.

"That must be a very interesting book to capture your attention so thoroughly."

She held it out for him to examine. "It is. I first read it two years ago, at my aunt's insistence. I enjoyed it so much that I decided to read it again."

"*Notre Dame de Paris*," he said, looking at the title. "Written by Victor Hugo. So you read French? A fine accomplishment for a woman."

She glared at him. "As well as French, I speak Spanish and English—and I speak them all very well. Would you like to check my teeth? I have all of them, you know."

He smiled. "I've examined most of your body, and I found no flaws."

"Oh, but there is a flaw, Ian." She slammed her hand against the book. "I have a temper! I do not want any man to think he can intimidate me, and I will have no man as my master."

"Is this the way it is to be between us, Emerada?"

She slid her hand nervously over the leather-bound book. "I do not know what you mean."

"I never want to cause you pain, Emerada. I suppose I have been feeling guilty because it's my fault you are having a baby. I can never tell you how sorry I am."

"Your fault?" Her breath caught in her throat. Had he guessed that the baby was his? "What makes you think you are responsible?"

He touched her cheek. "You were chaste when I made love to you. I know you must despise me for what I did to you. Even if the baby is Santa Anna's, he didn't take your innocence from you, as I did."

"I do not hate you, Ian. You are a good man, an honorable man. And what happened between us was as much my fault as it was yours, perhaps even more so."

301

Emerada caught Ian's soft expression, and her heart throbbed. His eyes reflected the glow of the flickering flames in the fireplace, and the blue shimmered with golden light, giving them the appearance of being made of exquisite glass.

He tilted her face upward. "I only wish I could take the sadness from your life. I want to make you happy."

"That is not a role I expect you to fill, Ian. We both have our troubles, and I am determined to face mine alone."

He sat down on the bed, and she panicked. Just the touch of his hand had awakened her yearnings for him. When he was this close, she couldn't reason.

"I will take very good care of you until the baby comes." He pulled her into his arms, and she melted against him. "My fiery-tempered little wife. God knows I'll never win you or tame you."

"Do you want to?" she asked, feeling his warm breath against her neck and going weak inside.

"Emerada, I have thought of nothing but you all day. I couldn't even conduct my business with the banker without wondering what you were doing, thinking, feeling."

So he had thought of her, as she had of him. She couldn't help feeling thrilled by his confession. Hoping her voice sounded normal, she asked, "You saw a banker?"

He straightened up and reached into his breast pocket, handing her a document. "This assures Molly a pension. You didn't say how much you wanted to give her."

With trembling fingers, she opened the written document. It stated that Molly would be paid the sum of six hundred dollars each year for the remainder of her life. She looked up at him with misty eyes. "It is too much."

"One can never put a price on a faithful servant."

"Thank you, Ian."

He brushed her tears away with his thumb, then bent his head, his lips settling on hers, and she slid her arms around his neck.

Oh, she did love him so!

Chapter Twenty-five

Much to Emerada's disappointment, Ian untangled her arms and stood up, moving away from her.

"I'm sorry," he said, looking guilty. "I didn't mean for that to happen. It's just that when I am around you, all I can think about is—"

She opened her book with a snap, hoping her heart would return to normal. "You have nothing to apologize for. What is so surprising about a husband kissing his wife on their wedding night? I am sure you enjoyed it quite as much as I did."

His laughter surprised her. "Emerada, you are the most amazing woman I've ever met. No other female of my acquaintance would ever say the things you do."

"I only say what I think. You already know this about me. If it offends you, be warned that I do not intend to change."

"I wouldn't change anything about you. I hope you will always speak your mind with me."

She laid her book aside and sank down onto her pillow. "I find I am very tired. I am going to sleep."

He came forward and blew out the lamp. "Sleep well, Mrs. McCain. I doubt I will."

It took Emerada a moment for her eyes to adjust to the darkness. She watched Ian remove his shirt, then turned her head into the pillow, aching to be in his arms.

"Good night," she whispered, wishing he were in bed with her. She yearned to feel his muscled body against hers, his lips on hers, his hands finding places on her body that excited her beyond endurance.

She heard him lie down on the daybed. "Good night, Emerada," he replied.

The next few days passed in a flurry of activity. The house had to be closed and most of the furnishings shipped to the town house in Paris. Emerada could not bear to part with all of her aunt's possessions. It was decided that Domingo would remain in New Orleans until the house was closed and Molly was settled in her sister's home.

Emerada was in the attic going through her aunt's trunks, which were filled with beautiful and expensive costumes. She removed a heavy, red velvet gown that shimmered with gold inlay.

Her mind reached backward to the time she had first seen her Aunt Dilena in the red gown. Her aunt had been like a sparkling jewel and so very beautiful. Emerada remembered asking her aunt how she could dance in such a heavy costume, and she could still hear the sound of her aunt's voice.

"Yes, Emerada, it is heavy and most uncomfortable, but I owe it to my audience to give my best performance, so I do not mind the discomfort. This will be true throughout your life in many different situations. You will find satisfaction and comfort in knowing you have done your best at whatever you do."

At the time Emerada hadn't understood her Aunt Dilena's reasoning, but it was perfectly clear to her now. She was so unsure of the future, but those words were a beacon of hope, giving her strength for what she must do. She would remain with Ian until the baby was born and then leave for Paris, as she had originally intended.

"Were you daydreaming about when you wore that beautiful costume and stole men's hearts, Emerada?"

She had not heard Ian come up the stairs. "No," she said, lovingly placing the gown back in the trunk. "This was my Aunt Dilena's gown. I was remembering the night she wore it."

He glanced about him at all the trunks, some packed, others spilling over with items. "Does this all go to Texas?"

"Most of it will go to Paris. Of course, most of the furniture will be sold with the house."

"If this house means so much to you, why not keep it? I'll have it restored for you, if you'd like."

She fastened the leather strap on the trunk before moving to another. "The person who made this house a home was my aunt. Now that she is gone, it is just a house—no, I do not want to keep it."

"And the one in Paris?"

"I will never sell that house. My aunt loved it too much."

"Is that why you can't part with her costumes?"

"I suppose. Perhaps someday I will be able to let them go." She turned to Ian. "I do not know if I can make you understand. You see, I have nothing left from my father, since everything was burned in the fire." She flicked open a green ostrich-feather fan. "This represents my past."

"You have been so alone." There was compassion in his voice. "I know what that feels like."

She smiled slightly, responding to his kindness, "I have had my moments."

"Will you be ready to leave tomorrow?" he asked, abruptly changing the subject.

"Must we go so soon?" She was almost afraid to leave her safe haven and live in Ian's world.

"I have stayed away too long now, Emerada. There is so much to do to help form the new republic, and Houston needs all his loyal friends at this time. We have to make Texas so strong that Mexico will never again move against us."

"Mexico will hesitate to take Houston on again. But the time will come when they will test him, Ian. They will have to. They were humiliated by losing the war and by Santa Anna's disgraceful actions."

It suddenly struck Ian that he enjoyed discussing politics and the welfare of the new republic with Emerada. She was intelligent and had a firm understanding of the situation in Texas. She understood about the fledging nation and many of the difficulties it would face. And she had done as much as any man to bring about an independent republic. Although she had not yet admitted it to herself, she had been instrumental in toppling Santa Anna.

"There have already been several skirmishes near the border. We have to make certain that they don't escalate into another war."

Emerada shuddered. "I pray that I will never have to witness another war."

Ian glanced at the heavy trunks, which would take hours to pack. "Shouldn't you have someone help you with this chore?"

"No. This is something I must do myself."

She lifted a shimmering black mantilla and

ran her fingers lovingly over it. "This belonged to my mother." She placed it over her head, and the folds fell across her cheek and down her back.

Ian drew in his breath. She was so beautiful it hurt to look at her. He took a step toward her and stopped himself. He didn't want to do anything that would make her reconsider going to Texas with him.

"I hope you're going to take that. It is very becoming to you."

She removed the mantilla and gently laid it aside. "*Si*—this I will take with me."

"I still have several arrangements to make." He walked to the stairs. "I will send Domingo to you. I don't want you to lift any of those heavy trunks."

Emerada waited for him to leave before she let out her breath. Whenever Ian was near her, it was difficult to pretend indifference to him.

Would he learn to care for her, just a little? No. He loved the woman in Virginia.

Perhaps when they reached Tejas—she heard his footsteps fade down the steps. No, she must not give herself false hopes. Perhaps it was enough that she loved him.

Ian had made sure the coach that would take them to Texas was well sprung and the seats comfortable, since it would be difficult for Emerada to travel in her condition.

As the coach bounced over the rutted road,

Emerada had to brace herself by gripping the leather handhold. Ian was sitting across from her with his hat pulled down over his face and his booted feet resting on the seat beside her.

Suddenly the coach hit a deep rut, lurched, and she went flying out of her seat to fall against Ian.

When he finally untangled her from a flurry of petticoats, he held her to his side. "Are you hurt?"

"No, not at all."

"The ride will be smoother when we get to the dryer region. The recent rains have caused deep ruts in the road here."

Emerada laughed as she remembered their first meeting. "It seems I am always falling into your arms."

He pressed her head to his shoulder. "Let it always be so," he said beneath his breath.

She pulled away. "What did you say?"

"It's of no importance. I will remark, however, on what a charming traveling companion you are. I have not heard a complaint from you, although the going has been rough at times. Especially for a woman in your condition."

Emerada yawned and laid her head against Ian's shoulder. She felt his deep intake of breath, and his arm settled around her. She was content to rest against his chest, listening to the steady beat of his heart.

She loved his courage and his commitment to what he believed in. He was a man who would always do what was right, not because others expected it of him, but because he expected it of himself.

Her eyes drifted shut, and she fell contentedly asleep.

Emerada didn't know when Ian laid his cheek against her head, nor did she feel his lips rest against her cheek. She didn't know his muscles tightened and he held her, loverlike, in his arms.

Chapter Twenty-six

When the coach reached the outskirts of San Antonio, Emerada was surprised to see all the new buildings. Of course, when they entered the town, she saw the same destruction she'd seen before.

"I always loved San Antonio, Ian. It is a pity that the town was so ravaged by war, and so many people were left without a place to live."

"The aftermath of war is never a pretty sight, Emerada."

She glanced over at him. "I know the war was necessary, but the people, Ian—what about them?"

"I was told that many of the Mexican families followed Lieutenant Castañeda back to Mexico. Juan Seguin reports that there are

312

only fifty people now residing in San Antonio. As time passes, more will come, and those who fled will return."

"I suppose."

It was stiflingly hot, and Emerada held her lace handkerchief to her nose, praying she was not going to be ill.

Ian saw her pallor and took her hand. "I will soon have you settled so you can rest."

She nodded, wishing she were lying down.

"Shall I get the doctor for you?"

"No. As you said, I merely need to rest."

"Did I make a mistake in bringing you here?" His jaw tightened. "There is not a proper doctor here, nor any of the comforts you're accustomed to."

"As you very well know, I have slept on the ground and in a stable. I am not one of your soft Southern women, Ian. I do not want to be pampered, so say no more about it."

He grinned. "How could I have forgotten for a moment that you have fire in your spirit?" His eyes gleamed when he looked at her. "You are like no other woman, Emerada."

She wondered how he would compare her and his intended bride. That woman was most probably a proper lady who would never have done any of the outrageous things Emerada had.

The coach came to a halt before a boardinghouse so recently built it didn't even have a sign. She could smell the scent of new lumber

313

and fresh paint. Emerada saw several work-men on ladders hammering and sawing. Apparently the building was not yet finished.

Ian smiled apologetically. "I'm sorry about the noise. As you see, out of the ruins, new life teems."

Emerada stepped down from the carriage with Ian's help, and her gaze went to the Alamo. She stood as if turned to stone, a lump lodged in her throat. "I never thought to look upon that sight again."

Ian hurried her into the boardinghouse and spoke to the man at the desk. "I will require your best rooms for my wife. Can you have them ready immediately?"

"Yes, sir, Colonel McCain," said the ruddy-complexioned man with a ready smile. "Your missus will have the best rooms in town."

"Very good," Ian said. "And your name is . . . ?"

"I'm Hank Glover, Colonel." He tugged at his earlobe nervously while his gray eyes sparkled with admiration. "I rode with you at San Jac-into, and proud I was to do it. Me and the other men saw as how you had no fear, sir, and it made us feel like we were gonna win—and that's the gospel truth."

Ian smiled. "I remember you, Sergeant Glover. As I recall, you made a good showing of yourself that day at San Jacinto."

"I'm not in the army now, sir. I bought this place, and I aim to settle down right here in San Antonio."

Ian glanced about the small common room. "Is there a store where you can purchase bedding and other necessary items for my wife's comfort?"

The man cleared his throat and crossed his arms as if he didn't know what to do with them. His gaze rested briefly on Emerada, taking in her condition; then he glanced back at Ian. "Well, sir, Javier's Mercantile ain't much, but it has some comforts. Javier said he got a nice shipment of goods in yesterday from New Orleans."

Ian laid several bills on the table. "Buy whatever you think it will take to make Mrs. McCain comfortable. If you need more money, let me know."

"Yes, sir. I'll see to it right now." The man rushed toward the door. "It's a delight to do anything for you, sir."

Emerada watched in amazement as the man sprinted out the door. She managed to recapture some of her good humor. She saluted Ian and imitated the man's voice. "Yes, sir, Colonel, sir, I'll do anything for the fearless warrior who seems to have won the war single-handedly."

Ian looked at her with irony. "If he but knew it, you are the one he should pay his respects to. Poor man didn't realize that he was in the presence of the celebrated San Antonio Rose."

Emerada moved to the window and stared at the market vendors near the square. "The San Antonio Rose is dead," she said with finality.

315

* * *

Emerada watched as the hot breeze stirred the curtains at the window. She imagined that she was the only person in town with lace curtains. She wondered what Hank Glover had had to do to get some poor woman to hurriedly sew them for him.

She walked across the braided rug onto the new plank floor, feeling confined in the small space, which consisted of a bed and a small table with two wooden chairs.

Emerada longed for the cool breezes of Paris, but she did not wish herself there. Here she could be near Ian if he ever got back from the border, where he'd been sent the first day they'd arrived in San Antonio.

That was five days ago. In that time she'd hardly left this room because she couldn't face the reminders of the destruction. She even had her food brought to her by an obliging Hank.

If she closed her eyes, she could still hear the awful sounds of the dying, the ground-shaking cannon fire, the rifle shots, and the horrible sound the cannonballs made when they exploded against the mission walls.

Leaning her forehead against the window, she looked out, knowing that from this vantage point she would see only the two new shops across the street.

Her eyes widened, and her heart quickened. Ian had just ridden up with several other soldiers. Her gaze devoured him. She had missed him so desperately! He was dressed in his uniform and wore his hat with one side of the brim turned up and held in place with a red cockade.

He dismounted and glanced up at her window, but she didn't think he could see her through the lacy curtains.

His voice drifted up to her.

"Get some rest," Ian told his men. "We have to ride for Victoria early in the morning."

Emerada's disappointment was sharp. He would be leaving again tomorrow. She hurried to the small mirror that hung on the wall and patted her hair into place.

An hour passed, and then two, and Ian still had not come to her room. She was beginning to wonder what could be keeping him so long. It was obvious that he hadn't come running home to her.

At last there was a light tap on the door, and Ian entered. His hair was still damp, and he was clean-shaven. She realized that he must have bathed before he came to her.

For a breathless moment they stared at each other.

After a moment he said, "You didn't have the door locked."

She blinked, slightly confused. His first words to her after being gone for so long were to reprimand her for not locking the door. "I did not think it was necessary," she answered stiffly.

He unbuttoned his jacket and placed it and

317

his hat on a chair. "Promise me that you will always lock the door when I'm not here. Remember, until Domingo arrives, or I am with you, you are a woman alone and susceptible to danger. There are many who know you as San Antonio Rose. I wouldn't want some enamored admirer storming your room one night."

He looked thoughtful for a moment. "I'll leave you a gun, too. I'm sorry I didn't think of it before."

Emerada felt the strain between them. "You shouldn't worry about me. But if it would make you feel better, you may leave the gun."

He looked her over from head to toe. "You are like a breath of spring." He glanced down at his boots, which were still dusty. "I must have swallowed a pound of trail dust between here and the border."

She took his jacket from the back of the chair and hung it and his hat on a hook. "You must be hungry. I'll have Hank bring you something to eat. The stew at the Iron Kettle is edible."

He smiled. "It's nice to come home to such a dutiful wife."

She gave him a haughty glance. "I live for nothing but to please you, Ian McCain."

His laughter followed her out the door.

Ian sat across the small table from Emerada while Hank cleared away the remnants of their meal. "Mrs. McCain tells me that you have looked after her, Hank. I want to let you know how much I appreciate it."

"Colonel, for your pretty missus, it's a real pleasure." He grinned broadly and left, a blush on his ruddy face.

"Another conquest, Emerada?"

"No. I would not say that. Hank has been very helpful. He lost a brother at Goliad, and his other brother lives in Georgia. He wants to bring his brother's family to Tejas as soon as he feels it is safe. He's lonely, Ian. I feel sorry for him."

"It will be a comfort to me knowing he will be looking after you." He reached across the table and caught her hand in a firm clasp. "The new republic is called Texas now, Emerada."

"*Sí.* I know this, but I sometimes forget." She noticed the tired lines around his eyes. "When did you sleep last?"

He rubbed his hand over his eyes. "I don't remember. I have been twelve hours in the saddle and changed horses three times. The last poor animal I almost rode to death."

"But why?"

He stood up and stretched his broad shoulders. "We chased several Mexican soldiers nearly to the border."

Her mouth opened in horror, and she grabbed his arm. "You were in a battle?"

"Of a sort. But it was of short duration. The Mexicans don't really have the stomach for fighting, and were soon heading back across the border."

Emerada stood and moved to the bed, turning down the covers. "You must get into bed now."

He smiled down at her. "Is that an invitation, Emerada?"

Her cheeks flamed, and she walked across the room to pull the curtains together and close out the glow of the sunset. "There is only one bed, and we will have to share it. But I have issued you no invitation."

He dropped down on the bed, yawning as he tugged at his boots. "I suppose I'll have to work on my charm," he said, standing up and slipping out of his trousers.

Emerada turned away, thinking he already had more charm than one man had a right to. She blew out the lamp, casting the room in shadow. She heard the bedsprings creak when Ian lay down.

There in the darkened room, she sat in a chair, her hands folded in her lap, listening to his breathing. He was so tired that he'd fallen asleep almost immediately. She didn't know how long she sat there, just listening to his steady breathing. She heard the sounds outside the window of people closing up their stores and going to their houses.

A feeling of loneliness washed over her, and she wanted to strip off her clothing and climb into bed beside her husband, to be in his arms, to have him make love to her.

He might tease her and pretend that he wanted to make love to her, but he must be disgusted by her because he thought she carried his enemy's baby. She had no one to blame but herself for the situation she found herself in. She had built a wall of deception between them, stone by stone. It stood there, impassable, and she didn't know how to tear it down. It was too late to tell him the truth about his baby. Anyway, it would be better if he never knew.

Somewhere, in one of the other rooms, she heard a clock chime the midnight hour. She stood up and went to the chest where she kept her nightgown. In the darkness, she quietly undressed and climbed carefully into bed, lying close to the edge.

Her body was rigid at first because she feared any movement might awaken Ian. But soon drowsiness descended on her and she fell asleep.

Emerada awoke and realized that someone was in her bed. Her sudden panic brought her fully awake until she remembered it was Ian. For a time she lay there, desperately wanting to touch him.

Finally she inched her hand slowly across the distance between them and touched his arm, feeling the muscles there. Since he didn't move, she dared to go further—he would never know.

Her hand moved lightly to his chest and rested against the mat of soft hair. Raw yearning raced through her, leaving her weak and faint.

Emerada gasped when Ian's hand clamped over her arm and he pulled her to him. "I have been lying here, listening to that damned clock tick away the hours, wishing I could touch you," he said hoarsely. "But I didn't dare."

His lips touched her cheek and slid past the opening of her gown to her breasts. He licked one nipple and then the other until she groaned with pleasure. Her legs intertwined with his, and she strained to be closer to him. She thought she would faint when she felt him swell against her.

Roughly he turned her onto her back and pushed her gown upward. "For so long now I could have you only in my dreams or in my memory." He hardened and throbbed to enter her hot, moist body. "I want you, Emerada."

She raised her head, pressing her mouth against his, and she felt intense satisfaction when he groaned her name.

He entered her with restrained passion, careful not to hurt her or the baby. She clung to him, meeting his passion with her own.

"Sweet little wife." He spoke against her lips, his breath becoming raspy. "You feel so good."

"Ian," she uttered breathlessly. "Oh, Ian!"

She ran her tongue over his lips, invoking a deeper passion in him. His engorged manhood seemed to reach into the far recesses of her trembling body.

"Say you want me," he urged, withdrawing and holding himself back with such willpower that his whole body trembled from the force of it.

"Ian, I want you," she admitted in a choked voice, squirming to take him back into her.

The gossamer kisses Ian sprinkled across her breasts were like an aphrodesiac to her already inflamed body. He gathered her to him and rolled to his back, holding her firmly on top of him.

Emerada bit her lip and threw back her head when he eased her down onto his arousal.

Their lovemaking became frantic, as it always did. She rode the tide of ecstasy with him, cried out his name, and reached a bone-melting climax with him.

Her energy spent, Emerada collapsed beside him, and his hand moved soothingly up and down her back, while he placed feather-soft kisses on her cheek.

For now, for this moment in time, Emerada

felt as if she had sole possession of him—of his mind and body. She had inflamed his desire, and she was his wife.

The other woman was far away, and Ian belonged to her . . . at least for tonight.

Chapter Twenty-seven

"You amaze me, Emerada," Ian whispered in wonder.

She nestled her head on his shoulder. "In what way?"

"Each time I take you, it's better than before. If I could, I would spend my lifetime in bed with you, making love."

She smiled against his neck. "Even when I am heavy with child?"

She felt him stiffen, and his whole attitude changed at the mention of the baby.

Ian firmly moved her away from him and sat up. "I had forgotten about the baby. Oh, God, how could I?"

She opened her mouth to tell him that the

child was his and that he had done no harm to it, but he moved even farther away from her.

"You must think I'm an insensitive beast," Ian said in an impassioned voice. He ran his hand through his hair. "I'm sorry, Emerada. I never meant for this to happen. I promised myself it wouldn't." He dropped his head into his hands. "Can you forgive me?"

She was still feeling the glow of their love-making, and his sudden regret was like a dash of cold water in her face. She couldn't find words to answer him.

Her spirits plummeted.

Ian moved off the bed and walked to the window. She watched him as silvery moonlight fell across his naked body.

He swiveled around to face her, and although she couldn't see his expression, she could sense his troubled thoughts. "God forgive me if I have hurt you or the baby . . ."

She came to her knees, reached out her hand, then let it drop helplessly to her side. "No, Ian, you have not hurt me or the baby."

He took several steps toward her. "I always prided myself on being able to command my own emotions. But when it comes to you, I have no control at all."

"You have nothing to blame yourself for, Ian. I was a willing partner in what happened between us."

He sat down beside her, struggling with what

he wanted to say. "It was my fault. I am experienced enough to make you want me, and I did just that. I should never have let it go so far." As if against his will, he reached out and touched her cheek. "I always seem to lose control when I'm near you."

She shook her head, her pride coming to her rescue. "There is no reason for you to torment yourself over me. What happened between us was nothing more than lust. We have talked about this before."

He sucked in his breath. "Yes, I do lust for you." Even now, just being this close to her, he swelled like a sex-starved youth, wanting to crush those lips beneath his and feel the velvet recesses of her body. He tried to ignore his urges and moved away from her. "You are in my blood, and I can't shake you loose."

By now the first glow of the morning sun pierced through the lace curtains, casting a golden pattern on the plank floor. Emerada felt so cold inside. She fought to suppress the trembling in her body. Ian wanted her, all right, but he loathed himself when he gave in to that temptation. This must be what happens when a man lusts without love, she thought sadly, or frequents a whorehouse.

A frown curved Ian's lips and deepened the tired lines about his eyes. "You have such a serious expression on your face. Will you not share your thoughts with me?"

San Antonio was coming to life. Emerada

could hear the sound of the street vendors setting up their stalls, and the stagecoach stopping just below their window.

"What should I think, Ian?"

He raised his shoulders in a shrug. "I don't
know. You tell me."

She moved out of bed and slipped into her
nightgown, which lay crumpled on the floor. "I
have some thinking to do. I will let you know
when I have reached a decision."

His smile was pleasant enough, but didn't
reached his eyes, which were hard and unyielding at that moment. "Any decisions you come
to will involve me, Emerada. Don't ask me to
let you go." He pulled on his pants and then his
shirt. "Not until the baby is born."

"There is no reason for this farce to go on
any longer. You have given my baby a name,
which is more than could be expected of
anyone."

He placed his hands on his hips and
glanced upward. "I understand how you feel,
but there is no time to talk about this right
now. I hate to leave it like this between us, but
I have to go to Victoria this morning, and I'll
be gone several days. We'll talk about this
when I get back."

She nodded her agreement. "You will eat before you leave?"

"Yes, of course, if you'll eat with me."

* * *

Ian had dressed in his uniform and was strapping his gun belt about his waist. "If you need anything, let Hank know."

I will. Do not be concerned about me while you are away. Just take care of yourself." Saying good-bye had always been difficult between them, as it was now. "Will you be . . . is there danger?"

"Not unless Houston loses his temper. Then who knows what could happen. As well you know, he's—"

There was a soft rap on the door, and Ian crossed the room. "Probably Corporal Dooley, reminding me I have tarried too long."

He opened the door and Emerada saw him freeze. In the next moment a woman threw herself into Ian's arms and kissed him soundly on the lips. Ian untangled her arms and held them in a firm grip, looking sheepishly at Emerada, then back to the woman.

"Pauline, what are you doing here?"

Emerada heard the woman speak in a soft Southern drawl. "You wouldn't come to me, so I came to you in this dusty, desolate old Texas that took you away from me."

The woman had a soft beauty, white skin, rosy cheeks, hair the color of wheat; she was slender, dainty, and petite. Emerada had hoped she would never meet this woman, but here she was in the flesh, looking more beautiful than any woman had a right to look.

Ian took Pauline's hand and led her forward to be introduced.

"Emerada," he stammered, "eh, Pauline. This is my—"

Ian was having a difficult time, and the last thing Emerada was going to do was make it easy for him. She stared at the woman he loved, wishing her in hell, or at least back in Virginia.

Pauline Harlandale glanced from Ian to the dark-haired woman. The man downstairs hadn't told her there was a woman in Ian's room. She knew men did this sort of thing—her mother had explained to her about mistresses—but she never thought she'd have to face the situation.

Pauline sized up the woman, who was not even properly dressed, but wearing a dressing gown. Pauline blushed and clung to Ian's arm. "I should have written that I was coming, but I wanted to surprise you." She released his arm. "It seems I'm the one surprised," she murmured, backing toward the door.

Pauline had to admit the whore was beautiful, with the darkest hair and eyes she'd ever seen. She glanced up at Ian, who was looking more uncomfortable by the minute. Pauline gave the woman an icy stare. "Ian, perhaps I should wait downstairs until you get rid of this . . . creature."

"Wait," Ian said, taking Pauline's arm and leading her back to Emerada. "Pauline, this is my wife, Emerada de la Rosa. Emerada, this is Pauline Harlandale. She's an . . . er . . . old friend from Virginia."

Emerada managed to hold her hands steady. "Actually, I am Emerada McCain, Señorita Harlandale. It is a pleasure to meet any of my husband's friends."

It took Pauline a moment to recover. She would have accepted the woman if she had been just a mistress—but a wife! Fury tore through her and she clutched her hands tightly.

"Your . . . wife?"

Ian looked to Emerada for help, but she only gave him a half smile. "Pauline, I had no idea that you would come to Texas. I should have written to you about Emerada."

"It was obviously a mistake for me to come." Her anger was directed at Emerada. "No one told me about her. I'm sure your mother doesn't know; or she would have advised me not to come."

"I have not written her about the marriage." His gaze went to Emerada. "It happened so quickly."

For the first time Pauline noticed the swell of the woman's stomach. "I can see why."

"Pauline," Ian said quickly, almost too quickly, saying the first thing that came into his mind. "Surely you didn't travel to Texas alone?"

"No. My cousin, Sara, came with me. You remember her, Ian—she's my older cousin, who never married. She would have come with me to say hello, but I wanted to see you alone." Pauline looked as if she might cry. "I couldn't wait to see . . ." Her voice trailed off.

Emerada moved to the window and opened it to allow a breeze to circulate, and because she needed something to occupy her hands. "Why do you not take your . . . friend to her room, Ian? Perhaps she has not yet had breakfast, and you can see to it for her."

"Oh, yes, Ian," Pauline said eagerly. "Everything is so primitive here." Her glare bore into Emerada as she spoke. "The town, the people, the women."

Ian glanced down at the woman he'd been betrothed to, feeling like the worst kind of cad. Pauline deserved better than he'd given her. Why hadn't he written to let her know he was married?

"I will see you settled, and then I have to leave, Pauline."

Pauline placed a gloved hand on his arm. "Must you leave?"

"I'm afraid so." He glanced at Emerada. "My wife will see to your comfort—won't you, Emerada?"

"I will do whatever I can," she answered,

damning Ian in her mind. She wanted to rip that woman's hand off her husband's arm. Didn't Ian see that Pauline was being deliberately vicious? She forced a smile. "I hope you are not of a delicate nature. As you said, Texas is a dusty, desolate place, and the women here are of hardy stock."

Ian frowned. There was friction in the room, and it was between the two women. He was almost glad he had to leave. He led Pauline to the door and spoke to Emerada as he went. "I will see you next week."

Emerada sat down in a chair to consider what had just happened. How could Ian love a woman who was so spiteful? Why did she have to be confined in the same boardinghouse with Pauline Harlandale?

She propped her elbows on her lap and rested her chin on her hands. Ian was to be pitied. He'd done a good deed in marrying her, and now he had to explain everything to the woman he should have married. Would he tell her the whole truth? she wondered.

Emerada sighed. She could have made it easier for him, but she wasn't feeling charitable at the moment, at least not toward the golden-haired woman with the soft Southern manners and asplike insinuations.

She touched her stomach, loving the baby who nestled there. "It looks like it is going to be just the two of us, little one," she said aloud.

"Your father has done more than anyone could ask of him. He must be free to marry the woman he loves."

She stood up and went to the trunk, removing her prettiest gown. She had to rally her courage. It was up to her to set things right between Ian and Pauline Harlandale.

She owed Ian that much.

Chapter Twenty-eight

Pauline paced the floor, stopping to kick at a hatbox and send a feathered and beribboned bonnet flying across the floor.

"It's insufferable!" she raged. "Ian is mine! He always has been. Everyone knows that!"

Sara Harlandale was of a lesser-known branch of the Virginia Harlandales. She reclined on the bed, fanning herself with a silk fan, watching her cousin's tantrum. "As I recall, you told me that Ian never actually asked you to marry him. It was more that everyone imagined he would one day."

Pauline glared at Sara, who was thirty-three and slender as a rail. Her brown hair was pulled away from her face in a matronly fashion, and she was pale from years of lung sickness. "What would you know? You have never gotten a marriage proposal, real or imagined."

Sara hid her face behind her fan until she could control her anger. Three weeks of being cooped up with Pauline in a public stagecoach had frayed her nerves beyond endurance. "That's true. But then I'm not a beauty like you, Pauline. In fact, I believe I have heard you refer to me more than once as rather plain. How many proposals had you received at last count—a dozen, fourteen? It seems that every eligible bachelor in the county has asked you to marry him—every one except the one you wanted," she said, glad when she heard Pauline gasp.

"What do you know? You have always lived in my shadow, and you resent me for it."

"You couldn't be more wrong, Pauline. I have kept quiet for years and taken all the abuse that you've thrown at my head, but there seems to be something in this Texas air that helps me find my voice."

She wondered who the woman was who had stolen Ian away from Pauline. He'd been the catch of Lee County, and many a young girl had pined when he'd gone away to military school and then set out for Texas.

"Shouldn't we be making plans to return home?" Sara asked, feeling exhilarated by a rush of newfound independence. "I don't think we are needed here."

"Little you know, you scrawny old maid.

And what gives you the right to say these things to me?"

"Yes, it must be something in the Texas air," Sara repeated with a smile. "I guess it fills a person's mind with thoughts of independence."

"You don't know anything. Ian didn't marry that woman out of love. She's having his by-blow. He married her out of a sense of honor."

"If it gives you comfort to think so."

Pauline rounded on her cousin. "Why are you talking to me in this insulting manner? If it weren't for my family's charity, you would have no place to live. None of the other relatives would take in a skinny old maid."

"I know. I have heard this same speech every day for the last ten years. Maybe I won't go back with you. Perhaps I will remain here in Texas. It's a new country, bursting at the seams with men, and women are scarce here."

"Not that you would find anyone who'd want you," Pauline taunted.

"And you speak from experience?" Sara was amazed by her own daring, but she couldn't seem to stop. "You came to Texas intending to take Ian home like a trophy on your arm. I'd like to meet the woman who took him away from you—not that he was ever truly yours. I always saw more interest on your side than on his."

"How dare you! After all I've done for you."

Sara moved off the bed. "I have been reborn. Have you noticed that I haven't coughed once since we got here? I haven't even taken my medicine in days. The fresh air must have cured me."

Pauline's eyes narrowed. "Never mind about that. I'm going to visit Ian's wife. It's time I found out just how she trapped him into marrying her."

Sara knew just how destructive her cousin could be, so she went to the door to block her path. "You said she was going to have his baby. Don't do anything that might make her lose the child. Leave them alone, Pauline."

Pauline shoved Sara out of the way and wrenched the door open. "I know he couldn't love that woman—she's not like us. She looks foreign, and speaks English with an accent. Ian's mother would never approve of such a wife for her son."

Pauline was out the door and rushing down the hallway before Sara could say anything further.

Sara gathered her shawl about her and went down the stairs. Someone had to help Ian's wife. Perhaps the man who ran the boarding-house, Mr. Glover, would protect her from Pauline. He seemed a nice enough fellow.

Emerada was packing her trunks. She would ask Hank if he would store them in his back room until she could send for them. She had just buckled the strap on the last trunk when the door handle rattled and someone pushed the door open. She had forgotten to lock it as she'd promised Ian. It didn't matter now anyway. She would be leaving today.

Emerada watched Pauline advance into the room, leaving the door ajar. She straightened so she could give the woman her full attention. "I am glad you are here, Señorita Harlandale," Emerada said. "I wanted to speak to you."

"I'm sure you do." Pauline strolled closer to Emerada. "And for your information, I am not a señorita—you are!"

"No, *Miss* Harlandale, I am a señora, since I am married to Ian." Emerada didn't like the woman at all, and she couldn't see how Ian could love someone so obviously hateful.

"You stole him from me, you know."

"It was never my intention to—"

"Suppose you just be quiet and listen to what I have to say."

Emerada was trying not to lose her temper, but the woman was testing her. "Will you not be seated?" she asked, biting her lip to keep back the angry retort that begged to be spoken. She must get through this for Ian's sake.

"I'm not staying long enough to get comfortable. I just want to know one thing—how did you lure Ian into marriage?"

"My personal life is my own. I will not discuss my relationship with my husband with you."

Pauline walked around Emerada, looking her over critically. It infuriated her that this dark, mysterious woman was almost too beautiful to be real. "Did Ian ever tell you about us? Did he tell you we were supposed to be married?"

"*Sí*, he did."

"And it made no difference to you that you were taking him away from the woman he loves? He does love me, no matter what he's said to you."

"I am sure he does, Miss Harlandale. Surely you do not need me to confirm what you already know."

Pauline was confused. "Did he tell you he loved me?"

"He is too much a gentleman to say such a thing in my hearing. But if you know him well, you are aware that he is a man of honor."

"Yes, and you took advantage of his honorable creed. What did you do, lure him into your bed and force him to marry you when the damage was done? Or, more probably, Ian gave his name to someone else's brat!"

"Pauline, how could you!" Sara appeared at the door, with Hank beside her. "How dare you speak this way to Ian's wife?"

"I'm going to have to ask you to leave, ma'am, if you pester Mrs. McCain again," Hank said, walking to stand beside Emerada, as if his presence would protect her. "Get out of here," he said with more authority.

Emerada placed her trembling hand in Hank's large, comforting one. "Please have them leave, Hank. I need to speak to you alone."

"You heard Mrs. McCain. She wants both of you to leave."

Pauline looked as if she might object, but the threatening glance Hank gave her made her reconsider. "I'll leave this room, but I won't leave town. I'll be here when Ian returns."

In a move that surprised both Pauline and Sara, the older woman grasped Pauline's shoulder and hustled her out the door. When Pauline stormed down the hallway, Sara turned back to Emerada.

"I'm sorry you had to go through that. You have to understand she's always had her eye on Ian as her husband."

Emerada nodded. "I understand."

Sara looked uncomfortable. "I can't apologize enough for my cousin's behavior. I am going to urge her to return to Virginia. Anyway, I don't think she'll bother you again."

"No. She will not bother me again," Emerada said, liking Sara Harlandale's straightforward manner.

Sara gave Emerada and Hank a sad smile and left, closing the door behind her.

Hank realized he was still holding Emerada's hand and he let it go, patting it kindly. "You said you wanted to talk to me?"

Emerada turned to the window, giving herself time to put her thoughts into words. She felt turmoil boiling inside after the unpleasant encounter with Pauline Harlandale.

"I will be leaving this afternoon, Hank. I

was wondering if you would store my trunks for me."

He was obviously distressed. "Ma'am, you aren't going to let what that woman said drive you away, are you?"

"No. It's not that, Hank. What you may not know is that I have a ranch nearby. I have been neglecting it lately."

"Yes, I know," he said, wishing he could make her feel better. He realized that the shrewish woman had hurt her. "Your ranch is Talavera."

"How did you know?"

"I knew your father and your brothers. I also know that you are the San Antonio Rose. I saw you twice with General Houston. Some of us figured out you was helping him catch Santa Anna."

Her mouth opened in horror. "Hank, have you told this to anyone?"

"Now, ma'am, don't fret none. I've never told another soul, and I never will."

She nodded, knowing he would keep his word to her. "Will you have the livery stable sell me a horse and saddle? And I'll need supplies— some to take with me, and the rest I will want delivered later. I will be leaving today."

"But Talavera was burned to the ground, and all your family's dead. Surely you can't stay there alone?"

She was touched by his concern. "I can manage quite well, Hank. Now, if you will send

San Antonio Rose

someone to the livery stable, I will make a list of the supplies I need. And there is something more I would like you to do for me. My friend, Domingo, might come looking for me. Tell him where I have gone."

He looked troubled, but it wasn't his place to tell her what to do. No one would convince him that she wasn't leaving because of the vicious woman in room seven. And Mrs. McCain was going to have a baby. It wasn't safe for her to be out at Talavera alone.

Colonel McCain was going to be damn mad when he came back.

Chapter Twenty-nine

Ian didn't spare his horse when riding back to San Antonio. He'd spent four days listening to men bicker over every fine detail of drawing up a working document for governing the new republic. The horrible truth was that Texas was broke. There was very little money in the treasury. The men who'd met to find answers for the problems couldn't even agree on how to put on their boots!

The one bright spot in it all was President Houston. He'd managed to calm everyone's temper, and in the end, most of them had rallied behind him.

Houston's popularity was running high, and no one else came close to his stature in Texas.

When Ian arrived back in San Antonio, it was after midnight, and the streets were deserted. He left his mount with a corporal and entered the boardinghouse, his footsteps hurried. He'd been a fool to leave Emerada without settling this thing between himself and Pauline. What worried him most of all was that Emerada had not defended herself when Pauline hurled insults at her head—but then, he hadn't defended her either. He didn't profess to know the workings of a woman's mind, but he was beginning to know Emerada. With her lightning-quick temper, she could strike back at the least provocation—but she hadn't.

There was no one at the front desk. Hank must have gone to bed hours earlier. Ian took the steps two at a time, Pauline's last words ringing in his ears.

You are mine, you always were, and you always will be.

He knew that something was wrong. Why hadn't he put Pauline on the coach and sent her back to Virginia? Knowing her past behavior, and her fits of jealousy when any woman had shown him the slightest attention, he was certain she had tried to cause trouble between him and Emerada. And, God knew, they had enough trouble already.

Perhaps he'd worried for nothing. After all, Emerada could certainly take care of herself.

He tapped lightly on the door, hating to wake

345

Emerada. Turning the knob, he discovered it wouldn't open. Good. She'd taken his advice and locked the door.

"She's not there, Ian," a silken voice said behind him. "There's some man in the room now, and I don't think he'd want to be disturbed."

Ian spun around to face Pauline. "What do you mean? Of course Emerada is in there. This is our room."

"If you ask me, Ian, your wife's kind of flighty. Can you imagine? She just left." Her hand covered his, and she moved closer to him. "I would never leave you if you belonged to me, as I thought you did."

He gripped her arm, his fingers biting into the tender flesh, and she squirmed to get away from him. "What are you talking about—tell me?"

At last she extracted her arm from his grasp, and she rubbed it gingerly. "I don't keep up with lost wives."

He took her hand and pulled her down the hallway, throwing open her door and pushing her none-too-gently inside. "Now, tell me where Emerada went, and what you had to do with her going."

Pauline dropped her gaze, and her bottom lip quivered, a ploy that had gained sympathy from other gentlemen in the past. "Why do you think I would know where she went?"

For the first time Ian noticed Sara sitting by the window, her glasses resting across the bridge of her nose and a book across her lap.

"Forgive me for disturbing you, Sara," he said. "I'm worried about my wife."

Sara laid her book aside. "You should be, Ian. She left the same day you did. That would be six days ago."

Ian looked at Pauline, feeling guilty for being so rough with her. "I ask your pardon, Pauline. I should not have taken my concern for Emerada out on you. Of course you had nothing to do with her leaving."

"Of course I didn't." She laid her hand on his arm. "Sara, why don't you leave us for a while. I need to speak to Ian alone."

"No," the older woman said. "I think I'll just stay right here until you tell Ian about your talk with Mrs. McCain."

Pauline glared at her cousin. "You'd better not say any more. You'll have Ian thinking the worst of me."

"He should," Sara said bluntly. Her glance went to Ian. "Ask her what she said to Mrs. McCain, Ian. Ask her why your wife left."

Ian shifted his gaze to Pauline's face. "What is Sara talking about? Tell me, Pauline," he insisted, with a sinking feeling in the pit of his stomach. "What did you say to make Emerada leave?"

Pauline was always at her best when defending her own actions. She raised her head and glared at Ian. "If you ask me, the woman you married isn't quite right in the head. If she's run away, I had nothing to do with it."

Ian stared at Pauline, realizing for the first time that he could never have married her—he'd always known it deep down. Pauline had one big flaw: she couldn't see anything past her own image in the mirror. She was selfish and vindictive. Emerada was as different from Pauline as night was from day—Emerada, his fiery little wife, who would take on the world's problems and make them her own. Why, then, had she allowed Pauline to drive her away? It just wasn't like her.

Ian's eyes narrowed, and he seemed to loom over Pauline. "Tell me about your conversation with Emerada."

"Tell him, or I will," Sara said threateningly.

Pauline turned on her cousin. "You beast! How can you care about me when you side with that woman against me?"

"The truth is," Sara said sadly, "you're not an easy person to love. The same traits that made you adorable as a child have turned you into a selfish, demanding woman now that you are grown. If you had intelligence to match your viciousness, you'd be dangerous. As it is, you are just pathetic."

Ian stood, silently listening. If what Sara said was true, and he believed it was, Pauline had driven Emerada away.

Pauline clutched at Ian's coatfront. "Are you going to let her say those hateful things to me?"

Ian shrugged off her hand. "I am interested only in my wife. Your troubles are your own."

348

Pauline was so near him she almost felt faint. It wasn't just Ian's wealth she wanted, although Ian had plenty of that; she wanted him. "You were supposed to marry me!"

The muscle in Ian's jaw tightened. "I have a wife."

At this point Sara saw the futility of the conversation. Ian wanted answers, and Pauline had no intention of giving them to him. "I don't know where she went, Ian, but Mr. Glover does. He and I tried to get your wife to stay until you returned, but she was determined to leave."

"Yes, I'll talk to Hank," Ian said, moving to the door. "He'll know where she went. She must be at Talavera!"

"Ian," Sara said, stepping between him and Pauline. "There was some man, a big Mexican gentleman who came looking for your wife. Hank told him where to find her."

Ian held his breath. "Was the man's name Domingo?"

Sara nodded. "Yes, that was his name."

"Thank God he's with her," Ian said with relief.

"What about me?" Pauline asked, her mouth turned down in a pout.

"I suggest you get to Galveston and take the first ship for home. There is nothing for you here," Ian told her, rushing out the door with every intention of waking Hank.

* * *

It was the first time Emerada had realized that silence had a sound—a deep, empty sound like echoes from an endless void.

She dipped her bucket into the well and let it fill with water while she stared at the charred remains of Talavera. The grizzly sight was always there to remind her how her family had died.

She struggled with the water bucket as she carried it toward the stable. Her back seemed to ache constantly from the weight of the child she carried. She had to find a place to have her child, but not in New Orleans, because Ian would find her there.

As Emerada passed the family grave site, she wished for the hundredth time that she knew where her father and brothers had been buried. She needed a place to go to make peace with them—to grieve for them—to say goodbye to them.

When she reached the stable, she set the bucket down and rubbed her aching back. She looked with satisfaction at the scrubbed floors. She had brushed the cobwebs away and had pitched hay to the horse. She had made herself a comfortable bed in the stall next to her horse, needing to feel the presence of another living, breathing thing.

Loneliness hung heavy over her, and she watched the road every day, waiting for Domingo to come. Emerada realized she couldn't stay at Talavera much longer or Ian would find her.

She knew him so well, and there wasn't a doubt in her mind that he would come after her. When Ian made a commitment, he would honor it in spite of any feelings he had for Pauline Harlandale.

The sun was setting when she poured the bucket of water in the horse trough. She would spend another lonely night listening to the howl of the coyote and the crickets chirping their age-old song.

She latched the barn door, knowing the flimsy lock wouldn't keep anyone out if they wanted to get in badly enough. But if trouble came, she would hear it and get her gun.

Emerada was not usually afraid of anything, but she'd had the strangest feeling for the last two days that someone was watching her. She hadn't seen or heard anyone; it was just an intuition she had—a feeling that made her skin prickle.

She fluffed up the hay and laid a thick blanket on top of it. Then she lay down fully clothed and listened to the lonely night sounds.

"Where are you, Domingo?" she said aloud, causing her horse to whinny. "I need you here with me."

Emerada awoke with a start. Someone was pushing against the stable door, making it creak and rattle. She glanced at the upper window—it was almost dawn.

Inching forward, she slid her gun from the

holster that hung over the railing and moved to a position where she could easily see whoever came through the door.

Again the door rattled, and she spoke to the person on the other side. "Who is there?"

"Emerada, let me in—it's Domingo."

A wave of relief washed over her, and she pulled the latch and swung the door open. She rushed to the big man, and his arms enveloped her in a protective hug.

"Oh, Domingo, I thought you would never come!"

Chapter Thirty

Domingo patted Emerada's shoulder comfortingly. "Everything has been taken care of in New Orleans. When I got to San Antonio, a man named Hank Glover told me where to find you."

He looked at her questioningly. "Why did you come back here—and alone?"

She walked along beside him as he led his horse inside the stable. Now that Domingo was there she felt safe, and she slid her gun back into the holster. "I'll explain everything to you while I make coffee. Are you hungry?"

He nodded. "You make the coffee, and I'll do the rest," he answered, seeing that the shelves were stacked with an ample amount of supplies. "It looks like you intended to stay here for a while."

Emerada stacked wood and twigs on the embers of the cookfire while she explained to Domingo what had happened with Pauline Harlandale, and why she had left Ian.

Domingo shook his head. "You should have waited to talk to Ian. I have never known you to run away from trouble. And if this woman is as bad as you say, Ian would not love her."

"You do not understand. He does love her. By my foolish behavior I may have prevented Ian from marrying the woman he loves."

"You have your life in a tangle, Emerada. It would have been better had you told Ian the truth about the baby. Why did you let him think Santa Anna is the father?"

She didn't answer while she filled a pot with water and scooped coffee into it before placing it among the glowing embers. "I do not know."

"Go back to San Antonio; tell him the truth. A man should know when he is to become a father."

She added more wood to the fire, then looked at Domingo. "I will never do that. I did not want him to feel obligated to stay married to me. But I wanted desperately for the child to have its father's name." Her shoulders hunched, and there was misery in her eyes. "I compromised Ian's future happiness by my own selfishness."

Domingo was placing fatback in an iron skillet. Then he sat back and looked at her carefully. "How do you know that you are not his future? I have seen how he looks at you, Emerada. He loves you. A man can tell these things about another man."

She stood up, dusting off her skirt. "You see only what you want to see, Domingo. I do not want to talk about it anymore. I need your help in deciding where we should go from here."

For the first time Domingo could remember, he lost his temper with Emerada. "Where you should go is back to the baby's father. Think of the baby. You will need a doctor when the time comes. I do not believe you have thought this through."

"I still have at least a month before the baby will be born, Domingo. But I am so confused. What do you think I should do?"

"There is only one thing for you to do. Go back to Ian. He is a good man and deserves better than silence from you."

She didn't want to talk about Ian, so she decided to tell Domingo her fears. "There is something that has been troubling me. For the last two days I have had the strongest feeling that I'm being watched. I think we should leave as soon as—"

Without any warning the stable door suddenly slammed open, and three men entered, their guns pointed at Domingo and Emerada.

Domingo jumped up and pushed Emerada

Constance O'Banyon

behind him, glancing at his gun leaning against the wall, just out of reach.

"Who are you?" Domingo asked in a threatening voice. "And what are you doing here?"

"You should recognize us," one of the men said with amused laughter. "I have seen you before, and the beautiful señorita." He aimed his rifle at Domingo's head. "Let me introduce myself and my friends to you. I am Ortega, this is Chavira, and there stands Martinez."

Domingo squinted in the growing light. "*Sí*, I know you. You were with Santa Anna."

"And you are the servant who followed like a burro behind the San Antonio Rose." Ortega grinned and bowed to Emerada. "Twice I have had the honor of seeing you dance."

Domingo glanced once more at his rifle, knowing that if he dove for it, he would leave Emerada unprotected. "You have not told me what you want here," he said, reaching for Emerada's arm to keep her behind him.

Emerada recognized the men, although they weren't in uniform now. The leader, Ortega, had never been far away from Santa Anna's side and had always been rushing about to do the dictator's slightest bidding. He was a lean man, with a long, narrow face and deep-set eyes. His two companions she had never seen before. They were both heavyset, and one had a long scar from forehead to chin, making him look sinister. All three wore leather trousers and vests and wide-brimmed sombreros.

She stepped from behind Domingo, knowing the men were up to nothing good. She didn't want Domingo to be hurt. "Have you come for me?" she asked, pretending a bravery she was far from feeling. If she could only distract them, Domingo might be able to get to his rifle.

"*Sí, señorita.* It seems Santa Anna has some unfinished business with you. He asked us to bring you to him unharmed, but if you make trouble, we will take him your dead body instead," Ortega said. "Pity Ian McCain is not with you. Santa Anna wants him real bad."

Emerada cringed, knowing these men had been watching her for days. They had probably waited to show themselves, thinking Ian might come to Talavera. Santa Anna had a lot to hate her for, and he neither forgot nor forgave a grievance. "Shoot me then, because I will not willingly come with you."

One man shrugged and smiled. "Then we will have to take you by force."

At that moment Domingo made a dive for his rifle. One of the men raised his gun and fired. Emerada screamed as Domingo crumpled to his knees and then tumbled forward.

Emerada cried out his name and ran to him, going down on her knees and lifting his head. She saw with horror that blood was soaking through his shirtfront, and she ripped his shirt open.

"Oh, Domingo, what have they done to you?"

She pressed her hand against his wound, frantically attempting to stop the flow of blood.

His eyes were glazing over, and he was having trouble keeping them focused. "So weak . . . need to help . . . you."

She glared at the three men, who were now standing in a circle around her. "You must help him. Take the bullet out—bandage him!"

"Sorry, señorita, his life is not important to me. You will come with us now."

The man named Chavira gripped her arm and jerked her to her feet. "Santa Anna is impatient to see you."

She struggled to get back to Domingo as she was being led away. "Please let me help Domingo. I cannot leave him to die!"

With a laugh, the man forced her through the door. "He is in no condition to follow us and will probably be dead before we ride out of sight."

Ian halted his horse and glanced at the ruins of Talavera in the distance. He saw no sign of life and wondered if Emerada had moved on. It would be just like her to do that.

With his jaw clamped shut at an angry angle, he rode down the hill and dismounted in front of the stable. He heard a horse whinny and felt encouraged that Emerada was there after all. The door was standing open, and he stepped inside, waiting a moment for his eyes to adjust to the darkened stable.

A groan came from the shadows near the

hayloft, and Ian eased his gun out of the holster. "Emerada?"

Again the groan, this time fainter than before.

Moving forward cautiously, and knowing something was very wrong, Ian found Domingo sprawled on the floor. He quickly bent down to examine him. When Ian saw the blood, fear for Emerada coiled inside him like the tightening of a mainspring. "Domingo, what happened here? Where's Emerada?"

Domingo was losing consciousness. "Sorry . . . shot me. Could not . . . help Emerada—"

Ian raised Domingo's head. "Talk to me— where is she? Don't pass out on me now. I have to know about Emerada!"

But Domingo did not respond. Ian placed his head on the big man's chest and was relieved to hear a heartbeat. He laid his gun nearby and rolled up his sleeves. Domingo couldn't tell him anything if he didn't get that bullet out of him.

An hour later Ian tied a bandage across Domingo's shoulder. The big man had lost a lot of blood, and Ian wasn't sure if he would live. He wasn't even sure if he'd regain consciousness. He willed him to wake up, so he could find out about Emerada.

Desperate, Ian bathed the big man's face, and Domingo stirred.

"Can you talk?"

"Emerada," Domingo said weakly. "Help . . . her!"

"What happened to her?" Ian asked, fearing Domingo would black out again before he could tell him.

"Santa Anna sent men." Domingo licked his dry lips. "They took her. I could not . . . stop them."

"Santa Anna won't hurt her. Not when he finds out she's carrying his child. I know he was halfway in love with her. Perhaps he can forgive her for humiliating him at San Jacinto, if she'll tell him about the baby."

Domingo rolled his head from side to side. "You fool. He never touched . . . " He stopped to catch his breath. "She never let him touch her."

Ian shook his head. "You don't know what you're saying." He laid his hand on Domingo's forehead. "It's the fever talking. You're confused."

"The child she carries is yours! That's why she married you, so . . . " He paused again until a spasm of pain passed. "She wanted the baby to have its real father's name—your name!"

Ian closed his eyes as realization ripped through him. He should have known—the truth was there before him all the time. She would never have allowed the man responsible for her family's death to touch her.

"No time to . . . lose," Domingo said weakly. "You must save her—I cannot."

Ian stood, removing his revolver and checking to make sure it was loaded. He had loaded his rifle before he'd left San Antonio.

"Which way did they go, Domingo?"

"They would take the shortest way to the border. You have the advantage—they think I am dead, and they will not expect anyone to be following them."

"Why would they not expect someone to follow them?"

Domingo pushed his pain aside so he could help Ian. "Emerada told me that she thought she was being watched for several days. Those three men thought she was alone, but for me."

Ian was anxious to leave, but he had to make sure Domingo was taken care of. He placed a canteen of water and a pouch of dried meat within Domingo's reach. He also laid his rifle beside him. "I have to leave you, and I don't have time to send help."

"Do not think about me. Go! Find her. And be careful; those three men are as mean as they come. Santa Anna wanted them to bring you." Domingo paled as pain stabbed through him. "Do not take chances—you must kill them, or they will kill you."

"I'm going to take your horse, since it's fresher than mine."

Domingo nodded and closed his eyes.

After circling the area for a few minutes, Ian picked up the trail of four riders. Urgency drove him, but good training kept him cautious. If the men discovered they were being followed, they would probably kill Emerada.

361

They didn't expect to be followed, so they wouldn't be in any hurry, and he could overtake them before morning. Chances were that they'd make camp for the night.

Anger coiled inside him like a poisonous snake. Sometimes he would lose the trail and have to stop and retrace his tracks.

But always he pushed onward. The one thought in his mind was to save the woman he loved and his unborn child.

Chapter Thirty-one

Emerada was tiring. For the last hour she'd felt an occasional sharp pain in the lower part of her back. She was relieved when they finally stopped. She was so weary that when she dismounted, she dropped to her knees, rubbing her back.

Ortega chose to make camp in a canyon that was protected on two sides by high cliffs. It would be an easy place to defend. By placing a guard on one of the cliffs, they could observe the whole valley.

Of course, the men knew, as she did, that no one would come to her rescue. Grief and outrage numbed her—Domingo was dead—they hadn't even given him a chance. They'd just shot him down as if his life didn't matter!

Emerada was trembling violently when Ortega spread a blanket under an oak tree and motioned for her to lie down. With her hands bound in front of her, it was difficult for her to accomplish, so he eased her down, his hand deliberately brushing against her breasts while his gaze lingered on her lips.

Emerada fearfully watched him as he went to his horse and got another blanket. When he stood over her, she shuddered with revulsion. "What are you going to do?"

"Do not fear me, señorita. It will mean my death if you are not delivered to Santa Anna unharmed." His eyes lingered on her lips. "Have a care, though; some things are worth dying for."

She was afraid to trust him, but she held her hands up to him. "Please loosen the ropes. They are cutting into my wrists."

"No, no, San Antonio Rose. I will take no chances that you can escape. The ropes stay."

"If you will help me escape, I will see that you are paid. I can make you a wealthy man."

He laughed and shook his head. "What good is wealth to a dead man?"

One of the men laid a campfire, while Ortega sent the other one to stand guard atop the cliff. Emerada twisted and turned, attempting to find a comfortable position. Being heavy with child didn't help, and the hard ground bit into her delicate skin. The pains had returned. They came in waves, and she sometimes had to bite her lip to keep from crying out.

Later Ortega knelt beside her with a plate of beans. "Since your hands are tied, I will have to feed you, San Antonio Rose."

She shook her head. "I do not want anything."

"Santa Anna will not be happy if you become ill." He nodded at her swollen stomach. "And I do not think he will be happy about that either."

She met his gaze. "I hope you are not under the mistaken assumption that I care what Santa Anna is happy or unhappy about. I loathe the man."

Ortega dipped the spoon into the beans and held it to her mouth. He laughed when Emerada turned her head away. "I can see why you have been so much on Santa Anna's mind. No man could easily forget you." He took a bite of the beans and smiled at her. "Take me, for instance. Perhaps I will change my mind and keep you. We could hide, and Santa Anna would never find us."

"That would not be wise, Señor Ortega. Because if Santa Anna did not kill you, I would, the first chance I got."

He shot her a furious glance and stood up, throwing down the plate of beans. "So be it. You have just sealed your own fate."

Emerada was so miserable she wanted to cry, but she would not give those men that satisfaction. She watched the sunset until it was no more than a splash of crimson that lingered against the western sky.

Ian crept up the side of the hill, taking care with each step. He didn't want to start a rock slide that would alert the three men that he was there. His gaze moved over the scrub bushes until he spotted the man on guard. Ian slowly moved back and flattened his body against the cliff.

Domingo had said that there were three of them, so the other two must be with Emerada. He didn't think they would hurt her, since they were taking her to Santa Anna, but he couldn't be sure, so he had to act quickly.

Taking particular care where he placed each foot, he inched closer to the guard. Suddenly the man called down to the others, and Ian crept back into the shadows.

"Hey, *amigos*, when do I eat? No one is following us—why do I have to stay up here?"

Ian heard the faint reply. "Martinez will take his turn after he eats. Just keep watching, Chavira."

He was within a few yards of the man now. The most critical part was yet to come—to dispatch the man before he could alert the others. Ian was within reach of the Mexican now, but he waited until the man's attention settled on the fading sunset.

Ian lunged forward, clamped his hand over the man's mouth, and drove his knife into the man's heart, all in one quick motion. Ian kept his hand on the man's mouth until he crumpled to his knees and pitched forward on his face. Then he wiped the blood off his knife before sliding it into the scabbard.

Good, he thought. *There are only two now.*

Ian knew that he must act fast, because time was against him. Soon the other man would climb the hill to take his turn at guarding the camp. He dropped down on his stomach and crawled to the edge of the cliff. Emerada was there on a bedroll, apparently unhurt. His lips thinned in anger when he saw that her hands were tied. She was too far away for him to see her face clearly, but he knew she was frightened.

The remaining two men would pay with their lives for this, just as their companion had.

By now darkness had fallen, and that was to Ian's advantage. He could stay in the shadows while the campfire illuminated the two Mexicans.

Carefully he shouldered his rifle and aimed it squarely in the middle of one man's forehead—he wasn't going to risk only wounding either of them. With practiced accuracy, he pulled the trigger. The man jerked backward, then crumpled in a heap.

He heard Emerada's muffled cry, and the third man drew his gun and kicked dirt onto the fire, casting the camp in darkness.

* * *

Emerada pressed her back against the tree, thinking they were being attacked by Indians or outlaws. The night was so dark. She could see nothing but the smoldering ashes from the campfire. A hand touched her shoulder—it was Ortega.

"It seems I did not kill your watchdog, after all. The fool comes for you."

"It is not Domingo," she whispered, wondering whom she feared the most—Ortega or the unknown assailant.

Fearfully, Ortega's eyes searched the darkness. "Then who can it be?" He called out, "Chavira, if you are there, answer me."

Silence was his only answer.

"Please," Emerada said, holding her arms out to him, "cut me free and give me a gun."

He shoved her aside. "Whoever it is has killed Chavira and Martinez, and they will kill us, too. If only I knew how many there were." Fear caused his voice to tremble. "What do they want with us?"

They both heard the sliding stones that alerted them that someone was coming down the cliff. Emerada braced herself against the tree and rose unsteadily to her feet. She inched in the direction of the horses, knowing that Ortega's entire attention was focused on the unknown enemy who stalked them from the darkness.

* * *

Ian watched Emerada mover toward the horses. She was out of the line of fire, so he didn't have to worry about a stray bullet hitting her. He heard a horse gallop away—she had managed to escape. He'd catch her later.

"What do you want?" Ortega called out. He was also moving toward the horses. "Show yourself so we can talk. I can offer you gold. I am a friend of Santa Anna's."

"A questionable honor." A cold voice spoke from the darkness at Ortega's right. "If you believe in God, start praying."

Ortega went down on his knees, trying to conceal his gun in the folds of his shirt. "Do not kill me, señor! We are not enemies."

Ian stepped into the faint light given off by the coals that had reignited the dry wood. "You are mistaken, Ortega. You are my enemy—you took my wife."

"You're the Raven's Claw!" He looked confused. "San Antonio Rose is your wife?"

"That's right."

Beads of sweat formed on Ortega's upper lip. This was Houston's man—he was dangerous and not to be underestimated. Not even Santa Anna's threats would have made him take the woman if he'd known she was Ian McCain's wife.

Ortega knew in that moment that if he didn't act quickly, he was a dead man. The hand that held the concealed gun trembled as he pulled it out of his shirt and fired.

Ian laughed as the shot went wild. "It seems you missed. Now it's my turn, and I almost never miss."

With anger in his heart, he raised the rifle and fired. Ortega was yanked backward as if by some invisible hand and slammed against the oak tree. He slid forward and lay still, his life blood spilling into the dirt.

Ian moved quickly toward the Mexican's horse, knowing there was no time to lose if he was going to catch Emerada.

Emerada was having a difficult time staying astride the horse with her hands tied. She heard the two gunshots, and a sob caught in her throat. They would be coming for her soon, and she could not outrun them with no saddle or bridle to guide the horse.

A few moments later she heard a rider coming—only one, from the sound of it. No matter who had won the gun battle, none of them would be a friend to her. She kicked the horse in the flanks and gathered the flowing mane in her fingers. Brambles cut into her face, and once she was almost unseated by a heavy branch, but she ducked just in time. She could barely make out the fallen tree trunk just ahead, and there was no way to guide the horse around it. The rider was getting closer now, and she closed her eyes, hoping the horse could make the jump across the wide trunk.

The horse did take to the air, but Emerada's hands slipped and she was falling. She covered her stomach in an attempt to protect her unborn baby. She hit the ground hard. Pain so sharp she could not breathe cut through her body like a knife.

The last thing she remembered was the sound of the rider getting closer, and then blackness engulfed her.

Ian saw Emerada fall. Had he saved her from the men, only to lose her now?

Chapter Thirty-two

Ian leaped from his horse and knelt by Emerada, lifting her head. When it fell limply back against his arm, he feared she might be dead. Pain hit him like shards of glass. He lowered his head to her chest and was overcome with joy when he heard the strong rhythm of her heart.

He gently examined her for injuries. He knew by the twisted position of her right arm that it was broken. He swore under his breath. Both he and Emerada had ridden bareback. He had nothing with him to set her arm.

He had to think clearly. He couldn't move her until her arm was set. He couldn't even build a fire.

With the need to hurry, he used his knife to hack two limbs from the fallen tree. Ripping his shirt into strips, he was ready. He was glad Emerada was unconscious.

Feeling gently along her arm, he located the break. Grasping the upper and lower arm, he yanked hard and heard it snap into place. Emerada screamed, her eyes opening wide. He would rather have ripped his own arm off than cause her pain.

"No." She moaned. "Why are you hurting me?" She closed her eyes and grabbed her stomach. "No. Not my baby."

That was the first time since finding her that Ian had thought of the baby. "Emerada, I had to set your arm. It's broken."

She tried to rise, but fell back against the ground. Her eyes were glazed with pain, and she didn't seem to know him.

"Don't move, Emerada. I have to make a splint. Do you understand?"

She went limp again, and he hurriedly placed the splints on either side of her arm and bound them tightly with the strips from his shirt. When he was satisfied that the splints would hold until he could get her to a doctor, he fashioned a makeshift bridle out of the rest of his shirt and slipped it over the horse's head. He had to have some control over the animal. If only he'd gone back to get his own horse! But there wasn't time now.

Ian mounted the horse with Emerada in his arms and rode in the direction of Talavera.

Suddenly Emerada twisted in his arms and cried out in pain.

He drew her closer to him, cradling her lovingly. "I know it hurts, my love. Try to bear it if you can."

She looked up at him, but it was plain she didn't know who he was in the darkness. "My baby, I am going to lose my baby!" Her hand went to her stomach, and she moaned as another pain hit her. "Help my baby," she whispered.

Ian felt as if his heart twisted violently inside him. "Oh, God, no—not the baby!"

He would ride the horse to death if he must. He had to find help for Emerada!

As the first streaks of gold touched the eastern horizon, Emerada was lost in a world of pain. She forgot about the pain of her arm because it felt as if her insides were being ripped out. She bit her lip to keep from crying out, but it didn't help. Her cry blended with the morning wind.

Ian watched the woman he loved more than life experience unspeakable agony, and there was nothing he could do to help her. They were still at least two hours from Talavera. He had heard of women dying in childbirth, and that was with a doctor in attendance.

He placed his hand on her stomach and felt it move and ripple from the child inside.

374

"Emerada, can you go on?" he asked, knowing the movement of the horse must be adding to her torment.

She finally focused her eyes and recognized Ian. "I cannot go on. Please put me down."

Ian nodded. He would have to deliver the baby, and he knew nothing about it whatsoever. On occasion he'd helped a mare give birth to a foal, but this was the woman he loved and his firstborn child. What if he did something wrong? And wasn't it too soon for the baby to be born?

He dismounted and carried her to a patch of green grass and laid her down carefully. "Emerada, I'm going to help you. Don't be afraid," he assured her.

She nodded, just as her body was gripped by another pain.

Ian glanced upward and silently begged for divine guidance.

Emerada stiffened and gripped his hand so hard that her fingernails dug into him. She moaned and tried not to scream, but the pain was excruciating.

"Go ahead," Ian urged her. "Scream if you want to. No one but me will hear."

And she did. She screamed when it felt like someone had crammed a hot poker through her body.

Tears blinded Ian, and he knew he would never forget the sound of Emerada's scream—

not as long as he lived. It tore him apart inside, and he prayed the birth would not last long. The heavy hand of guilt settled on him. He was responsible for her pain because it was his baby that was causing her pain.

When she pushed until her body trembled, he hurriedly brushed the tears from his eyes. He didn't even have water to dampen her dried and cracked lips.

Ian had been so absorbed in helping Emerada that he hadn't heard riders approaching. When horses neighed behind him, he jumped to his feet and saw three Indians!

He felt a flood of relief when he saw Chief Bowles with two Indian women.

"Is this your woman, Raven's Claw?" Chief Bowles asked, dismounting.

"Yes. She's having her baby here!"

"Help my baby," Emerada said in a whisper. She was so weak. She could hardly voice the words.

The chief said something to the women, and they went to Emerada. Then he motioned for Ian to follow him. "My wives will help your woman. Let us leave the birth to them. This is no place for warriors."

Ian was doubtful about leaving Emerada with the women. "She might be afraid."

"Not that woman, Raven's Claw. I hear things. Your woman is not soft, like other white women."

* * *

In her world of constant pain, Emerada vaguely saw the Indian women, but she didn't care who they were; she welcomed the helping hands.

"Please save my baby," she said weakly.

One of them lifted her skirt and positioned her for the birth. By now the baby's head was visible, and the other woman took Emerada's hand and spoke to her soothingly, while her companion waited for Emerada to push.

With the next agonizing push, the baby emerged into the Indian woman's capable hands. She deftly wiped the baby's face with the edge of a cloth and turned the child over her shoulder. The baby was so blue that the two women exchanged glances, fearing it might be dead.

Suddenly Ian heard a small cry, and nothing Chief Bowles could say could keep him from running to Emerada. As he knelt beside her, the baby's cries became stronger, and unashamed tears moistened his eyes.

Emcrada's eyes were closed, and he quickly looked at the Indian women. "Is she all right?"

Sensing his distress, they smiled and nodded. One of them handed him the baby. He glanced down at the now rosy infant and saw that he had a daughter!

Lovingly he raised the child to his face,

amazed by how tiny she was, and stunned by the sudden love that washed over him. She had come into the world kicking and screaming. She was her mother's daughter.

Chief Bowles glanced at the child and frowned. "Do not feel bad that it is only a girl. Next time you will have a son."

While Ian held the miracle in his arms, the chief set about fashioning a crude *travois* while his wives wrapped the infant in a bright yellow cloth. Chief Bowles offered Ian a leather skin of water and some dried meat. "Take your wife home, Ian McCain." Then he and his wives mounted, and the three of them disappeared as suddenly as they'd appeared.

Emerada opened her eyes and stared at him. "Ian?"

"Yes, my darling," he said, holding the child out for her to see. "We have a daughter. And she is as high-spirited and beautiful as her mother."

She shook her head. "Did I dream it, or were there Indians here?"

He laid the baby against her good arm. "You did not dream it. Our daughter was helped into the world by Chief Bowles's wives."

She looked down at the baby. "I thought I would lose her."

"Emerada, do you think you're strong enough to travel?"

She nodded. "I am strong."

He laughed as he lifted her onto the *travois*,

which he had tied behind the horse. "Oh, yes, you are, Emerada McCain. I don't know anyone who has your strength."

Her mind was muddled, and she just wanted to sleep. "Did you say we had a daughter?"

"I did." He supported the baby's head, since Emerada was beginning to go limp against him. He had to get them both to Talavera as quickly as possible. He still didn't know how badly Emerada might be hurt.

Ian reined in his panic and urged the horse forward, dragging the travois behind. He had to get help for Emerada.

It was hours later when they reached the ranch. He saw a wagon at the stable, and Domingo was mounted on a horse. When Ian reached the stable, the big man dismounted and walked toward him in astonishment.

"Is she all right?" Then Domingo saw all the blood. "What happened?"

"As amazing as it sounds, Emerada gave birth to my daughter. Take the child, Domingo. I'll bring Emerada inside."

Tenderly the big man took the tiny infant in his arms and stared at her in wonder. "I was just leaving to hunt for Emerada."

Emerada opened her eyes and stared at Domingo as if she'd seen a ghost. "You are alive!"

"It takes more than a bullet to kill me," he said, grinning down at the baby as if she was the most precious creature in the world.

Tears crept from between Emerada's eyelids and slid down her cheeks. "I thought you were lost to me, Domingo."

At that moment Hank and Sara came out of the stable, and Ian explained what had happened. "I'll have to lift her carefully. Her arm's broken."

"It's lucky for everyone concerned that I chose today to deliver the supplies Emerada ordered," Hank said in amazement. "I can't wait to hear what happened, Colonel."

Sara took the baby from Domingo and walked toward the barn. "Men," she murmured. "Make me a bed for Emerada, and I'll want lots of water, warm enough to bathe them both." She turned around and looked at the three men. "Well, what are you waiting for? Do it now!"

Ian glanced at Hank, and the innkeeper grinned. "I found me a gem in her. We're gonna get married."

Ian nodded wearily. "I believe we'd better do what she asked. You know how women are when they're riled."

Since Emerada couldn't be moved again, a bed and mattress had been brought from town for her. Sara had taken over her care and that of the baby.

Ian sent for a doctor from Victoria, and he pronounced both mother and daughter healthy. He told Emerada that Ian had done well in setting her arm. He laughingly told her that if word got around about the Indian women delivering babies, he might lose his practice to them.

Emerada had not seen Ian to thank him for all he'd done for her. He'd been gone for three days and was supposed to return to Talavera today.

Emerada glanced down at her daughter, happy to acknowledge that she had Ian's blue eyes.

"She is a miracle, Sara," Emerada said, kissing the soft cheek of her sleeping daughter.

"That she is," Sara agreed, "and not the first babe to find shelter in a stable. I can't imagine what you went through, delivering this child under such primitive circumstances. I don't know if I could be that strong."

Emerada smiled at Sara. In a very short time, they had become fond of each other. "If you do not have a choice, you can do anything, Sara."

Sara had been brushing Emerada's hair, and she laid the brush aside. "You haven't asked me about Pauline, and I know you must be curious."

"I have not asked because I do not want to know."

"She went back to Virginia."

"Oh." Emerada lay back against the pillow.

381

Now that the baby was born, she would give Ian his freedom, and he could go to Virginia to get Pauline. Emerada heard the sound of wagons and men talking, and she was confused.

"Sara, what is happening out there?"

"Why don't you ask your husband?" Sara answered, smiling and moving away as Ian approached.

Ian's eyes were so brilliant that Emerada lowered hers. "Ian, I'm glad you came so I could thank you for all you did. My daughter and I owe you our lives."

He knelt down beside her and placed his hand on the small head that was covered with black hair. The baby looked right at him, and he felt a lump forming in his throat. "She is so amazing, this daughter of mine."

Emerada glanced up at him. "You know I wasn't truthful to you about—"

He reached forward and placed a kiss on her lips, silencing her. "Let that be the last time either of us is not completely honest with the other."

She was puzzled. "Very well." At that moment there was a loud noise just outside. It sounded like someone stacking lumber. "Ian, can you tell me what's happening out there?"

"Of course. Workers are unloading supplies."

"What kind of supplies?"

"To build a house."

She tried to sit up, but she turned her arm

wrong and decided to remain still. "I gave no such orders."

"I did. Let me tell you about what I want to do for you. If you approve, the building will begin immediately."

The baby grabbed the finger Ian held out to her. He laughed and kissed the tiny hand. Emerada's heart swelled with love for the man who had given her this daughter, and it seemed he loved the child.

"Tell me what you are doing with the lumber," she said in a voice that trembled with emotion.

"I reasoned that you wouldn't want to build a house where the first one burned. So if you have no objections, I thought we could have a garden there—a place with flowers and fountains. A place dedicated to the memory of your family."

Her eyes widened. "Why would you do that for me?"

"Let me finish. Do you know that place on the hill with all the oak trees, where you can see the entire valley?"

"*Sí.* I know the place."

"What would you think about our building the house there? I have brought plans for you to look at. But I thought we'd keep to the Spanish style. What do you think?"

She wrinkled her brow in thought. "Ian, we said that we would always be honest with each other, and I will not have this lie between us. I know that you love Pauline, and that the two of you would have been married if not for me. I do not want you to devote yourself to a life you would grow to detest. I want you to have your freedom."

He scooped up his daughter and carried her outside to Sara, who was supervising the men. Then he came back, and shut and locked the door. He sat down beside Emerada and took her hand. "There are too many people around here, and I want to talk to you undisturbed."

She knew what was coming, and she dreaded hearing it. *Please,* she thought sadly, *don't let him tell me how much he loves Pauline.* "I know you are an honorable man, Ian. And I know that you would stay married to me for the baby's sake. But I do not want to have a husband who loves another woman."

He raised her hand to his lips and kissed it. "Would you have any objections to having a husband who can't think of anything but you from sunup to sundown? Would you object to having a husband who loves you with every breath he takes?" He raised her chin and gazed deeply into her eyes. "Would you mind that so much, Emerada?"

"But I thought . . . " She shook her head. "I thought you loved the golden-haired American."

"You couldn't be more mistaken," he said, his gaze sweeping across her face, his eyes moist.

"God help me, because I lost my heart to a dark-haired, dark-eyed beauty who is obstinate, brave, stubborn, compassionate, and very, very desirable."

She was still afraid to believe him. "We said we would be honest with each other."

"I have just opened my heart to you, Emerada." His voice deepened, and he lay down so he was beside her. "I don't know if I fell in love with you that first day you landed in my arms, or the night you danced your way into my heart. I only know that I love you, Emerada."

A lone tear trailed down her cheek. "How can that be?"

He breathed in the fresh scent of her and took her in his arms. "You know I love you, but I don't know how you feel about me."

She moved back so she could see his eyes. "Oh, Ian, I have loved you for so long—at least it seems a long time. I know the seeds of love began to grow in my heart that very first day when I stumbled into your arms. Each time I saw you, the love became deeper and deeper. Then I learned I was going to have your baby."

She attempted to put her arms around him and then laughingly drew away when the splint on her broken arm became wedged between them.

His voice deepened. "Hurry and get well, Emerada. I want to show you just how much I love you."

385

She laughed, feeling happiness for the first time in so long. "Ian, I wonder what they are all thinking out there with us locked in here?"

"They're thinking I'm one damned lucky man. I have captured the San Antonio Rose for my wife." He pulled back and looked at her. "From now on, you dance only for me—understood?"

She parted her lips and waited for his kiss. "Understood. I dance only for my husband."

Epilogue

Emerada stood beneath the spreading branches of a live oak tree, gazing lovingly out on Talavera. From her vantage point, she could see fat cattle grazing in the pasture and spirited horses galloping around a fenced grassland.

A warm breeze touched her cheek and rippled through her hair. Talavera had come back to life—Ian had done that for her.

Her gaze went to the garden, where the previous ranch house had stood. The blackened ruins no longer scarred the land. In the garden were exotic trees and plants and flowers of every color. There were three fountains, many marble benches, and a giant angel monument like the one that stood guard by her Aunt Dilena's grave in New Orleans. On the base of the monument the names of her father and brothers were carved. Ian had kept his promise to her. He had given her a place to heal, a place to sit and remember the wonderful things about her father and brothers, and not how they died.

She turned to the huge, white, Spanish-style hacienda that sprawled among the trees. With its fountains, courtyards, and cool tile floors, it was so beautiful. But more than that, it was a home where love dwelled.

She could hear her daughter laughing in the courtyard while she was watched over by her *niñera*. No doubt Domingo was keeping a watchful eye on the child as well, just as he'd done with Emerada.

Life was good. Her days were filled with such happiness that she could hardly bear it.

She heard footsteps behind her and turned to see Ian approach. She rushed into his arms, and he held her to his heart.

"Mr. McCain, shouldn't you be supervising the branding?"

"I'm no use to the foreman. I can't keep my mind on what I'm doing."

She gazed into his wonderful eyes. "And why is that?"

He looked at her rakishly. "Because I was thinking how I'd like to take you to bed."

She laughed and turned back to gaze at the valley. "What a wonderful mind you have, Mr. McCain."

He rested his chin on the top of her head. "I had a letter from Mother today."

"How is she?"

"She wants to come for another visit," he said hesitantly, not knowing how Emerada would feel about another visit, because it would be his mother's third in two years. "It seems she has a great fondness for Texas."

"Why do you not have her move here? She needs to be near her family, and we need her. I love your mother, Ian."

He looked at her in surprise. "Do you really mean that?"

"I can assure you that I do. She is so gentle, and life has not always been kind to her."

He laughed to hide the tightness in his throat. "What were you doing when I came up, Emerada, surveying all your kingdom?"

"I was numbering my blessings. I have so many."

He smiled down at her. "Am I one of your blessings?"

She pressed her lips against his, and his arms tightened. "You are the most important one," she said in a throaty voice.

He gazed at her in wonder. "Why is it, Emerada, that all you have to do is look at me with those melting brown eyes and I want to take you to bed?" He pressed her tighter to him, and she laughed, pulled away.

"That would explain why I am expecting again."

He pulled back, his eyes glowing with warmth. "Are you sure?"

"Of course. A woman knows these things."

He placed his hands on each side of her face and drew her to him, kissing her gently.

They had built a home and a life on this Texas land. They would have strong sons and happy daughters. Their roots would reach deep into the soil and heal all old wounds. Their love would nourish and grow beneath the blue Texas sky.

TEXAS PROUD
CONSTANCE O'BANYON

Rachel Rutledge has her gun trained on Noble Vincente. With one shot, she will have her revenge on the man who killed her father. So what is stopping her from pulling the trigger? Perhaps it is the memory of Noble's teasing voice, his soft smile, or the way one glance from his dark Spanish eyes once stirred her foolish heart to longing. Yes, she loved him then . . . as much as she hates him now. One way or another, she will wound him to the heart—if not with bullets, then with her own feminine wiles. But as Rachel discovers, sometimes the line between love and hate is too thinly drawn.

___4492-7 $5.99 US/$6.99 CAN

SEVEN BRIDES
LEIGH GREENWOOD
FERN

"I loved *Rose*, but I absolutely loved *Fern*! She's fabulous! An incredible job!"
—*Romantic Times*

A man of taste and culture, James Madison Randolph enjoys the refined pleasures of life in Boston. It's been years since the suave lawyer abandoned the Randolphs' ramshackle ranch—and the dark secrets that haunted him there. But he is forced to return to the hated frontier when his brother is falsely accused of murder. What he doesn't expect is a sharp-tongued vixen who wants to gun down his entire family. As tough as any cowhand in Kansas, Fern Sproull will see her cousin's killer hang for his crime, and no smooth-talking city slicker will stop her from seeing justice done. But one look at James awakens a tender longing to taste heaven in his kiss. While the townsfolk of Abilene prepare for the trial of the century, Madison and Fern ready themselves for a knock-down, drag-out battle of the sexes that might just have two winners.

___4409-9 $5.99 US/$6.99 CAN

SEVEN BRIDES

LEIGH GREENWOOD

VIOLET

Broken and bitter, Jefferson Randolph can never forget all he
lost in the War Between the States—or forgive those he has
fought. Long after most of his six brothers have found wedded
bliss, the former Rebel soldier keeps himself buried in work,
until a run-in with Yankee schoolteacher Violet Goodwin
teaches him that he has a lot to learn about passion. But Jeff
fears that love alone isn't enough to help him put his past
behind him—or convince a proper lady that she can find
happiness as the newest bride in the rowdy Randolph clan.

___4494-3 $5.99 US/$6.99 CAN

Dorchester Publishing Co., Inc.
P.O. Box 6640
Wayne, PA 19087-8640

Please add $1.75 for shipping and handling for the first book and
$.50 for each book thereafter. NY, NYC, and PA residents,
please add appropriate sales tax. No cash, stamps, or C.O.D.s. All
orders shipped within 6 weeks via postal service book rate.
Canadian orders require $2.00 extra postage and must be paid in
U.S. dollars through a U.S. banking facility.

Name_____
Address_____
City_____State_____Zip_____
I have enclosed $_____ in payment for the checked book(s).
Payment must accompany all orders. ❑ Please send a free catalog.
   CHECK OUT OUR WEBSITE! www.dorchesterpub.com

CONNIE MASON

BOLD LAND BOLD LOVE

New South Wales in 1807 is a vast land of wild beauty and wilder passions: a frontier as yet untamed by man; a place where women have few rights and fewer pleasures. For a female convict like flame-haired Casey O'Cain, it is a living nightmare. And from the first, arrogant, handsome Dare Penrod makes it clear what he wants of her. Casey knows she should fight him with every breath in her body, but her heart tells her he can make a paradise of this wilderness for her.

___52274-8 $5.99 US/$6.99 CAN

Dorchester Publishing Co., Inc.
P.O. Box 6640
Wayne, PA 19087-8640

Please add $1.75 for shipping and handling for the first book and $.50 for each book thereafter. NY, NYC, and PA residents, please add appropriate sales tax. No cash, stamps, or C.O.D.s. All orders shipped within 6 weeks via postal service book rate. Canadian orders require $2.00 extra postage and must be paid in U.S. dollars through a U.S. banking facility.

Name_____
Address_____
City_____State_____Zip_____
I have enclosed $_____ in payment for the checked book(s).
Payment <u>must</u> accompany all orders. ❏ Please send a free catalog.
        CHECK OUT OUR WEBSITE! www.dorchesterpub.com

Golden Man

Evelyn Rogers

Steven Marshall is the kind of guy who makes a woman think of satin sheets and steamy nights, of wild fantasies involving hot tubs and whipped cream—and then brass bands, waving flags, and Fourth of July parades. All-American terrific, that's what he is; tall and bronzed, with hair the color of the sun, thick-lashed blue eyes, and a killer grin slanted against a square jaw—a true Golden Man. He is even single. Unfortunately, he is also the President of the United States. So when average citizen Ginny Baxter finds herself his date for a diplomatic reception, she doesn't know if she is the luckiest woman in the country, or the victim of a practical joke. Either way, she is in for the ride of her life . . . and the man of her dreams.

____52295-0 $5.99 US/$6.99 CAN

Love, Cherish Me

Rebecca Brandewyne

The man in black shows his hand: five black spades. Storm Lesconflair knows what this means—she now belongs to him. The close heat of the saloon flushes her skin as she feels the half-breed's eyes travel over her body. Her father's plantation house in New Orleans suddenly seems but a dream, while the handsome stranger before her is all too real. Dawn is breaking outside as the man who won her rises and walks through the swinging doors. She follows him out into the growing light, only vaguely aware that she has become his forever, never guessing that he has also become hers.

___52302-7 $5.99 US/$6.99 CAN

LINDA WINSTEAD

From the moment Dillon feasts his eyes on the raven-haired beauty, Grace Cavanaugh, he knows she is trouble. Sharp-tongued and stubborn, with a flawless complexion and a priceless wardrobe, Grace certainly doesn't belong on a Western ranch. But that's what Dillon calls home, and as long as the lovely orphan is his charge, that's where they'll stay.

But Grace Cavanaugh has learned the hard way that men can't be trusted. Not for all the diamonds and rubies in England will she give herself to any man. But when Dillon walks into her life he changes all the rules. Suddenly the unapproachable ice princess finds herself melting at his simplest touch, and wondering what she'll have to do to convince him that their love is the most precious gem of all.

_4223-1 $5.50 US/$6.50 CAN

Dorchester Publishing Co., Inc.
P.O. Box 6640
Wayne, PA 19087-8640

Please add $1.75 for shipping and handling for the first book and $.50 for each book thereafter. NY, NYC, and PA residents, please add appropriate sales tax. No cash, stamps, or C.O.D.s. All orders shipped within 6 weeks via postal service book rate. Canadian orders require $2.00 extra postage and must be paid in U.S. dollars through a U.S. banking facility.

Name_____
Address_____
City_____ State_____ Zip_____
I have enclosed $_____ in payment for the checked book(s).
Payment must accompany all orders. ☐ Please send a free catalog.

NIGHT WALKER

Sylvie SOMMERFIELD

He calls her Morning Sun, for she first came to him in a vision . . . misty and golden. But does her appearance at his village signal good fortune or disaster? Harsh experience has taught him there can be no union between his people and hers, yet her sweet kisses heat his blood until it flows like honey, until he knows that like two halves of one whole, she will always be the morning sun of his midnight desire.

___4359-9 $5.99 US/$6.99CAN